Praise for *The*

'A brilliant, twisty thriller tha[...]
warnings out loud to the c[...]
Peter James, author of the bestselling Roy Grace series

'Paced flawlessly from the start to the barn-burner of a finale,
I gobbled this up in two days and can still hear the hum of
insects and feel the heat on my skin. An absolute must-read
for your summer – Nikki Allen is one to watch'
Sarah Goodwin, author of *The Yacht*

'With shades of *The White Lotus*, *Apple Cider Vinegar* and
Agatha Christie's *And Then There Were None*, this Costa
Rican-set thriller is an accomplished white-knuckle ride
from start to finish'
Kate Riordan, author of *The Heatwave*

'The perfect destination thriller to lose yourself in this summer'
Natasha Boydell, author of *The Fortune Teller*

'I really enjoyed this twisty debut from Nikki Allen . . . the
brilliantly visceral way Nikki brought it to life: the heat,
the crawling insects, the danger!'
Amanda Reynolds, author of *Close to Me*

'*The Hideaway* is THE thriller debut of the summer! Filled
with tense twists and turns, it will keep you guessing – and
distrusting everyone – until the very end!'
Sara Ochs, author of *The Resort*

'Dangers and secrets lurk in the shadows in this
unputdownable destination thriller'
Allie Reynolds, author of *Shiver*

ABOUT THE AUTHOR

Nikki is a former journalist and copywriter, and a qualified therapist. A voracious reader, Nikki was inspired to write *The Hideaway* after reading true stories of people disappearing in the Costa Rican rainforest. Nikki was born in Holland, grew up the only Jewish kid in her Worcestershire village, and now lives in North London with her family. *The Hideaway* is her debut novel.

THE
HIDEAWAY

NIKKI ALLEN

PAN BOOKS

First published 2025 by Pan Books
an imprint of Pan Macmillan
The Smithson, 6 Briset Street, London EC1M 5NR
EU representative: Macmillan Publishers Ireland Ltd, 1st Floor,
The Liffey Trust Centre, 117–126 Sheriff Street Upper,
Dublin 1 D01 YC43
Associated companies throughout the world

ISBN 978-1-0350-7197-5

1 3 5 7 9 8 6 4 2

A CIP catalogue record for this book is available from the British Library.

Illustrations © Arina Ulyasheva/Shutterstock

Typeset in Sabon MT Std by Palimpsest Book Production Limited, Falkirk, Stirlingshire
Printed and bound in the UK using 100% Renewable Electricity by CPI Group (UK) Ltd

Visit **www.panmacmillan.com** to read more about all our books
and to buy them.

For Leila and Raphael, who will write their own stories.

PROLOGUE

Beneath the canopy of the rainforest, the ground is alive. Leaves move seemingly of their own accord as the mammals of the tropical wilderness – spiny rats and coatis and agoutis – shuffle across the forest floor. Armies of ants march with purpose, swarms of beetles scuttle over the fallen branches and rotting vines.

Today, they are unified: they move as one, with a single mission, each organism compelled like a zombie army in the same direction. They advance towards the motionless figure lying under a hasty scattering of leaves and mulchy earth, a body so broken that it seems beyond all repair. The foliage beneath her head is gradually turning a deeper shade of crimson as the blood oozes through the back of her scalp, soaking through her hair, making it dark and matted, before it seeps into the damp earth.

Her hands unfurl from the tight fists they have been curled into, revealing a crumpled photograph inside them. A deep crease runs through its middle, and the face of the person in the picture is slightly faded, as though fingertips have caressed its outline, tracing the image over and over until the colours have begun to wear away.

The jungle's creatures are curious; greedy, now that they have found her. Their steps are careful at first. But soon they will rush in with wildness, with abandon. After that, a wake of vultures will begin to form, circling overhead. When they have waited long enough for her, when they are ready to devour her, they will swoop down, one after the other, over and over, leaving nothing but a heap of bones scoured clean by fast beaks.

Her eyes loll open, glassy, unfocused. But she is not dead; not yet – she is hanging to life by a scrawny strand.

I want to live, her desperate eyes tell the animals and vegetation around her, attempting to communicate her anguish in the silence.

Her eyelids flutter closed, open again, each movement laboured. Her breaths are shallow; they are becoming slower.

A croak emerges from her throat – a last, desperate call for help; a cry to the rainforest, to the creatures surrounding her. To anyone who happens to be out here in this wilderness with her.

But there is no one; not any more.

And even if there were, it is too late.

They can do nothing for her now.

FEBRUARY 2024

[Hannah looks to camera, smiling.]

Hello, my amazing spiritual seeking community – all ten million of you! How did that happen, right? Thank you so much for following me!

Now listen up, y'all, because the day has finally come. I am so excited to let you know that after two years of getting this incredible space ready for you, The Hideaway, my beautiful wellness lodge in the heart of the Costa Rican rainforest, will be launching in-person retreats in the next few months! Hold tight, because I'll be taking you on a virtual tour of the space in my next reel.

But first, I have some exciting news and my heart is bursting to share this with you! To celebrate The Hideaway opening up, I want to offer an exclusive group of you beautiful people the chance to come and experience the healing transformation that this luxurious eco-retreat, nestled amidst hundreds of acres of rainforest, can give you!

A select number of you will get to spend a week here at the end of April with me, healing and rejuvenating on a tailored, personalized wellness retreat – for free! You'll get to stay in my stunning ecolodge for a week, getting gorgeous pampering and bespoke treatments. I'll spend the first twenty-four hours getting to know each of you on a deep, intimate level, so that I can then create a customized programme of healing just for you, designed to give you the transformation you've been seeking. For the lucky few who win a place, all of your flights, transfers and taxis will be paid for – though be warned, this place is a little off the beaten track, so prepare yourselves for a bumpy ride!

[Hannah pauses; her expression turns sombre, and her voice becomes serious.]

Now, I want to make sure I'm offering this experience to those of you who will benefit from it the most. So, to be eligible, you must be genuinely ready for spiritual growth, to going inward, and to getting vulnerable – even if it's hard. You must be willing to take part in rituals and activities that push you beyond what feels safe.

Y'all, this is not just a relaxation retreat, but an opportunity to dive fully into what's holding you back in your life so that it can be released! That's why I can only offer this experience to such a special, limited group – because we are going DEEP and you'll be working with me one-on-one! You must be prepared to leave here completely transformed. And if you're not ready for that at this stage in your journey, then sadly this retreat is not for you.

[Hannah smiles, her tone of voice becomes upbeat again.]

All right, I'm almost out of time, I'd better wrap this up! To be in with a chance to win this amazing opportunity, DM me a three-minute video telling me all about yourself and why you want to come and experience The Hideaway with me. And open up! Share what comes into your mind and heart, talk truthfully about who you are, your struggles, and the transform-ation you truly desire for yourself.

I can't wait to see all your faces, and to host my first little group of y'all here!

Until then, peace and love, spiritual seekers.

[Camera fades to black.]

MIRA

'*Mierda!*'

Mira startled at the driver's exclamation as the jeep rocked wildly on the uneven track, tracing a path through gigantic trees, splashing through puddles the size of small ponds.

Is this even a road? She wound her window down and poked her head out, looked upwards, took in the lush forest that rose so high it seemed to touch the lowering sun, the tops of the trees barely visible. Above them, grey-black clouds were starting to gather and swirl – the approaching storm that she'd heard murmurings of at the airport.

Without the buffer of the window, she heard a cacophony of squawks and chirps. On her left, almost buried by the lush greenery, she caught sight of a smart wooden sign with *The Hideaway* painted in a beautiful cursive script, then a second sign underneath: *PRIVATE PROPERTY: GUESTS ONLY.*

Mira exhaled a shaky breath, tried to quell the nauseating mix of excitement and nerves that were curdling in her stomach. There had been brief moments on her journey here when she had questioned her sanity in accepting this invitation; seconds of wondering what she was doing here.

Back in London, she'd felt confident that she could handle the physical aspects of this trip – the weather, the activities. It had been true, mostly, on the health and safety form that Hannah had asked her to fill in, when she'd said she was well enough to travel; to exercise.

But already, the reality of the sweltering Costa Rican climate was a shock. Within minutes of getting off the artificially cool plane – first, the eleven-hour flight from Heathrow with the smell of *challah* still clinging to her maxi skirt, then the quick internal hop from San José to Puerto Jiménez – she was uncomfortable. Barely out of the airport terminal and she was swatting at insects keen to feast on her pale flesh. Then on the drive here, sweat from her thighs had soaked the ripped leather seat of the four-by-four taxi as it took her high into the hills of the Osa Peninsula, further from the sparkling turquoise sea lined with palm trees and white sand. A hot dampness itched at her scalp as they wove deeper into the jungle, further from the towns and beach resorts buzzing with ecotourists.

But then the doubts released her again, and her excitement returned, especially now that she was actually, finally, *here*. The same buzz of anticipation she'd felt the day she saw Hannah's video swept through her now. As soon as Mira had heard about this retreat – the way Hannah had *guaranteed that everyone who came here would leave totally transformed* – she knew it was the sign she'd been looking for. She was going, and no one – not even her husband – would stop her.

Mira drew in a breath as the taxi pulled into a clearing – a sudden reprieve from the thick canopy – and slowed as a large, open-sided wooden pavilion with a triangular, thatched roof and polished floorboards came into view a few metres ahead. Two huge fans dangled from its ceiling, their silent blades stirring the humid air; thick wooden benches piled with fat white cushions lined the structure – and a tall, curvaceous woman in her mid-twenties stood at its centre, dressed in immaculate white trousers and tunic, and holding a platter of exotic fruit.

This wasn't Hannah. Mira recalled the numerous photos and videos she'd seen of the glowing thirty-something: long, dirty-blonde plaits, bronzed from head to toe, face full of piercings and often sitting in the lotus position. Quite different from this statuesque brunette, her dark hair pulled back in a high, smooth ponytail, a pair of bronze hoops dangling from her earlobes.

'*Gracias.*' Mira stepped out of the taxi, waited for the driver to lift her suitcase out of the boot and wheel it towards her. She took it from him, felt it sag into the soft earth. The humidity clutched at her throat, so fierce it almost knocked her petite frame to the ground. She sucked in a breath, steadied herself, and said a quiet prayer of thanks that she was here; that she wasn't at home, muted by the safety of her comfortable but stifling semi-detached house in Golders Green, the salty sting of brisket in her mouth; her mother-in-law, uninvited, at the kitchen table gossiping about the neighbours.

Mira climbed the three polished steps to the pavilion and was enveloped in a rush of enthusiastic chatter in heavily accented English. The woman smiled at her as she spoke, full lips parting to show neat white teeth in perfect rows.

'Welcome to Hannah's Hideaway. I am so happy you are here!' she said. 'I am Luisa – I am the assistant to our main housekeeper, and will be helping to make sure you have everything you need during your stay. You would like some passionfruit?' She held out the plate towards Mira. 'Or a glass of iced water, perhaps?'

Mira smiled at her warmth, her enthusiasm. 'Thank you,' she said. 'I'm Mira. And yes, I'd love both.' She put her luggage down, resisted the overwhelming urge to scratch at her scalp, then reached for the plate of green and yellow fruits. She took a glass of water from the side table next and glugged half of it down before digging her thumb into a ripe passionfruit. She devoured its soft, sweet flesh; it was delicious.

'Mira, yes, we are expecting you. Please, take a seat,' said Luisa. She gestured to the bench at the edge of the pavilion; Mira walked over and sat down. The fingers of her right hand began tapping on the wood at her side, knocking out some long-forgotten melody; her pianist's fingers now slower, but still practised. She could play almost anything she'd heard just once: it was her party trick, her one special gift.

She surveyed the empty space. *Where are the other guests – and our host?* 'Am I the first to arrive?' she said. 'And what about Hannah – I thought she'd be here to greet everyone?'

Something passed across Luisa's expression, a brief darkening of her striking features – but it was fleeting. Her beaming smile returned.

'Ah, yes,' said Luisa. 'You are here first, but the others will arrive soon. And Hannah will be here any minute – Paola will be here in a moment too. When she arrives, I will ask her, she will know everything . . .'

Paola, Paola . . . Mira recognized the name; Hannah had mentioned her in the welcome email, perhaps. *She must be*

Luisa's boss – the housekeeper. She opened her mouth to check, but Luisa interrupted her before she could speak.

'Look, someone else comes now!' she said, pointing, that gleaming smile lighting up her face again. Another four-by-four taxi was lurching its way down the track, its brakes squealing softly as it came to a halt by the pavilion. A buzz of excitement grew in Mira's stomach, spread upwards to her chest. *Perhaps Hannah is in there? Am I really about to meet her?*

Or it could be one of the other guests. In her emails, Hannah had said she'd tried to arrange for them all to come in the same taxi from the airport, but it turned out they were all arriving at different times, so she'd asked them to make their own way to the retreat today.

Mira got to her feet, walked back towards the steps and shaded her eyes from the lowering sun as she watched two men climb out. The first was a thirty-ish, muscular, handsome blond in smooth linen trousers; the word *jock* sprang to mind, quite unexpectedly – though it did seem to suit. The other man was one of the tallest people she'd ever seen. He looked about her age – early forties – attractive, greying, with a warm, kind-looking face, and wearing a baseball cap, T-shirt and shorts that looked slightly too small. Watching him almost bump his head on the taxi door as he got out, she felt a rush of affection for him.

'G'day,' said the tall man, lumbering up the steps, ducking to avoid hitting his head again on the pavilion roof. 'Name's Scott. Good to meet you.' For someone so large, his voice was surprisingly gentle. Mira warmed to him a little more.

'And I'm Ben,' said the blond man in a thick southern drawl, staring at Mira. She caught him eyeing her hair with obvious curiosity before he seemed to realize his rudeness and abruptly averted his gaze. She smiled, shook his outstretched hand. 'Good to meet you.'

'So, are you Australian?' said Mira, turning to Scott, after Luisa had rushed towards the men, handing over slices of fruit and tumblers of water.

Scott nodded. 'Yeah, I'm born and bred in Melbourne,' he said. 'We're heading into winter over there soon, so this temperature's a bit of a shock. How about you? Or maybe I can take a guess from the accent – are you British?'

'Yes – I'm from London. And my name's Mira, by the way.' She paused to take him in, realized she was craning her neck just to look up at his face and, embarrassingly, standing on tiptoes – she'd not even realized she was doing it. She lowered her feet, but not before Scott noticed.

'It's OK – I get that a lot,' he said, smiling, bending down towards her a little. 'One of the hazards of being six foot six, I guess.'

'Are you really? Wow. Well, I'm five foot nothing, so we can be this retreat's little and large,' said Mira. Both men laughed; she knew it hadn't been that funny, but she appreciated the kindness. 'Did you two travel here together?' she said.

'Only from the top of the track there,' said Ben, pointing behind him. 'It was a stroke of luck – Scott was just coming down the pathway when we turned in.'

'I hiked most of the way here from Playa Blanca,' said Scott. 'I wanted to see as much of the area as I could before we start the retreat. I'm so happy to finally be here, though – I can't wait to see the place, and to meet Hannah, of course.' He was practically vibrating with excitement: bobbing up and down on the balls of his feet, eyes darting around, as he said: 'She's changed my life.'

'Yeah, Hannah's the best,' said Ben, nodding rapidly. 'I literally cannot wait to see her either.' He looked around the pavilion. 'Where is she, anyway? I thought she'd be here to meet us.'

'Hannah will be here any moment,' said Luisa. 'She is so excited to meet you too.'

'I hope she's not been caught up in the storm somewhere,' said Scott. 'The driver just said the rain has already hit the other side of the peninsula and it's causing all kinds of havoc to the traffic.' He paused to grab another thick slice of mango from the plate in Luisa's hand.

'Any more of those mangoes?' came a new voice with a Welsh lilt from behind them. Mira turned to see a tall, athletic-looking redhead in skintight leggings and a matching vest jog up the stairs, her high ponytail swishing as she moved, one side of her mouth turned upwards, teasingly. 'Hey, everyone,' she said. 'I'm Carly.' She moved around the group, shaking hands, smiling.

'Welcome!' said Luisa. 'Of course, Carly, we are so happy you are here!'

'Me too – and just in time,' she said, smiling. 'I was dying to get here before it got dark and the rain kicked in.' She raised her eyes heavenwards. 'It's starting to look pretty bleak, isn't it?'

Luisa looked up, nodded. 'I think the storm will come soon,' she said. 'I'll get Paola, and we will go to the house, OK?' But just as Luisa turned to leave, Mira heard something. A soft, swift *ding*: a text message. She rooted through the pockets of her backpack, found her phone. As she reached to swipe the screen, a series of similar *dings* echoed around the pavilion.

'Did we all just get a message at the same time?' asked Mira. 'Maybe it's . . .' She swiped at the screen, tapped the green icon, opened the text. It was a message from a number she didn't have saved, starting with the digits 506 – *is that the Costa Rican dial code?* – but next to it was a little icon with a picture of a smiling blonde woman she recognized. *Hannah.*

'Yes, it's her – did you all get one too?' The three of them nodded; Luisa turned back to the group to listen as Scott read the message out loud, Mira's eyes following the words on her own screen at the same time:

'Hey, everyone! Welcome to The Hideaway. I'm so happy you're here, but I'm sorry I'm not there right now. Earlier today, I took a boat to Golfito to pick us up some special supplies for our retreat. Now the weather has taken a turn for the worse and none of the boats will take me back! But I'll be with you just as soon as I can – the second the storm passes and these boats start up again, I'm out of here. In the meantime, enjoy a gorgeous evening of pampering at my Costa Rican home! I'll see you very soon – I can't wait! Love, Hannah.'

Scott finished reading and looked up at the group, his eyebrows drawn slightly together. Just then, Mira caught a flash of movement along the track, where a dark green jeep was jerking its way along the uneven ground. *I wonder who this is?* She peered over, tried to make out the features of the person inside before it came to a halt.

'Ah, Paola is here,' said Luisa.

She muttered something in Spanish, then jogged down the

steps towards the jeep, calling, 'Paola, Paola!' She opened the driver's door, leaned over and spoke rapidly. A slight, grey-haired woman who looked to be in her late fifties, with narrow features and a pinched look to her face, wearing faded jeans and a T-shirt, stepped out of the jeep and walked towards the pavilion.

At the top of the steps, Paola offered each of them in turn a brief smile and a nod. '*Hola*, welcome to you all, our guests. I am Paola, The Hideaway's housekeeper – I look after Hannah's *casa*, and I will look after you all,' she said. 'I am sorry I was not here to greet you – I wanted to get to the store in the village for some fresh milk before the storm, but I was too late – it looks like the track will flood quickly in this rain.' She turned to Luisa, spoke in Spanish; Mira caught mention of Hannah's name, but not much else.

'Luisa has told me about your message from Hannah,' she said. 'She has taken the boat to Golfito, yes? She must have needed some extra things for our retreat – we were just with her this morning, weren't we, Luisa?' Luisa dipped her head in agreement. 'She was so excited to meet you all. I will call her now, to check what time she'll be here.'

Mira and the others watched as Paola pulled a mobile from her pocket and called Hannah on speaker for everyone to hear. But Hannah's phone was switched off; it went straight to voicemail, Hannah's chirpy Texan drawl asking the caller to leave a message.

Paola shrugged and hung up. 'OK, never mind,' she said. 'The weather sometimes affects cell service out here, and the storm is already starting further down the peninsula. She'll be back soon, I am sure.' She slipped the phone back into her pocket, looked around at the group, properly, for the first time.

Then she seemed to register something; her eyes roamed around the four of them, back and forth. They widened a touch, then narrowed. 'Wait a moment – there is a problem,' she said. 'There—'

But whatever Paola's problem was, they didn't get to hear it: a crack of thunder erupted, so loud it was as if the sky above Mira's head was being ripped in two. Seconds later, fat droplets of rain began to plummet from the sky, lashing through the open sides of the pavilion into their faces. Mira had never been in a tropical storm before, and the mixture of heat and rain was strange. A bit like being in a warm shower, but out in the open air. She felt irrationally naked, exposed; she moved a hand quickly to her hair, held onto the top of her head. It was OK, everything was still in place.

Luisa fired some more rapid Spanish at Paola, who hesitated, looked at the group again, then glanced at the rain. She nodded, said: '*Sí, sí*. Everybody, let's get to the house – we can work this out when we get into the dry.'

Mira tugged her jacket out of her suitcase and threw it on, then lifted it onto its wheels and followed Paola and the others down the stairs of the pavilion, shielding her face with her hood.

She shivered and tried to shake off a prickle of unease. It was probably just her body reacting to the sudden rain, the violence of the storm, the darkening of the clouds. She pushed away the thought that her disquiet was because of something else. Like the expression she'd seen pass across Paola's face as she looked around the group of people gathered here.

She'd looked confused, thought Mira.

Understandably so, perhaps — it sounded like she'd not expected Hannah to take a last-minute boat trip just before the storm.

But it was more than that. She'd looked *afraid*.

SCOTT

Scott shielded his face from the pummelling rain and forced himself to focus on the movement of his shoes on the earth. It would be easy to lose his grip here, especially while he was so giddy with excitement. The last thing he needed was to fall on his face and make an ass of himself before they'd made it as far as Hannah's lodge.

The trees were thick and high on both sides of the narrow track as they walked, the branches waving wildly as the wind and rain picked up speed, obscuring their view of what lay ahead of them. The chirps and croaks coming from the dense jungle were loud even through the storm, nature's symphony blaring over the thunder and rain. The air smelled damp and earthy. In the shadows, swinging between branches, Scott thought he could make out the silhouettes of two small monkeys. Perhaps they were weaving their way back to a comfortable branch, somewhere to spend the night and shelter from the storm.

His eyes had just started to adjust to the gloom when there was a thinning in the canopy above them. With the relative shelter of branches and leaves removed from above their heads, the black, rumbling clouds came into stark view, and the rain slapped his hood with the force of a shower on full blast.

Then – its slate walls and floor-to-ceiling glass so out of place in the middle of this lush forest – there was Hannah's Costa Rican home.

Holy shit. Scott shielded his eyes from the storm to get a proper look in front of him. He'd never seen anything like it; not even Hannah's online tours had done it justice. He remembered her saying in one of her videos that she had bought the land and then got some hotshot eco-conscious architect from San José to design the place, bringing together 'the environmentally friendly and the luxurious'.

Well, the luxurious part had clearly come to fruition. Even now, in the near dark, with the rain lashing down and those bruise-coloured clouds overhead, the place was superb. Sharp, clean lines and the combination of sleek grey walls and glass made it look like it had fallen from the pages of a design magazine. Pulling the hood of his waterproof further down to shield his head from the rain, Scott noted a stone footpath leading neatly through some gardens to the front of the house. It then split into two: one path leading to the house's front door, the other to a sharply rectangular infinity pool surrounded by bright green tiles. Dark mahogany loungers the size of double beds lay around its edges, loaded with thick cream mattresses and bright turquoise pillows, the whole pool area protected by a sloping roof of glossy wood.

The place was perfect. It was just missing one thing: *Hannah*. Scott was surprised she was running late. It seemed out of character somehow. He didn't *know* Hannah, of course, but the impression he'd always got of her was that she was reliable, consistent. That she generally did what she said she was going to do – upload a video on a certain day, respond to viewers when she said she would, talk about a subject she'd promised to talk about. Be on time to greet her guests at her first ever in-person retreat.

Still, everyone was allowed a slip-up – even Hannah. And he could already tell this trip was going to be more than worth the inconvenience of her late arrival.

Paola and Luisa ushered the group along the neat stone path to shelter under the porch outside the house's doorway.

'Welcome to Hannah's *casa*, where you will stay for your retreat at The Hideaway – the most beautiful house in the whole of Osa!' said Paola, beaming as she looked around the group, then flinching as another clap of thunder struck. Raising her voice, she said, 'Please, come inside, now!'

As Paola turned to the door and pressed a code into the keypad to the side, an unfamiliar voice reached their ears, loud enough to pierce the battering rain.

'Hey, *attendez* – wait for me!' Scott turned to see a brown-skinned woman, with loose tendrils of corkscrew curls escaping from the hood of her anorak, dragging a sodden suitcase along the path towards them. She was panting and flustered, water running in rivets off her lightweight black jacket. *Whoever this is, she's gorgeous.*

'I'm Naya – I'm here for the retreat.' Her accent was French; her voice was breathless. 'With – with Hannah? Is this not – am I in the wrong place?' She started rifling through her bag, then stretched her arm out, phone held towards Paola's face, wiping streams of water from its screen.

Paola glanced at the phone, frowned. 'Naya, yes, of course –

21

it's OK, thank you. My name is Paola, I look after the house, and all of you until Hannah arrives.'

'Oh, thank goodness! But . . . arrives?' said Naya. 'Is Hannah not here?'

Paola gave a quick shake of her head, glanced again around the group, then, muttering in Spanish, opened the door and began to usher everyone inside. Scott hung back, waited for the others to head in before him; he noticed Naya was lingering at the door too, looking baffled.

He leaned towards her, ready to explain that Hannah had just been delayed, that she'd arrive any minute, but before he could speak, Paola walked over to him and placed a hand near his elbow. 'I need to speak with you – straight away.' Her voice was stern, and he saw she had a clipboard, giving him the unwelcome impression of a schoolteacher taking the register. *Have I done something wrong?* Had he ballsed up, somehow, without even realizing it?

He felt a flush of anticipatory embarrassment. *How am I doing this already? Assuming I've screwed up before the thing has even bloody started?*

Keep it together, Scott. Hadn't Hannah talked about exactly this 'false belief', the crap he kept getting stuck on like a broken record – that his past would always dictate his future? That just because he'd always felt like he messed things up, that meant he always would? Hannah said that wasn't true – people could change; they could be different, with a bit of help. That's why he was here, wasn't it? He'd get to work one-on-one with Hannah, in this amazing place, and he'd go home a new man.

He looked at Paola. 'Of course.'

She eyed him. 'Can you please tell me your full name?'

'I'm Scott – Scott Harris.'

Paola gave him a curt nod. 'Can I see your passport, please?'

'Sure, just let me get it out,' he said, setting down his rucksack, unzipping the pocket at the front where his passport was neatly tucked into its special case. 'Here you go.' He opened it to the page of his unsmiling photo – a picture he'd had taken two years ago, right when things with Justine were at their worst, which looked disconcertingly like a prison mugshot.

'OK, now I will speak to the other man,' she said, turning away from Scott and towards the others, who were still gathered near the doorway, chatting and taking off their wet jackets and shoes. 'Please, everyone, go and take a look around,' she said. Then, addressing Ben: 'I need to talk to you.'

Leaving Ben and Paola to their conversation, Scott followed Luisa further into the building; as she moved, a sequence of lights sprang to life, illuminating the vast room. A gleaming white and silver kitchen with breakfast bar and stools was tucked to the left; in the centre was a sweeping wooden dining table, complete with six purple velvet-covered chairs.

To the right was the living area with a curved, cream sofa made of impossibly soft, silky-looking fabric, burnt orange cushions scattered across it, and a thick oak coffee table in front. Carved wooden ornaments sat on the surfaces; bright works of abstract art lined the walls; tall vases stuffed with vibrant red, orange and yellow hibiscus adorned each table. Through the sliding glass doors at the front of the house, he could make out the glassy surface of the pool.

'Welcome to the *casa*,' said Luisa, beaming. 'We will make everything perfect for you!'

Scott closed his eyes briefly, pictured his front room with

its dated lino flooring and battered leather sofa. Every surface cluttered with paperwork and books and tools and all the things he had nowhere to bloody put.

I couldn't feel further away from my life if I tried – and it's great.

Raised voices tugged him from his thoughts. He glanced behind him, where Ben and Paola were deep in conversation – but this didn't look like small talk, or clearing up some admin. Paola's brows were knitted together, her eyes narrowed. Ben's arms were folded across his body, and he was shaking his head – his whole posture looked defensive. Scott thought he heard Ben say, 'It's not my fault if she didn't give you the right infor- mation,' before Paola shushed him, and they continued in raised whispers. He could no longer make out what they were saying. Scott turned back to the group, noticed Carly also looking in Ben and Paola's direction. He caught her eye. *She'd heard it too.*

'The *casa* uses only drip technology to water the beautiful gardens outside.' Luisa's voice floated towards him. 'And as you can see, our pool is truly one of a kind – under the surface of the pool there are loungers to lie on, and it even plays relaxing music underwater when you swim!' she said.

Music – under the water? Now that, he needed to check out.

'And here is the Wi-Fi, in case any of you need it. The code is written here, but a big storm like this might stop it from working so well. Shall we go upstairs? You will see when we show you your bedrooms, each room has its own special and unique design, inspired by the rainforest – bamboo ceilings, teakwood panels and giant beds. You will even find hammocks and your own cedar hot tubs outside on your personal balcon- ies, where the views of the rainforest will take your air away!'

Scott smiled at Luisa's mistake, and at her excitement – she was right to be this enthusiastic. This place, everything about it, was exceptional.

'And dinner will be served once you're all unpacked. We use only the freshest, finest local ingredients to make your meals,' said Paola, walking towards the group with Ben trailing behind her, a terse smile on her lips. 'Come, now,' she said. 'We will show you to your rooms.'

An hour later, unpacked and refreshed by a dip in his hot tub followed by a long stint in the high-pressure rain shower, Scott was shovelling forkfuls of *gallo pinto* into his mouth, his taste-buds exploding with spicy sweetness. He hadn't realized how hungry he was until Paola had filled his plate with rice, beans and picadillo, the aromas making his mouth water.

'So, what made you all want to come here, on the retreat?' said Carly. 'Have you been fans of Hannah for a while? How long have you been following her online?'

Well, this is an easy one.

'I've been following her for years – I've probably watched all her videos,' said Scott, laughing. 'My mates think I've lost the plot, but she really helped me – I've not always felt like I fit in, and Hannah gave me a community. She made me feel . . . understood.' *When for so much of my life, I've felt like a mystery to everyone – including myself.* 'I couldn't believe it when she announced the competition – the chance to come and actually *meet* her,' he went on. 'I fully poured my heart out in that video.'

He stopped himself from saying the rest: that he'd told Hannah all the things he didn't want anyone else to know in that video: the cruel voice that lived inside his head, the judge-ments it made about everything he said and did. He told her about the way he went through life always *looking* as though he was fitting in – saying the right things, doing what other people thought he should, with his mates, in his job as a park ranger – but that underneath, he was exhausted from the effort. It was as though he was wearing a bodysuit made of malleable plastic that he could only take off when he was at home, alone, with his apartment door closed.

He'd said all that, and then he'd sent the damn video, tried to forget about it and let it go. 'I thought it was a total long shot,' he said. 'So, when I got the email telling me I'd won a place – well, I almost keeled over in shock. Now here I am.'

Here I am. There was a silence around the table. He'd been talking for too long, hadn't he? He felt himself flush. He'd already made a fool of himself, no doubt. Said far too much. *Bloody hell, Scott. All mouth, no brain.*

'OK, me next.' Naya cleared her throat; Scott smiled at her gratefully. 'I started following Hannah about a year ago. Someone recommended her to me – suggested I start watching some of her videos, in case they could help me.' She paused, looked at the others. 'And she did – help me, that is. You remember when she made that series about how we shouldn't always take medical diagnoses at face value – that there is so much that can be done to heal the mind and body when we work with the spirit?'

Scott nodded; he'd watched all Hannah's videos five times at least. 'Western medicine gets so much wrong,' he remembered Hannah saying. 'What so-called doctors call *disease* – everything from dementia to cancer to schizophrenia to Covid – are simply energetic blockages, usually from negative emotions trapped within the body. Once you release these through deep energetic cleansing, you will achieve perfect health.'

'Well, it was just what I needed to hear,' Naya was saying. 'Especially these last few months, when I've been having a hard time – with my kids, working long hours in my nursing job, parenting alone since I split up from their father.'

Her voice wobbled then, and she broke off. Scott felt a pang of something in his chest; he rubbed at his breastbone until it went away. 'I could feel myself slipping down into something . . . somewhere bad,' she said. 'But Hannah, everything she has taught me – she's helped me so much. The idea of having some one-on-one time with her – her making a dedicated programme just for me, helping me find ways to improve mine and my kids' wellbeing – and in such a beautiful place, no expenses spared – well, it was too amazing to miss. Even if . . .' She tailed off again, looked down sadly.

'Even if what?' said Carly, her tone gentle.

Naya met her eyes. 'Even if I've had to leave my young children behind with my mother for the week. That was hard – I've never left them for so long before. In fact, I've never left them at all.'

'Oh, well, I understand that perfectly – it's not stupid at all,' said Ben.

Naya looked at him, eyes hopeful. 'You have children too?'

'Ah, no, not exactly,' he said, looking embarrassed. 'In fact, I'm sorry, it's not the same at all – but I've had to leave my dog Blondie behind. She gets mad when I'm away!'

Naya laughed. 'Well, then, it's almost the same.' Her laugh faded then, and she looked away. 'It feels extra hard, though, leaving my kids – they are autistic,' she said softly. 'I'm honestly not sure how they'll manage without me for a week – even though I know my mother will take good care of them.' Scott heard her voice catch.

'You didn't leave them with their dad?' asked Ben. It sounded blunt to Scott's ears, though he'd been wondering the same thing.

A flash of anger passed across Naya's lovely features, before she said tightly, 'No, I'd never leave them with him.'

'That must be tough for you,' said Carly. 'I've worked with parents of neurodivergent children in therapy, and it's not easy – especially not when you're doing it on your own.'

Naya gave a quick, grateful smile, then seemed to force herself to brighten. 'All the more reason for me to be here – I'm sure Hannah will give me some ideas to help me support them, ease some of the things they struggle with. She seems to know how to deal with anything and everything.'

She turned to the person sitting next to her. 'So, Ben, you next. What made you want to come here?'

Ben leaned back in his chair, shrugged. 'Well, Hannah is something pretty special, I guess,' he said. 'And so is this place – I've always wanted to come to Costa Rica.' He paused, seemed to deliberate over something, then: 'I gotta say, I don't agree with everything she believes in – like some of the stuff about spirit guides is a little far out for me.' Scott bristled at that; why did Hannah want him here if he didn't even believe in all of her teachings?

'But I feel like I've been stuck on the same issues for so long – so when she said that thing about how we would leave here transformed?' Ben said. 'That's what I've been waiting for. I can't carry on the same way. I can't change by myself, so . . .

yeah. I'm here hoping she can help me.' He looked at Mira. 'So, how about you?'

Mira smiled. 'Yes, I loved what she said about leaving here transformed too,' she said. 'In my video, I talked about what a hard time I've been having over the past year or so. About how I'd never travelled outside of Europe, let alone somewhere like Costa Rica. I told her it would be the chance of a lifetime for me, and I'd be open to doing whatever exploration – whatever work – she wanted me to do. And I am – I really am.'

Mira's voice was so gentle, but the passion in her dark eyes, and on her quietly pretty, delicate features, burned through. 'Wow,' said Scott. 'She's made quite an impact on us, hasn't she? Same for you as well, Carly?'

'She changed my life,' said Carly. A shadow passed over her face then, her bright expression faltering. 'I went through something – something hard – a couple of years back. Things with my ex-girlfriend . . . they didn't end well at all. But following Hannah, listening to her – it's what's kept me going.' She smiled. 'And I'm a therapist; I've worked with so many people who are struggling with their mental health.' She sighed. 'Hannah has such a unique take on dealing with things like depression and anxiety. So, everything I learn from her, I can pass on to my clients as well. I can spread Hannah's message.'

Ben shifted in his chair. 'You could spread it more easily if she was actually *here* to teach us, though, right?' he said, his tone harsh.

Scott was starting to get riled up; irritated by Ben's negativity. 'I'm sure she'd be here if she could,' he snapped. 'You've seen the weather outside – it wouldn't be safe for her to try and travel back here now, in that.'

Ben arched an eyebrow. 'Well, sure, but everyone knew the storm was coming – so why did she head out in it right before we were due to arrive?'

'I'm sure she had good reason,' said Carly.

Ben opened his mouth, looked like he was about to protest some more, but was interrupted by Paola's brisk tone from the kitchen area, where she'd been perched on a high stool. 'I will try to call Hannah again,' she said, tapping her phone, holding it to her ear; then a moment later, 'It is still turned off.'

'What?' said Ben. 'Isn't that weird? Why would she turn her phone off?'

Paola shrugged. 'It must be the storm – or maybe she didn't take her charger. All right, she will be back first thing tomorrow morning, then. In the meantime, you can enjoy the relaxing treatments we have prepared for you, and make the most of Hannah's beautiful home.'

'I'm not sure,' said Mira slowly. 'I was looking forward to getting the one-on-one time with Hannah. It seems a shame to miss even these few hours with her, to be honest.'

'But she'll be here when we wake up tomorrow, won't she?' said Scott. 'And maybe there'll be something good to come out of being here, just for the first night, without her. You know, for our own . . . exploration. Our healing? And I mean, look at this place. I still feel like I'm dreaming, being here.'

'Me too,' said Naya. 'I mean, I'm really excited to see Hannah – she's the main reason I'm here – but this house is amazing, Paola – you've done an amazing job for all of us. And Costa Rica is a wonderful country, it's paradise here.' She paused, took a sip of water – she was the only one not drinking wine, Scott noticed.

'Exactly,' said Carly. 'We can relax, enjoy ourselves, make the best of it without her. We need to think positive, not grumble about what's gone wrong.'

Mira looked startled for a second; then she sighed. 'You know what, you're right. This is a once-in-a-lifetime trip. We're so lucky to be here – think of all the thousands of people who applied, and she picked us. I promise I'll stop complaining now and start enjoying myself.'

'Yes, you will all enjoy yourself. I will make sure everything is perfect,' said Paola. 'Now – Luisa will show you around, you will have a relaxing treatment with our personal masseur this evening, and you will all sleep well – then Hannah will be back in the morning.'

She took a moment to look around the group in turn.

'Everything is going to be wonderful,' she said.

Scott knew she was right. This retreat – Hannah – all of it *was* going to be wonderful.

So why, then, did Paola sound like she was trying to convince herself?

BEN

Hannah's place was *insane*.

Ben had stayed at some expensive resorts in his time; one of the perks of travelling so much for work – but this was something else. The attention to detail, the little touches – like the petals arranged across their beds; the homemade soaps with *H* stamped in the middle; the exquisite hand-bound journals for recording their wellness journeys – Hannah had thought about everything, and it showed.

Like he'd admitted at dinner, he didn't agree with *all* the things Hannah talked about – like some of the wacky spiritual stuff, and her insistence that modern medicine couldn't be trusted, that natural, holistic treatments were the answer; Ben was only too aware of the benefits of American pharmaceuticals. But this place, The Hideaway – this was one thing she'd got just right.

They'd finished up their food – Paola bringing them freshly made *tres leches* for dessert, its texture almost unnaturally light and fluffy. It was a Costa Rican speciality, and even now, a half hour later, its sweet creaminess was sitting pleasantly on his tongue. Carly and Scott had headed up to their rooms, but he'd taken a post-dinner *digestif* outside and was now sitting on one of the bed-sized recliners near the pool, Mira and Naya settled on the one next to his, and all of them sheltered snugly under the extending roof. Solar-powered lanterns shaped like perfume bottles dotted the terrace around them, giving the space a warm glow. Above their heads hung three ceiling fans, their gold blades whipping a welcome breeze – even in the storm, it was humid; Ben's skin was damp to the touch.

'This is the life, isn't it?' said Mira. 'It's still so warm out here – and it's kind of soothing, listening to the rain hammering on the roof.'

'I know. I can't believe how relaxed I feel already,' said Naya.

Ben smiled at her, let his gaze linger on her face, her eyelids gently closed, long lashes flickering slightly, lips settled in a sleepy, relaxed pout. Naya was sexy, for sure, but not really his type; with the addition of two kids, even less so.

He made a soft grunt of agreement, then took a long, deep puff on his vape, blew it out of his mouth. Mira was right: this was the life. Already the worries of the past few days seemed like they belonged to another life – another person. Now, they just needed Hannah to get here, and everything would be exactly as it was supposed to be. He'd leave here just as Hannah had promised: transformed.

'And that food,' he said. 'Paola is a genius. I ate like a king at dinner – if we get fed like that every day, you guys are going to have to roll me back to the airport.'

Both women laughed, just as the sliding French doors whooshed open behind them. Ben turned and smiled at Luisa as she walked towards him.

'Sorry, Ben, you cannot smoke out here,' she said, with an apologetic bob of her head.

'Oh, I'm not smoking,' laughed Ben. 'It's just a vape.'

'Ah, no vaping either – I am very sorry,' Luisa said. 'This is Hannah's rules.'

Hannah's rules, huh? Well, in that case, he'd better do as he was told. 'No problem,' he said, flashing Luisa his broadest smile and tucking away his vape. He didn't need it now, anyway: at just the mention of Hannah's name, Ben felt the familiar buzz of excitement that she seemed to stir in him. He might not even need the pill packet he'd tucked carefully into the side pocket of his suitcase.

'Ben, I can take you for your treatment now?' said Luisa. 'We have prepared for you an aromatherapy massage with The Hideaway's personal masseuse, Isabel.' Luisa gestured inside the house. 'She is waiting for you in one of our treatment rooms.'

'Oh, lucky you, Ben,' murmured Naya lazily. 'I can't wait to have mine – that will be the perfect end to this evening.'

Ben felt another tingle of anticipation. This place got better and better. He'd never needed a massage more, after the stress of the past few days, plus that long-ass plane ride and the bumpy drive to The Hideaway. He stretched upwards on the sunbed, swung his legs to the floor and luxuriated in a long stretch, groaning as he did.

'It looks like you are already feeling relaxed?' said Luisa with a gentle laugh. 'I am happy to see this.'

He smiled and followed Luisa inside, registering the cold shock of the air conditioning as he stepped through the sliding doors. Its artificial coolness brought his high-rise office block in Silicon Hills to mind – the image slamming into his brain before he could stop it; and with it the memory of Trish, the way she'd looked at him across her mahogany desk just a few days ago, Ben staring at the floor, hands twisting in his lap.

No. Stop it, Ben. Put the thoughts away. He couldn't let them cross his mind now, distract him from such a great evening.

Luisa, walking in front of him through the house, came to a stop outside a door that led off the back of the main kitchen and living room area. It opened into a small, windowless, pure white treatment room with a massage bed in its centre, glass diffusers billowing out lemongrass fragrance on a corner shelf, gentle spa music playing from a cream, oval-shaped speaker. The woman standing in the room looked to be in her late forties, short and squat with bobbed black hair and strong-looking forearms emerging from her white tunic.

'This is Isabel,' said Luisa. 'Ben, you filled in the treatment forms, yes? Telling us about medical history, giving your consent for products. You did this when you arrived?'

'Yeah,' said Ben. 'And I'm good with anything – come on then, Isabel, do your worst on these aching muscles.' He gave her a wink.

'*Hola*,' said Isabel, returning his smile. 'Of course. Please, change into this robe, then lie down on your front and place your head into the hole here. I will give you a moment of privacy.'

Luisa and Isabel stepped outside of the room, closing the door gently behind them, and Ben did as he was told, stripping out of his shirt and shorts, slipping into the robe, enjoying the touch of soft fabric on his skin. A moment later, Isabel returned, lathered her hands with sweet-smelling oil and got to work, performing long, gliding strokes along the taut muscles of his back and shoulders.

'This pressure is good?' she asked, after a moment of kneading with increasing firmness.

'Mmm. Just right, thanks.'

As he lay there, lulled by the soft music and rhythmic movements, Ben's mind began to drift again, out of his control. The same memory that had been playing on repeat was coming back to taunt him, even here, blissed out on a massage table, hundreds of miles away from where it had all played out.

How could Trish have done it? How could she have believed what she heard – and acted on it so fast? She didn't even know the facts – the background. And even with what she knew, surely her decision was too rash. Ben had brought more new business to that overhyped fintech in the past two years than his predecessor had in the decade before. Ben lived and breathed that job: the high of new prospects, the rush of sealing deals. Now he was here, about as far from a client meeting in a hushed boardroom as he could get.

With the image of Trish in his mind – the memory of what had happened right before he'd come here – Ben's fingers curled themselves into fists.

'Try to relax, please, Ben,' said Isabel. 'You are tensing your whole body.'

'Ah – sorry. Of course,' he said, doing his best to breathe more deeply, to stretch his hands back out.

This wasn't the time, or the place, to go over all that.

It was in the past. While he was here, and with Hannah's help, he could start to properly put all of this behind him.

Yes, he reminded himself. He was here now. And he was going to get exactly what he came for.

CARLY

Carly's phone told her it was five in the morning. So she'd been trying to get some rest, on and off, for the best part of six hours, on a king-size four-poster bed that looked so new and expensive she felt weird disturbing it by *sleeping* on it.

It was pointless: her mind was alert, her legs twitchy. An hour or so ago, while she was downstairs refilling her bottle with filtered water, she'd thought about shoving her walking boots back on and letting her restless feet take her out into the elements. But the bucketing rain soon changed her mind; where would she even go? She'd taken her water and gone back to bed.

For fuck's sake, Carly, go to sleep. She was meant to be relaxing, wasn't she? And this place, tonight – well, it was the ideal time to chill out, get some proper rest before the real work began. She should be drifting off into blissful oblivion on her perfectly form-fitting mattress.

Insomnia wasn't normally an issue for her; she never struggled with either falling or staying asleep, even when things were tough. Amongst her sisters, her friends, Robyn – anyone who'd had the privilege of sharing a room with her – her ability to sleep like the dead was a running joke. A couple of years back, on a girls' weekend away for someone's birthday up in Chester, her mate Julie said she'd been doing an ear-splitting rendition of Katy Perry on the karaoke machine at the bottom of Carly's bed; Carly – like a Welsh, thirty-something Sleeping Beauty – didn't stir.

But here, in a tropical hideaway of all places, she was struggling. She was jittery, wired; her legs wouldn't stop fidgeting under the covers; she was tossing and turning non-stop. And it didn't help that someone – one of the other guests – kept walking around on the ground floor. She'd wondered at first if it was one of the staff, but then she remembered Luisa saying that she and Paola stayed in separate lodges behind the main building, so it could only be another guest. Carly couldn't hear them, but her bedroom faced the stairs which led to the open-plan room downstairs, and through the gap underneath her door, she could see the lights below flickering on and off. She'd tried to block it out with her eye-mask, but now the idea of a restless soul wandering about below had taken root, and she couldn't shake it off.

The tropical storm seemed to have died down now, after hours of violent winds buffeting the roof above her, sheets of rain battering the windows. At one point, it was so heavy she'd been worried the thick glass might shatter, with what sounded like pails of water smashing against her window. It was the loudest, longest storm she'd ever witnessed – not even the last time she was in a rainforest was there something like this – and she couldn't imagine how they'd even step outside in the morning.

This is no use. Carly whipped off her sheets, swung her feet down onto the cool marble floor. Her mind floated back to the evening: a peaceful, relaxing night punctuated by the sounds of thunder and the electricity going on and off as the relentless wind downed the pylons higher in the mountains. The sharp tang of Paola's *ceviche*; the pressure of Isabel's firm hands on her neck and shoulders, kneading away the discomfort of her long journey here.

She thought about her fellow guests. She noticed her mind making its usual quick assumptions about each of them – *addict, loner, trauma survivor, co-dependent* – the snap judgements that her training had taught her, and which now she found impossible to switch off. It happened every time she met new people, even though she knew it displayed a gross lack of boundaries, something she'd hate if anyone did it to her.

Focus, Carly – you're not here to be a therapist.

Apart from the storm, the evening had passed without drama; it had been nice enough. The conversation over dinner had been easy – chatting about where they were from, what they did, how they felt about Hannah, why they were here. They seemed like a good bunch of people: self-aware, kind, considerate, for the most part. Clearly Hannah had chosen her group well. And Naya was gorgeous; there was a warmth about her that reminded her of Robyn, even though they were nothing alike physically.

Draining her glass of water now, pushing thoughts of Robyn out of her mind – that was the last thing she needed, if she was trying to sleep – Carly stood up, stretched, felt her eyelids flicker; perhaps finally, she was ready to get some rest.

When her eyes opened again, she was surprised to see light trickling through the edges of the heavy silk curtains lining her bedroom window. She checked the time on her phone: it was gone eight. She'd had a few hours' sleep then. *That'll do.*

She got up, luxuriated in her rain shower for a few minutes, then dressed in a vest and leggings and opened her bedroom door, listening for the others; there was only silence. She slipped down to the kitchen, taking in the stunning view outside, the still waters of the pool, the lush green leaves and bright red and pink flowers at the garden's edge. On the dining room table was a spread of fresh fruit, filled pastries, brightly coloured juices and steaming percolators of coffee, their toasty scent reaching her nostrils. Her stomach rumbled.

'Ah, you are awake!' Paola strode into the kitchen, ushered Carly towards a seat at the table and filled her mug with coffee. As Carly took a sip, a clicking sound came from the front door. Luisa, dressed in the same crisp white linen tunic and trousers as yesterday, stepped inside the house, waved and gave Carly a broad smile.

'Good morning, Carly. I hope you slept well! Paola has made a delicious breakfast for you, of course,' she said. Then, looking around: 'Hannah is here now?'

Carly was about to respond, but she was interrupted. 'Well, if Hannah's here, I sure haven't seen her.' It was Ben, his voice coming from the bottom of the stairs. He ambled into the kitchen, yawning, plaid shirt undone, revealing what looked like a ten-pack of abs on a perfectly smooth torso – waxed, Carly assumed, to within an inch of its life – as he stretched his arms above his head.

'Anyone else up?' he asked.

'Nope,' Carly replied, with a shrug. 'Not yet, anyway.'

Mira wandered into the kitchen behind Ben, and Carly startled when she saw her: perhaps it was because she'd just woken up, but Mira looked paler and even more delicate in the morning light, and positively minuscule in an oversized blue sundress. And her hair – which Carly was sure, now, could only be a wig – was fixed at an angle, one side sloping down further towards her neck. She looked fragile, and Carly felt a sudden rush of care for her; a desire to wrap her up in a blanket, keep her safe, like she'd done with her most vulnerable clients.

Like she'd done with Robyn when they were having their difficult days, she realized, with a hot pang in her chest.

Paola shuffled somewhere near Carly's shoulder. 'No, Hannah is not back,' she said. 'Perhaps she is stuck somewhere on the road – it is probably not safe to come back by boat yet. But she will be here soon. At least the storm is over now, and it was not so bad as they said . . .'

That storm? Not so bad? Carly wondered what a *bad* storm here would be like, in that case.

'Ah, *sí*, she has probably got caught somewhere,' agreed Luisa. 'But the water will start to move away in the next few hours, I am sure.'

She paused and turned to wave at Scott as he arrived downstairs, with Naya a few steps behind him. Naya looked pale and washed out; perhaps she hadn't slept much, either.

'Good morning to you both!' said Luisa. 'Hannah will be here soon – until then, you can eat, drink, and we have a fabulous morning prepared for you all.'

'Hannah is still a little delayed by the weather,' explained Paola, in response to the questioning look on Naya's face. 'There's some flooding in the area that must be stopping her from getting back. But it is not a problem – you will still enjoy this morning with us.'

'Sounds great,' said Scott, and Naya nodded her agreement, as the five of them joined Carly at the table and filled their plates with various fruits, tortillas and *salchichón*.

'What's the plan for today then?' asked Scott, pouring coffee into a mug. 'Hannah emailed an itinerary, but it was pretty loose, from what I remember – just a couple of activities scheduled each day, with plenty of time left for our one-on-one work with her.'

'Didn't she put something about a waterfall in the email itinerary?' said Naya. 'I really hope so – the pictures of it looked incredible. I'm dying to see it and go for a swim.'

'Yes, this is true,' said Paola. 'But first for this morning, we have planned a sound bath, which our specialist practitioner Thiago will lead for you when he arrives, and then . . .'

Paola's words faded as a text bleeped on someone's phone.

First one; then another.

Then another.

All at the same time.

There was only one possible sender.

NAYA

Naya set down her fork and reached into her pocket for her phone. Truth be told, she didn't have much of an appetite – she was grateful for the distraction from her full plate of food. She'd surprised herself by managing to sleep deeply last night in spite of the storm, but the rest had done nothing to ease the queasiness sitting in her belly. She tried to shake away the tremor of anxiety she felt about what it meant.

'It must be Hannah,' said Carly.

Naya glanced at her screen. 'Oh yes, I have a text from her – did you all get it too?'

'Yes,' said Mira. 'Let's all read it together on my phone. Hang on, there's something else coming through, but it's a little slow to download – perhaps the Wi-Fi isn't back up to full speed after the storm . . . Paola, Luisa, do you want to look at this with us?' The two women came over to stand at Mira's shoulder, and they stared at the phone. A photo of Hannah's face filled the screen; behind her was a view of the beach, its white sand and balmy trees similar to the coastline the taxi had driven along yesterday.

Paola nodded. '*Sí*. She is in Golfito.'

Naya frowned, as the thought occurred to her: 'Hasn't she messaged you too, Paola? Or Luisa?' Both women shook their heads. Strange that she'd not been in touch with her staff – but somehow reassuring that she was contacting them directly. It showed how much Hannah cared about them and their experience here.

Mira scrolled to the message below, and they listened to her as she read it out, Hannah's way of writing sounding strange in a British accent. 'Hey y'all! Here I am at the beach, waiting for a boat to take me back to Osa after last night's storm. The water is still rough, the tide is high and there's not going to be a boat back for hours! I've tried to find a taxi to take me the long way around, but they're saying there's been a landslide on the road out of Golfito and it's too dangerous to drive. So it looks like I'll be held up a little longer.'

Another message dinged through on everyone's phones. Mira opened it and continued reading: 'I'm sorry I wasn't there with you last night, and that you've had to start the retreat without me. But I hope you'll still enjoy your experience at The Hideaway. Over the next few days, you will be healing and becoming the person you are meant to be in your very own, bespoke programme! In a minute, I'll send instructions for what you're doing today. I can't wait to see you all later – I'm doing everything I can to get back to you all. Bye, beloveds!'

Mira stopped reading. Ben set his glass down on the table with a thud. 'I guess we'll just wait here for her *instructions*, then,' he said, a throb of sarcasm in his voice.

'Let's try calling her,' suggested Scott. 'She must be online now – she just sent those messages.'

'Good idea,' agreed Paola, picking her phone up from the kitchen counter, scrolling, then holding it to her ear. She waited for a moment, the group watching her expectantly, then shook her head. 'Her phone is still turned off.'

'Well, let's send her a text, then,' said Ben. He picked his phone up, just as another message tone sounded.

'It's Hannah again. These must be the instructions for the day,' said Mira. She held the phone up for Paola to see; started to read it out loud.

'Now, even though I'm not there, you can start today's activities. I know this isn't going to be the same as it would be if I was there with you, and I'm so sorry! But it can still be a wonderful day.' That answered that then – they'd stick to Hannah's plan.

Another message pinged and Scott read it aloud this time: 'After this morning's treatments, you will take a walk to our very own private waterfall in The Hideaway's rainforest, where you can swim in the crystal waters. Paola will tell you how to get there – it's only a little over an hour away, and the walk is easy, even on wet ground. Before you leave, please turn off your phones, laptops, smart watches and tablets and place them inside the hallway cabinet – they'll be safe there until you return. It's so important to give yourselves this digital detox so you can benefit from being here! Take the map of the rain-forest from the cabinet near the front door, and the satellite phone, so you can contact someone in case of emergencies. You'll also find an eco-friendly spray paint – take that to mark the trees to help you find your way back. Have an awesome time, and see you later!'

Naya glanced around the group; she saw Paola frowning at

Mira's screen. 'Would you mind if I take a look at your phone, please?' asked Paola. 'I need to check something.'

'Oh, yes – sure,' said Mira, handing it to her. Paola held both Mira's and her own phone in front of her, her eyes moving back and forth between the two screens.

'Ah – it is not the same number,' said Paola in a low voice. She turned to Luisa, spoke quickly in Spanish; as Naya watched, Luisa's eyes widened briefly, but just as fast, she fixed her expression back to its usual smile. 'It must be a new phone,' said Paola. 'This is a Costa Rican number, but the one I have for her is American. She did say she would get a local SIM – I'm sure that's what she was doing in Golfito.'

A gentle knock at the front door interrupted her before anyone could respond.

'Good, Thiago is here,' said Paola. 'Luisa, let him in, please.' Naya watched as Luisa opened the door and a tall, attractive man with dark hair and piercing blue eyes stepped into the house, carrying a pile of mats, blankets and cushions, as well as a heavy-looking black holdall. He smiled at the group and gestured towards the roofed area next to the pool.

'Please, take your time with your breakfast,' he said, his voice deep and melodic. 'When you have finished, come and join me outside.'

They did as they were told; Naya even managed to swallow down a few mouthfuls of a sweet pastry, before her stomach started to curdle again. *You remember the last time you felt like this, don't you? You're going to have to find out for sure, sooner or later.* The words were a cruel whisper at the edges of her mind. She forced them away, tried to focus on taking small sips of water instead.

Oh God. Perhaps she shouldn't have come here, especially feeling like this. She thought she was doing this for all the right reasons – but was this just another one of her impulsive, reckless decisions? A decision that was impacting more than just her.

It's just a few days, she told herself. *And remember why you're here.* It surged through her again – the wild hope she'd felt that this trip might give her some of the answers she needed on how to better help herself and her children. That it was a chance for someone to take care of Naya for a change, instead of her looking after everyone else 24/7. And in the meantime, the kids would be having a wonderful time, being spoilt rotten by their *mamie*. This should be a good thing, truly, for all of them.

She was desperate to see their faces now, to hear their voices. She hadn't managed to call since she'd got here: they'd have been fast asleep back home when she arrived last night, and waking them just to FaceTime would have left both children unsettled for the rest of the day. They would be finding it hard enough without her as it was; she couldn't risk making it worse. She hadn't expected to sleep for so long on her first night here, but she was exhausted from the flight and the change in time zones, and her body clearly needed its rest.

So, when she'd got up this morning, she'd called her mother, but of course the kids were still at school – and soon she'd have to put her phone away and set off into the rainforest. She'd not get to talk to them until they were back at the house. '*Merde,*' she whispered to herself. Maybe she should have set an alarm and called home at midnight, while they were up and eating breakfast. *Why didn't I think of that?*

'Naya? Are you joining us?' Scott's voice reached her; his gentle eyes were searching her out.

'I just need a moment,' she said.

Scott looked at the others, then back at Naya. 'Can I wait with you?' he said.

She smiled. 'Be my guest.'

Scott took a seat at the table next to her; they sat there silently for a while, but it wasn't awkward. It was comfortable; natural, somehow. He made her feel quite at ease.

'How are you doing?' he said, after a moment. 'Is it hard, being away from your little ones?'

Her stomach clenched again at the thought of them without her – missing her, needing her. 'Yes, it is, to be honest – it just feels so strange, leaving them.' He nodded but said nothing. She appreciated that: too many people rushed to try to make things better, to offer solutions to problems they understood little about. But she rarely wanted that; she wanted someone to hear her. To give her the space to talk, to hold her emotionally – physically too, sometimes.

She swallowed down another rush of nausea, and turned to look at Scott then, really look at him. His eyes were a pale green with flecks of hazel and his face was tanned, weathered, as though he spent much of his time outdoors. The gentle creases around the sides of his eyes and his cheeks made his kind face look even kinder; it was the sort of face that belonged to someone who felt things deeply and kept smiling anyway. She liked it – him, perhaps – in a way that felt warm and good and unsettling all at once.

'What – is there something in my beard?' said Scott, moving a hand to his face.

Naya laughed. 'Oh no – I'm sorry, I didn't mean to stare at you like that. I was just . . .' She tailed off, feeling awkward suddenly, vulnerable. Her expression always seemed to give her thoughts away – perhaps he could sense that she was enjoying looking at him; that she felt the first stirrings of attraction towards him.

He smiled. 'It's OK,' he said, his gaze fixed on hers now, then quietly: 'I actually liked it.'

Naya sensed the heat rushing to her cheeks, and felt a sudden urge to move away from this unexpected intimacy.

'We should really go and . . .' She pointed to Thiago and the others outside. Scott nodded.

'Yeah,' he said. 'We probably should.'

They stood up and went to join Thiago outside.

'Welcome, everyone, to the deeply restorative experience of the sound bath,' Thiago was saying. 'For the next hour, I am going to make a variety of sounds that will create healing vibrations, while you lie down, relax and listen. Try to still your minds and focus only on the sounds. You will finish this session feeling relaxed, refreshed and calm. Now, please take a yoga mat, blanket and pillow, and get yourselves comfortable. When you are ready, I invite you to close your eyes and breathe deeply as the vibrations wash over you.'

The group did as he asked, and Thiago began making a soft, pulsating sound with a singing bowl, its pitch and volume rising and falling hypnotically. Listening to it, Naya felt herself drifting away. She was exhausted, drained – and she knew it wasn't just jet lag. An hour later, blissed out to the point of stupor, the sound bath was over; Thiago was asking them to come back to their bodies, open their eyes.

Paola was waiting for them by the French windows. 'OK, everyone? I hope you are relaxed. Now, take a cold drink, then you will go for a beautiful walk to the waterfall and bathe in the water,' she said. 'I have prepared some snacks for you to enjoy while you are there. You will have a wonderful time.'

'Oh, *sí*,' said Luisa, appearing behind Paola and beaming at them. 'It is one of the most stunning waterfalls I have seen in Costa Rica, and you can only get to it from Hannah's land – the pool at the bottom is so clear, you can see all the fish! When you come back, Isabel will come to give you a hot stone massage, then Hannah will be here for evening meditation, and we'll serve you another delicious meal.'

'I don't know,' Mira said, yawning. 'Shouldn't we have a guide, if we're going into the rainforest? Do any of us have experience trekking somewhere like this?'

'I do, actually,' Carly said, smiling. 'I spent a month in the Amazon, a few years back – plenty of walking in the wilderness. I'm happy to guide us.'

'Anyway, there is no need for a guide,' said Paola. 'The walk is not too far – like Hannah said, only a little over an hour to get there. The path is not very difficult. Everybody is fit and healthy, yes? This will be no problem for you all.'

Naya caught Mira's eye, gave her what she hoped was a reassuring smile. She felt drawn towards this small, gentle woman. There was a vulnerability to her, underlined with a quiet resolve. Naya needed more of her composure: Mira looked as if she knew how to hold herself together; she didn't look like the sort of person who was always running late, or who'd speak out of turn at work. She didn't look like the kind of woman who'd have a complaint filed against her for saying far too much, on impulse.

Unlike me.

Naya couldn't let herself think about that now. Mira still looked unconvinced about the idea of the hike, but soon seemed buoyed up by the others' excitement as they chattered about the delicious selection of treats Paola had arranged for them and whether or not to wear their swimsuits now or change at the waterfall.

Fifteen minutes later, her bag packed with water, the food Paola had prepared for her, plus a towel, her first aid kid, some insect repellent – and with her phone stowed in the hallway cabinet as instructed – Naya waited for the others at the front door. Carly and Scott came down next, then Mira.

For several minutes, there was no sign of their fifth companion.

'Ben? Are you nearly ready?' Naya called up the stairs. A moment later, they heard his footsteps on the stairs, and he emerged, a little red in the face.

'All OK?' Carly said. Then, without waiting for an answer, 'Everyone packed? I've got the map and the satellite phone.' She showed them the folded square of paper and a bulky black phone that looked like a cross between an ancient Nokia and a walkie-talkie. *Let's hope there are no emergencies, then.*

'I found some torches in the cabinet too,' said Scott. 'Shall we take them in case there's any plants or insects we want to get a closer look at?'

Naya smiled. 'Great idea,' she said.

'And shall we have a look at the route before we go?' said Scott.

'Yep, here we are.' Carly unfolded the simple black-and-white printed map, stamped with Hannah's branded logo in the bottom right-hand corner, and traced a line with her finger from the house to an image of a waterfall with a circle drawn around it in red. 'Just looks like one path the whole way. It should be straightforward.'

Naya swallowed back another wave of nausea. 'Great,' she said. 'Let's do this, shall we?'

BEN

As he stepped into the open, the humidity hit Ben like he'd opened the door to a steam bath, the air so thick you could cut it with a knife. With the damp heat came an explosion of sounds, kept at bay to an impressive extent by the house's thick glass. When ensconced inside The Hideaway, he'd almost forgotten they were in the middle of a jungle, but there was no escaping it now, as the trills and cries of a thousand birds and insects roared around him. The ground beneath his feet slipped and slid as he walked, last night's rain turning everything to mush.

He was a little out of sorts this morning, even after the highs of last night and the sound bath earlier: the beginnings of the itch he always needed to scratch, plus the memory of saying goodbye to Blondie yesterday – leaving her at the doggie boarding house, her chocolate eyes so liquid they looked like they were melting – sitting heavy on his chest.

And it felt strange that Hannah wasn't here. Leaving those messages, but her phone being switched off straight after. It was bothering him.

He shook the thoughts away. He was just too hot and

sweaty – the heat always made him cranky, and despite the clouds that still hovered above, it was hotter than hell out here, the humidity far more intense than back in Austin, the damp air cloying in his nostrils.

Once they'd reached the pavilion, passing Paola's jeep and the clearing next to it, there was a small wooden signpost bedded into the mulchy brown earth, pointing to a pathway through the forest.

'*To the waterfall*,' read Naya. 'Great, it's this way.'

They picked their way carefully amongst the branches, rocks and mud. Occasionally Ben paused to glance further up the path, trying to get a sense of the route. But the canopy of trees bathed the track in shade, the heavy foliage constructing a jade curtain that disguised anything more than twenty feet ahead.

His backpack snagged on a low-hanging branch; for a second, he thought it was going to tear away from his body altogether. A wave of panic ran through him, then passed. *It's OK; my bag is on my back.* In his room, he'd had no idea what to pack for the walk – he'd spent twenty minutes putting things in his bag and taking them out again while the others waited for him. In the end, he'd settled for a towel and a spare T-shirt, a bottle of water, Paola's food and some insect repellent – a hasty airport buy.

And one more thing. Something he'd grabbed from the kitchen while the others were busy in their rooms – something to protect himself in case they ran into a hungry predator of some kind – a jaguar, perhaps. Paola had assured them the route they were taking was safe, yes, but it was still a jungle; who knew what they might need to defend themselves from?

Bag packed, he'd heard Naya call out to him. He'd been

about to head downstairs when, at the last minute, he'd paused; and waited for the familiar, inevitable conversation, the eternal internal struggle to play out in his head:

Don't do it, don't do it.

But if I just take one . . . surely one won't hurt – one barely does anything.

You know where it leads, though. You can never just take one.

I know, but . . . fuck it, I'll just keep them in my bag – just in case.

And then he'd hurried back to his suitcase, taken out the foil packet tucked in its lining and shoved it into a side pocket of his rucksack before joining the others. At the front door, his eyes had landed on the hallway cabinet, where he'd dutifully placed his phone after breakfast. It didn't feel good – he'd have felt better if he could just have checked his emails, sent one more message to Trish before they left. But there was no time; the others were there, waiting for him. And besides – what more was there to say? He'd already spent too long hunched next to the Wi-Fi router in the middle of the night, walking up and down, triggering those goddamn lights on and off, trying to get enough of a signal to reply to Trish's email. The words swam in front of his eyes now:

I hope you're doing well, Ben. I'm sorry for what was said in our last conversation. I hope you know I want the best for you. I trust you'll do what's needed to put things right.

The *compassion* in her eyes when she'd told him to go and 'get himself together', that was the worst part. He couldn't bear the pity – he didn't need it. There was nothing that wrong with him. OK, he worked too hard. And yes, he liked a little boost now and then, a spur, something to help him to focus – to help him achieve his best. But it was because he was ambitious. He always had been; it was what growing up like he did had taught him: that success was everything, and financial success was the kind that mattered most.

Ben's cheeks felt warm; he didn't like going there – remembering where he'd come from. He brushed the thoughts away, focused on the rainforest. He was starting to enjoy the trek now. The downpour had made the ground slippery, and they had to be careful to navigate the fallen branches and vines underfoot, but it was sort of fun, too – splashing through puddles, picking across rocks and stones and mulchy earth. He felt like a kid, playing in the wild, exhilarated by mud and dirt and water; the kind of thing he'd never got to do when he was *actually* a kid. Perhaps he could make up for some of that now.

The wildlife along their walk was breathtaking: howler monkeys swinging from branch to branch, brightly coloured parrots and toucans nestled in the thick foliage above their heads. He even thought he saw a sloth in one of the trees, but it was too far away to make out for sure. As the track got narrower and the vegetation around them thicker, Scott had taken on the role of track marker: every few minutes, Ben saw him spray a trunk with a small speck of white paint.

'It feels wrong to spray these beautiful old trees with this stuff,' said Naya. 'Like you're desecrating them somehow.'

'Don't worry – this stuff washes off easily with a bit of water. We can do it on our way back,' said Scott, touching Naya gently on the shoulder – was that a touch of flirtation, perhaps? *Well, why not, I guess?* He'd probably try to turn on the charm with Naya himself, if he weren't so distracted by thoughts of Hannah and where she was. Or on Carly, who was hot too, although she'd mentioned last night that she was into women, hadn't she? A shame. He wasn't especially attracted to either woman, but he liked the thrill of it; the validation of someone wanting him.

After an hour or so of walking, they tuned into the sound of rushing water. 'I think we're almost there,' said Mira. Her voice was wistful, and now Ben looked at her and noticed something new. *She's different out here.* There was colour in her cheeks; and though she looked tired, there was something else: a sparkle to her since they'd come out into the rainforest, and it made her look alive – and something more. He searched for the word, landed on it at last: *ethereal.*

Soon, the space between the mammoth leaves that had been dripping fat raindrops onto their heads began to expand, the path widened and the rushing sound became a roar. The trees thinned out, gradually giving way to a solid bank of mud, engorged by the rainfall, and then . . . the most stunning view Ben had ever seen. A large clearing, where a tall, wide, torrent of water tumbled over rocks that had formed into an almost perfect staircase.

The waterfall frothed into a gorgeous, green-blue pool that looked as if it had been dramatically swollen by the rain, almost bursting out of its banks. From the pool, the water cascaded down a rushing stream and disappeared around a corner. Ben's jaw dropped as he spun around, taking it all in: it was breathtaking.

'This place is stunning,' said Carly, raising her voice over the crashing water. 'Look how clear the water is! Does anyone want to join me for a dip? Naya?'

'I'll come,' Scott said, smiling at Carly. 'If the invitation's open to me?'

'Of course!'

Mira shook her head. 'Are you sure it's a good idea?' she said. 'The current looks quite strong, and it might be deep, after the rain . . .'

'It'll be fine,' said Carly. 'The water's still pretty shallow – I reckon it'll only reach our knees – see?'

Ben watched as Carly and Scott picked their way across the rocky ground to the edge of the water, stripped down to their swimsuits and started to wade into the frothing pool, splashing and shrieking with laughter.

'It's gorgeous – you've got to come in, guys!' shouted Carly.

'Screw it,' said Ben. 'I'm doing it.'

'And me,' said Naya. 'Mira – will you join us?'

'Ah – I think I'll just stay here and watch you all,' she said, waving them off. Naya and Ben trod a careful path across the slippery rocks to the edge of the pool, took their clothes off and lowered themselves into the water. It was deliciously cool, and crystal clear – Ben laughed in amazement as a shoal of small red and yellow fish began circling his ankle.

'It's incredible here,' said Naya. 'I know it's not how we thought the first day would be, and it's a shame Hannah's not with us – but still. I'm so glad we're here, doing this.'

Ben turned to smile at her. 'Me too.' And he meant it; he was at ease. He was going to enjoy it here. He just needed to relax.

He felt a drop of water land on his head; at first, he thought it had reached him from the waterfall. But as he looked up, he saw it was raining. Small droplets at first. Then, so fast he barely had time to register the change, the drops turned into sheets, heavy lashings of water that slapped him so hard he could barely breathe.

'Quick, guys, let's get out of here and take cover,' he called to the others, helping Naya out of the pool and towards a dry spot under a nearby tree's branches, waving to Mira, then to Carly and Scott to join them. The five of them waited under the shelter of the tree for the heaviest of the rain to pass; for ten, fifteen minutes, there was no let-up.

Gradually, the thunderous pelting became a steadier shower. Next to him, Ben noticed Mira wobble and reach out a hand to the trunk of the tree to balance herself. The pelting rain and the walk in this heat and humidity – it seemed like it was a lot for her.

'I think we should head back to the house,' he said. 'The rain's letting up – we can start walking now, right? And Hannah might be back by now – I don't want to miss out on any time with her.'

'Yeah, I wouldn't mind getting back and having a sit down – or maybe even a nap,' said Mira. 'The jet lag's hitting me a bit now, I think.'

'Of course – let's just take the walk nice and slow,' said Carly, touching Mira gently on the shoulder. 'And hopefully when we get back, Hannah will be waiting for us.'

'Shall we eat something before we go?' suggested Scott. 'It might give you some strength, Mira.'

Mira nodded, and the group crouched over their damp backpacks, pulling out the selection of snacks and fruit Paola had provided, along with bottles of water, and began tucking in. Once they were done, they packed the leftovers away and stood up.

With Mira now leading the way and Ben at the rear, they stepped out from under the tree and headed towards the track. Seeing that the muddy bank had swollen even further, looked even looser, after this fresh bout of rain, Ben called out to warn the others: 'Make sure you stay away from the slope here – now there's been even more rain, it could be—'

But he didn't get to finish his sentence. Mira was a few steps ahead of the others now, and he watched, frozen to the spot, as she stumbled over a slippery rock on the path and threw a hand out towards the slope at the side of the path to steady herself.

And then there was a deafening roar, as a huge chunk of the earth next to them began to rumble and shake.

'Mira!' he yelled, willing her to move, to get out of the way, seeing that she was directly in the path of the rapidly plunging hillside, but for some reason he couldn't understand she stood stock still, as if her feet were locked in place – she looked as though she couldn't move a muscle, even if she'd wanted to.

Carly and Naya and Scott lunged towards her, Ben at their heels, as in unison they tried to reach her, attempted to yank her out of the way.

But they had to stop themselves before they got there. They could only look on in mute horror as the bank of mud rushed downwards and covered the chunk of track where, half a second ago, Mira had been standing.

MIRA

Her feet had refused to obey her brain.

The split second when Mira had heard the earth rumble, when she'd felt the bizarre sensation of the ground next to her slipping, sliding away – she'd tried to move. She'd known that was what she needed to do; her survival instincts were still intact. But she'd frozen, stuck to the spot, helpless as the tower of mud rushed towards her.

Then when it hit her, the sensation was something akin to standing next to the sea and being hit by a huge, crashing wave; at least, that was the closest comparison she could come up with. She was hurled backwards, flattened to the ground by the force of the sodden earth. And now she was under here, paralysed – yet, somehow, still able to take shallow breaths.

How am I breathing?

Vaguely, Mira was aware that the bulk of the sodden earth had covered her body, from her collarbone downwards. Perhaps it was the way she'd been standing; the way she'd fallen. Perhaps it was sheer, dumb luck. But her neck, her head, both were covered by only a thin layer of water; she could move her head from side to side a little. The tip of her nose could feel air; she could inhale it. She tried to open her eyes, managed to crack her eyelids apart; then promptly squeezed them shut again as trickles of stinging, filthy water flowed into her eyes.

A throbbing in her leg drew her attention to her body. It didn't hurt, exactly. It felt more like a deep pressure forcing her downwards. The weight of the mud on her chest, she realized, was what was making her breathing shallow. Her face could reach the air, but she couldn't take it in properly; her lungs were being crushed by the mass sitting on top of them.

What about talking – screaming? *Could I try that?* The others must be close by; even if they couldn't see exactly where she was under here, surely they'd be able to hear her?

She opened her mouth, managed to make a gurgling sound – not even loud enough for herself to hear, let alone the others – then immediately felt a rush of mud slide into it; she spat it out, coughed it up. *Was the mud still moving, then?* Was it still coming down onto her? If it buried her much more, if it reached further, covered her neck, then her mouth . . .

Well, then she was well and truly done for.

There is nothing like facing death to make you appreciate being alive.

Over the past two years, she'd heard that sort of thing more times than she could count, and every time she did it took all she could muster not to bloody well scream in the person's face. Apart from the fact that it was trite and Mira hated cliché, the real issue – for her, anyway – was that it was just plain *wrong*.

For Mira, getting diagnosed with slowly progressing bone cancer – having a ticking clock placed on her life, hearing doctors talk in hushed voices about *limited lifespan* and *experimental treatment options* – none of that had given her a new lease of life. None of that had made her want to live, to get better. She'd wondered if there was something very wrong with her inside: could she be the only person in the history of time not to be spurred towards survival by the fear of impending sickness and death?

Because when Mira found out she had cancer, her first thought wasn't *I need to live*. It was *I think I'm OK with dying*.

No one could understand it: Mira's placid acceptance of the fact she had only a few years left at best, that she would most likely die not long after she hit fifty. Her friends thought she was in shock; depressed, maybe. But Mira knew she was not. She was content, in many ways, with her life: she had a decent home in an area she liked and felt part of, she had her music, and a kind and attentive husband. It had been hard finding someone like Ezra, happy to agree to a life without children – but she'd known that was what was right for her, unlike many in her community. She'd never wanted children; had known being a mother wouldn't suit her. She relished the freedom the two of them enjoyed.

And yet underneath all that, she acknowledged, there had been a listlessness, a passivity towards life. A sense of having used up all her energy on the first half, then having nothing left in the tank for the second. After her diagnosis, Mira found herself researching life expectancy in Roman times, the Middle Ages, the Victorian era. She discovered that for vast spans of history, forty-five, even forty, was a perfectly respectable age to reach – certainly not one that would be proclaimed a tragedy.

The thought gave her comfort. In any other epoch, she'd

have been considered to have had a good innings. It was simply her time. So, when the second round of chemotherapy made her vomit until blood poured out of her throat, and forced great clumps of hair to fall out in the shower, she'd decided that it would be the last time she'd put her body through this torture.

The chance of an all-expenses-paid retreat in the Costa Rican rainforest with a famous wellness influencer who openly rejected modern medicine, who thought chemo was toxic and did more harm than good – it had been what Mira wanted to hear at that exact moment. And applying for a place had been a last-ditch attempt to do something – *anything* – with the time she had left, knowing that she wouldn't put herself through more chemo, knowing that the end was coming soon.

That was why she'd gone to all that effort when she made her video – piling on her niece's bronzer and blush to add colour to her cheeks, drinking three cups of coffee just before she filmed it so her crushing fatigue wouldn't give her away. She didn't ever *really* believe it would work, though. And if it didn't – well, then. She hadn't lost anything; she was slowly marching towards death either way.

But now, lying under the weight of the cold, heavy earth, for the first time Mira though she might be changing her mind. That she might truly – deeply – want to *live*.

As she lay there motionless, she wondered if she was – far too late – moving past what she'd convinced herself to believe for so long: that life was meant to be short, and death should not be resisted when it came. She wondered if she'd emerged into a new truth: that her mere existence was an ordinary miracle and something precious. Something to be fought for, to hold onto. That perhaps a part of her was hoping that Hannah's spiritual principles for healing might actually work.

Visions of the last time she had sat *shiva* flashed into her mind; of the matzah ball soup she'd made for last Friday night's dinner; the way the cool ivory keys of her mother's old piano felt beneath her fingertips. Of the look of despair on Ezra's face when she had told him she would not put her body through more chemotherapy.

She saw all of it, and every moment of it was beautiful.

Breathing was getting harder now. Every time she tried to inhale, the sludgy mass weighing on her chest constricted her airways, made it impossible to take the full, deep breath she was increasingly desperate for.

Why is it getting harder?

Could it be that something else – something more, not just mud and soil – had landed on her body? A rock, more than one rock, even? Was there any chance she was making it out of here alive – or was this how she would die? The idea that it might not be cancer that took her in the end, but standing in the wrong spot in a jungle after rainfall, was the kind of absurdity Mira might have laughed at if it had happened to a character in a book, or a play, or a movie. Not in real life – not if it happened to her.

Her breaths were coming shorter and faster now, and the movement of her lungs was beginning to hurt. An awful burning sensation was starting to move through her chest. She wanted to struggle in her panic, but the only thing she could move was her head, and even that was becoming almost impossible.

This is it. I will die here.

From far away, as if from an alternate plane, voices were drifting towards Mira's ears now: urgent, frantic voices that she could tune into, and then lost again.

'Mira! I think I can see her – I'm going to try and get her out from under there!' said one.

'Naya, you can't, it's way too dangerous. Another mudslide . . . any minute . . . we've got to wait for it to settle. If we don't . . .'

'She's going to die under there! Scott – come on, help me! We can still save her . . .'

'We have to make sure the ground is solid . . .'

'I don't give a shit about the ground . . .'

And then something moving now, closer to her. Then a voice, Carly's voice, yelling at the others, 'I've found her – she's here, everyone, I can see her!' And then a face – Naya's face, her expression a perfect snapshot of terror, and hope, all mixed together in one desperate look.

'Quick, move that earth away from her nose and mouth – help her breathe!'

Hands, then, pawing at her face, stripping away the mud and the soil, allowing her to taste the air with her tongue.

But still, she could not breathe.

'It's . . . my . . . chest . . .' she managed to gasp.

'What was that?' It was Carly, confident, competent Carly, right there in front of her. 'Your chest? Oh God, the weight on her – she can't breathe! We have to dig her body out . . .'

Their words were fading now; the pain in Mira's chest was becoming so strong, she couldn't think about anything else. The urge to struggle was leaving her body too.

'Mira! Stay with us . . .' *At least I won't die alone.*

Another voice. 'Please be careful . . . another landslide, and then we'll all be . . . no one to dig us out.'

'We can do it.' Naya, that time. 'Scott . . . get behind her, take her shoulders, and pull – then Carly, dig the earth off her chest . . .'

Mira tried to inhale one more time; realized she couldn't even take in the smallest gasp. There was no more air; no more breathing.

There was a moment of pure stillness; of silence.

And then – an end to her suffering that she almost welcomed – the others' voices melting away alongside the rasping of her breaths, the burning in her lungs, as Mira's world faded into a quiet stillness.

NAYA

'Keep going, we're almost there – come on!'

The length of Naya's arms, her legs all the way up to her shorts, were coated in thick, wet mud. She didn't care; if they could save Mira, she would happily spend the rest of her days here caked in shit from head to toe.

'Here!' yelled Ben, appearing suddenly next to her, brandishing something long and thin in his hand. *A knife* – a long carving knife, by the looks of it. *What is he doing with that?* 'Can we do anything with this – use it to dislodge the rocks, the mud, maybe?' His voice was desperate; he waved the knife at them frantically.

'Where did you get that?' said Carly.

'I brought it from the kitchen in the house – I just thought we might need it to get through—'

'Never mind that,' said Naya. 'Forget the knife, that's not going to help. Come on, we have to pull her out!'

Scott had hold of Mira, underneath her arms, was pulling, yanking her free of the tonne of sodden earth her body was encased in. Now, Naya, Ben and Carly stopped digging debris off the top of her chest and came to join him, helping him haul her out. For a moment, it felt like nothing was happening: she remained stuck, her body and the mud unyielding, and Naya wondered why Scott had called them away from their digging to help. But then she felt it – a tug, at first just the slightest shift – and then a sudden release, and she was tumbling backwards, they all were – falling into the earth behind them, caking their whole backs now in the same gunky soil. They all scrambled up to drag Mira away from the heap of mud and towards the clearing near the waterfall.

Carly placed her jacket onto the ground and Scott laid Mira down gently onto it. Naya bolted forward, shoving the others out of the way, muttering 'Sorry, sorry . . .' as she moved. 'I'm a nurse, remember? I told you last night – I know what to do,' she said, as she leant over Mira, started to rub away the mud covering her nose and mouth, checking her pulse at the same time. It was there, but it was faint – and even through the mud coating Mira's body, she could see the bluish grey tinge to her skin, the disturbing lack of movement in her chest, her limbs.

Naya placed her cheek over Mira's face, felt for breath coming from her mouth, her nose: there was nothing.

'She's alive, but she's not breathing – watch her chest, tell me if you see it rise and fall when I'm doing mouth to mouth!'

Naya tilted Mira's head back, pinched her nose closed, placed her lips over Mira's – they were cold, and now she could see they had the same bluish tinge as the rest of her – and blew a steady breath into her mouth. Then she stopped, waited to hear anything from the others, for them to see the rise and fall from Mira's chest she was desperate for.

'Nothing,' said Carly. 'I didn't see any movement.'

Naya wasn't giving up yet. She tried again, hoping, praying.

'I think her chest – I think it went up a little that time, I saw it!' called Ben.

'She's breathing – yes, Naya, look,' said Scott.

Sure enough, as Naya moved slightly away from Mira's mouth, she felt a whisper of air. There was breath; there was life. *I've done it. Thank God.* She turned Mira's body into the recovery position, sat herself close to her face, kept her eyes on her. Naya was hopeful: Mira's breaths were coming steadier now, and deeper.

They waited as Mira's breathing grew noisier, still a little rasping, but solid. Naya allowed herself to shift her gaze from Mira's face to look around the clearing; as she did, she felt a twinge in her stomach, reached her hand instinctively to massage the spot beneath her belly button. The motion made her think of the way she rubbed Elodie's tummy when it ached, which it seemed to on an almost daily basis.

Her little girl's face swam before her. Had she really done this? Left her precious babies behind – not with their pathetic excuse for a father, thank God; they only saw the man once every few months, and his idea of parenting was throwing some Chipsters in a bowl and letting them play *Zelda* until they passed out from sheer exhaustion at heaven knew what time. At least they were with Naya's *maman*, who she knew would take the same care of them as she had of Naya herself as a child – but for a whole week? All to go halfway across the world and hang out with a bunch of strangers in a rainforest?

And then she thought: *yes*. She really had done this. And *yes*, she'd needed to. She was exhausted; she was starting to burn out – though of course, some of her stress was self-inflicted. Loud-mouthing to a patient about the failings of the

French hospital system – not realizing the on-call doctor was standing right behind her, landing herself with a disciplinary hearing . . .

And that wasn't even the worst of it.

She was doing things without thinking; things she knew weren't right for herself or – even worse – for her kids. Right now, she was not the mother they needed her to be. She needed to take time for herself, get some space – to *faites le plein*, to replenish herself; that's what that support worker said the last time she'd come round. She needed to receive Hannah's healing, her wisdom, the tailored support that she had promised would make such a difference to their lives. If only Hannah were here to actually deliver it.

'Naya!' said Carly, stirring her from her thoughts. 'Mira's waking up.' Naya looked down, and sure enough, Mira's eyelids had flickered open; in the same instant she tried to lurch upwards, taking huge, rasping breaths. Naya gently moved her back down.

'You're OK, Mira – you can breathe. We're here with you. Just rest.'

Mira made a small noise, a slight nod of her head, closed her eyes again. When she opened them a few minutes later, there was a sudden look of panic, of horror, spreading across her face, as she lifted a hand to touch her scalp. Naya's eyes followed her motion; in the desperation to get her breathing, in the thick coating of mud and filth covering Mira's body, she hadn't noticed it, not fully, until now. Her hair was gone. Mira's bare scalp was now slicked with dark brown mud, like the rest of her body.

It was a wig. She'd suspected it was; she'd noticed the way

Mira's hair sat solidly on her head. She'd wondered, vaguely, what it might mean; she'd heard Mira mention over dinner that she was Jewish, and thought perhaps it could be related to that – she was sure some religious women covered their hair.

She stared at Mira. 'You look lovely without it,' she said, meaning it.

Mira's eyes filled with tears. 'Thank you,' she said, still slow with her words, still full of effort. 'I had . . . cancer – stage two – I've . . . finished my treatment.'

Naya nodded, clasped Mira's hand. *That makes sense.* She wondered, now, why she hadn't also considered that as a possibility. Her exhaustion; how pale she was. Naya had met cancer patients who took months to recover from chemo, even once the cancer had gone. She wondered if Mira had managed to disguise it in her video somehow – surely Hannah couldn't have known? She'd never have agreed to her coming here if she had – would she?

'I'm so impressed you still managed to come here,' said Carly, reaching a hand to Mira's shoulder.

'Thanks,' said Mira, her hand moving down from her scalp. 'And I'm glad the wig . . . is gone, actually,' she said, a small smile on her lips. 'I was never sure . . . it was because Ezra – my husband – he thought it would help me feel better, when all my hair came out . . .' She shook her head. 'But it always felt wrong . . . I feel more myself without it.'

'That's good you're having a break from treatment now – did you have to go through a few rounds of chemo?' said Ben, before tailing off. 'I'm sorry, I don't mean to pry – my mother had cancer, so I know a thing or two . . .'

'Yes, I did, and it was . . . brutal,' breathed Mira. 'But the last round . . . was the worst.' She stopped talking, tried to sit up again, then grimaced in pain and grabbed at her chest. 'My chest – it hurts so badly,' she gasped. Naya leaned forward, felt for Mira's pulse. It was weak, but steady.

'I don't think it's your heart,' she said. 'It's most likely bruising to your ribs from where the mud landed on you. One of us must have some painkillers . . .'

'I have some in my bag, hold on a second,' said Ben, unzipping the side pocket of his rucksack, rifling through the compartment. 'Here,' he said, brandishing a pill packet, holding it in Naya's direction. She reached for it, was about to pop one of the tablets from the pack. Then she looked at the label.

'These?' she said. She held them up. She saw Scott glance at the packet and frown, then Carly's eyes flicker towards it, both of them taking in the name on its side.

'These aren't painkillers,' she said, 'they're—'

Ben grabbed the packet back from her hand before she could finish her sentence. 'Sorry, not those,' he muttered. 'I've got too much shit in here. Look – I've got some Panadol, here.'

Naya took them from his outstretched hand; nodded. It was none of her business what medication Ben was on, but it was difficult to get hold of the kind of drugs she'd just seen – he must have had a good reason to be on them. She handed Mira two of the Panadol and her water bottle to swig them down.

'Thanks,' said Mira. 'I need to lie down – in a bed – can we walk back to the house?'

Naya nodded, smiled, her relief at Mira's rescue from the mudslide feeling doubly intense now that she knew she'd also survived cancer. She stood up – but she moved fast, much too fast, and a wave of nausea rose up and took her in its grip. *No, no, not now.* Naya turned away from Mira, away from all of them – she refused to vomit in front of the others, especially Scott; she did still have *some* dignity; she wanted to maintain some appearance of attractiveness near someone she was already feeling so drawn to.

She stumbled towards the waterfall, her hand covering her mouth, reached the tree where they'd taken shelter, just had time to lean over before the vomit started to rise. She threw up until there was nothing left but yellow bile; she wiped her mouth, tried to calm her heart rate.

Her hands moved, instinctively, towards her stomach, feeling for the scar that spanned its width, splitting her belly in two, the way the surgeon had when each of her children came screaming into the world. Their short lives flashed before her eyes like a movie reel: bawling red-faced babies, blundering toddlers, first days at school with uniform hanging off them like dolls playing dress up. Tears, hers and theirs; well-meaning but heart-rending *concern about their development* from doctors and teachers and, now, their family therapist.

And then the chaos of her own conflicted feelings. Because Naya wouldn't change her children. Whenever people asked her how she coped, that's the first thing she said. She meant it; she wouldn't. They were perfect. They were exactly as they were meant to be.

She'd change how hard things were for them, though. She'd take away their meltdowns and the way they suffered trying to do things that others took for granted, like going to a supermarket or making new friends. She'd change the fact that none of the things she'd tried – speech and language sessions, occupational therapy, social stories, everything the professionals recommended – none of them made much of a difference; nothing seemed to help much, or for long.

She would change the world around them too, if she could. And she'd change other people: the way they looked at Marcus when a car horn beeped and he fell to the floor, screaming, hands clamped to his ears. Or the way they treated Elodie when she was too exhausted to keep the mask up any longer, when it had to come off, and everyone acted like she was a different person all of a sudden. A person they didn't understand, or maybe even like, if they were being honest. But it was the Elodie without her mask – a nine-year-old girl who liked to mew like a kitten and spin in circles until she felt sick – the real Elodie, that's who Naya saw. That's who she loved. And yet it was hard – getting harder all the time, in a way. It must have been; she wouldn't have come here if everything was OK. If she was *coping*.

'Naya – are you all right?' Scott was standing next to her now, one large hand reaching to her shoulder.

Naya nodded, stood up. 'Sorry, yes – I think it was just the shock of it all, and I stood up too fast – I'm OK now.'

'Here,' he said, handing her his water bottle. 'Drink something.' Naya took a slow sip, waited for the liquid to settle in her stomach. She looked at the others; all exhausted, all covered in damp mud, leaves in their hair, bodies slumped, exhausted. She watched Mira, still recovering her strength. She'd need help if she was going to manage more than an hour of hiking; Naya wasn't sure she was strong enough to walk back herself now.

She felt a sudden flash of irritation. *Why are we doing this without Hannah, anyway?* Wasn't this supposed to be a guided retreat, helping them to learn how to heal, away from the trappings of rigid, traditional medicine? Teaching her some new techniques and ideas to help both herself and her children?

So why had Hannah decided to travel to another town on the very day they were arriving, when she knew a storm was coming? A DIY wellness experience and being out in a rainforest with no guide wasn't what any of them had signed up for; she might as well have stayed at home and hoped to achieve respite via the online forums for mothers of autistic children she sometimes visited. At least with those, she knew exactly what she was signing up for. She'd left her children behind, come all the way here; she deserved more than this. They all did.

'I wonder if we should use the satellite phone now,' she said, turning towards Carly. 'You have it, right?' Carly nodded, bent down to open her backpack. 'I'm just not sure Mira should try to walk back – she's weak still. I think perhaps we should call for help?'

'You're right,' said Scott, nodding. 'She should probably get checked over in hospital – do you reckon, Naya?'

Naya nodded. 'I think that's for the best.'

As she glanced at Carly, waited for her to dig out the satellite phone, she heard a quiet gasp behind her, a mumbled, 'Oh, holy shit.' *What now?* Naya turned; it was Ben. He was staring at the path from the waterfall that led back towards the house, a finger pointing towards it. She followed its direction.

'The rain – it must have dislodged more mud,' he said. 'The track is covered – there's no way we can use that now.' Naya squinted, then walked a few feet towards the track. Sure enough, a layer of mud, at least a metre high and almost four times as wide, had now gathered at the point where the path met the edge of the clearing.

'Fuck,' said Carly. 'It's totally blocked the pathway – we can't walk over it. It's way too dangerous – we might dislodge a load more earth.'

Naya wanted to protest, but she knew it was no use. Carly was right.

There was no safe route back the way they had come.

CARLY

What the hell are we going to do now?

Carly should have known better than this. She'd spent months in the jungle; OK, it was a few years back now, and yes, she'd got a bit distracted with meeting Robyn and everything that had happened out there. Carly had been ill at ease with so much of the wilderness – the intense swings of the weather, the insects, the general lack of comfort – but Robyn just seemed to throw herself into all of it; fearless, full of joy. It ended up rubbing off on Carly too.

Her time in Peru had at least taught her a few of the basics: she *knew* how risky it could be to trek near a hill or a slope after a decent dose of rain, to risk disturbing a mound of earth that had been pelted with water for hours on end. And despite what Paola had said about the storm being *not so bad*, she'd been up half the night; she'd heard the storm battering her window. Why had she thought they'd all be fine walking out here today?

They needed to get out of here; *she* needed to get out of here.

Come on. I said I'd be able to guide them. I need to stay in control.

'OK, everyone, let's try and stay calm,' she said. 'We'll just need to find a different way back – it might take us a bit longer, but we'll manage it.'

Naya shook her head. 'There's no way Mira can walk right now – especially if it's going to take longer to get back. I really think we just need to use that satellite phone and call for help. Carly, you were looking for it before – did you find it? That's our best option.'

Carly sifted her hand through her bag, her fingers curled around the hefty phone with its solid antenna. She pulled it out and waved it to the others.

'Thank goodness,' said Naya. 'Does anyone know how to use one of these?'

Scott nodded. 'I've used one before – on a work trip back home, monitoring conditions in a pretty remote area of one of the national parks. We just need to switch it on, and it should pick up a signal. Then we call 911 – that will get us through to the emergency services here.'

Carly nodded, held her finger down on the phone's red 'on' switch. After a moment, the screen lit up, flashed the word 'MENU'. Scott peered at the screen over her shoulder. He frowned.

'It's not showing any signal,' he said. 'Let me see . . .' He took the device from Carly's hand, started to walk away from the shelter of the tree where they'd laid Mira down and towards the open expanse of the clearing. He lifted the phone up towards the sky, squinting. 'I can't seem to find a bar. I don't get it – the thing should be picking up a signal outside the line of trees here – it must be the cloud cover.' Sure enough, despite the end to the rainfall, there were still thick, dark clouds swirling above the tops of the trees.

A loud, urgent beep emitted from the phone.

'Shit,' said Scott. 'It's saying it needs charging – that can't be right. Why wasn't it charged already?'

Fuck – we should really have checked it was fully charged before we left. Carly watched as Scott shook the phone, his fist wrapped around it. There were touches of pink on his cheeks; his brows were furrowed together.

'What a piece of crap!' he yelled.

'OK, deep breaths now,' she said, walking over to him, taking the phone out of his hands. She noticed the screen was off now; *how has it already lost its charge?* She groaned. 'Right, this is hopeless. If the satellite phone isn't an option, we need to try and find another way back to the house. It's not far – we'll be fine. Let's take a look at the map.' Carly reached down into her backpack, pulled the map out and unfolded it, started to study it.

'I'm sorry, Carly, but I don't think Mira can walk anytime soon,' Naya said, interrupting Carly's focus.

'Well, let's separate then – two of us can set off, find a way back to the house and get Paola to call for an ambulance? The others stay here with Mira and wait for help,' said Ben.

'I really think we should stick together,' said Scott. 'We're much safer as a group. I'd feel better if we were all in the same place, not stumbling around out here in pairs and threes. And we've got that knife that Ben brought – it'll help us, cutting back the branches on a different path.'

'No, Scott. Ben's . . . right,' breathed Mira. 'There's . . . no way I can walk. Scott, Ben – you two go, and the other two stay with me?'

Carly frowned. Mira was still recovering; it would be tough

for her to walk the whole way back this evening. But it was a basic rule of outdoor survival: safety in numbers.

'Well, how about this. I could carry you, or at the very least, prop you up,' said Scott. 'I'd need to rest now and then, but I'm strong enough . . .'

'No, that'll only slow us down!' said Ben. 'Surely the most important thing is to get back as fast as we can, so we can call for help for Mira?'

Carly felt herself edging backwards, map in hand, away from the group, closer to the water's edge. The last thing she felt like doing was diffusing an argument. There was a reason she'd never wanted to go into couples' therapy or group treatment – the dynamics between people were so *messy*. All that projection from past hurt, past trauma, past relationships – usually people's very earliest ones – muddying the water. It was way too much hard work.

People often assumed that, because Carly was a therapist, she lived and breathed other people's problems. That she'd automatically start analysing them from the moment they met, pulling apart their childhoods, their deeply buried neuroses. The assumption pissed her off for a whole bunch of reasons, but two in particular: firstly, the fact that it was wholly unethical, a breach of professional boundaries. To start digging around inside someone's head, working out how they ticked, when they hadn't agreed to it? Sometimes, yes, it happened instinctively – before she could stop herself, she'd start filling in the blanks about someone, like she had when she'd first met the others yesterday. But she never *meant* to.

And the other point was a more mundane one: people, for the most part, just really *weren't that interesting*. When you'd been in the healing field for more than ten years, like Carly had, the truth was that people tended to fit into certain patterns – the same patterns, over and over – based on how they'd been treated in the first two years of their life. *Anxious, avoidant or secure.*

You figured out which one of those styles they fit into, and you could predict how people would behave in almost any situation. From those earliest years of life, you could work out – with terrifying degrees of accuracy – whether or not someone would be likely to become a depressed alcoholic or a healthy, happy success. Marry young and live together blissfully to old age, or go through a bitter divorce. Have secure, well-adjusted children or unconsciously pass a heap of trauma onto the next generation. That sort of knowledge took the mystery out of life a bit. It was worth it when sometimes, if you were good at your job – and Carly very much hoped that she *was* good at it – you helped someone change and find ways to be happier. But really, no wonder she'd got fed up with her job; with people in general, sometimes. *It's all so bloody predictable.*

Robyn was the exception to that, of course. Fuck, she missed her so bloody much. They always had such a laugh together. They could crack each other up with a single look half the time – it was one of the reasons Carly fell for her, their sense of humour being so perfectly in sync.

It wasn't just that, though: Robyn had intrigued her, surprised her, even. From the first day they met, as well as fancying the pants off her, Carly had wanted to get inside her head, to understand how she worked. And it was different, so different to how she'd felt about all her ex-girlfriends: usually, as soon as she got to know someone better, she lost interest.

With Robyn, it was as if the more she knew, the more she *wanted* to know. She could never have known enough, really. That was how it felt.

Hannah was intriguing too, in a different kind of way. Her ideas about alternative medicine as the path to healing; about spiritual cures for physical and psychological ailments; everything she'd been able to create here and online to offer people that. Her charisma; the power she had over people. Carly wished deeply for a moment that Hannah were here now, so she could talk to her more about it, about everything she believed. Just like she'd said she wanted to do in the video she made.

'Carly?' Naya's voice came floating towards her.

She snapped back to the present. *Damn it*. They were still arguing about what to do – they needed her. Someone had to make a decision, and it seemed like no one else was capable of doing it. She rubbed at the spot between her eyes. She couldn't hang around over here, by the water, much longer; it was starting to look weird. She needed to stop worrying about whether they'd see her as therapist, friend or leader. She just had to do what needed to be done.

Carly headed back to the group. 'Guys, we've got no choice,' she said. 'We've got to try and find our way back – using a different path, if needs be.' Her voice sounded more confident than she felt, but she knew this was her role: she needed to be the one to hold it together. She looked down at the map, then back up at the clearing. The map only showed one main track, but there had to be another way back – a track that would join back onto the central pathway soon enough.

Her eyes scanned the edges of the clearing, landing upon a small break in the trees with what looked like a pathway – a small one, narrow, but a pathway nonetheless – that seemed to veer outwards from the waterfall and turn back on itself in the direction of their original track to the pavilion and the house behind it.

'Look, there's another track over there, a little further down the stream – can you see? It looks like it might lead in the same direction as the one we took here.'

'You think we should take it?' asked Naya, walking towards her. 'And all stick together – helping to carry Mira?'

Carly turned, felt her brows knit together. 'I think so, yes – no, actually, I'm sure. Sticking together is way safer. And from looking at the map . . . I really think that's our best shot.' Her voice betrayed none of her internal struggle, her terrified thoughts: *I don't have a bloody clue. Don't let them figure out this is all guesswork.*

'We just can't risk getting stuck out here at night,' said Scott. 'It's a dangerous place, the jungle, after dark.'

Oh, come on – don't make this any harder than it already is. 'There's no need to panic everyone, Scott – we should be back at The Hideaway in two hours tops, even if this track isn't the most direct. And besides, humans and the wilderness have lived side by side for thousands of years,' said Carly. 'Please, no one listen to him – we're far safer here than we would be in the middle of bloody Cardiff, especially with that knife in our hands!'

Scott looked shocked, and for a second she wondered if she'd gone too far. But really, she thought he must know what she was doing: trying to reassure everyone. Make them feel better. It was what she was good at.

'That way is our best hope of getting back,' she said,

pointing to the path. She looked at the four wary faces in front of her. 'We either all stick together, and walk this way back now, or we split up and leave some of us here. But if we do that . . .'

Carly's words tailed off. She allowed a beat of silence to fill the humid air, then continued: 'If we do that, I'm not sure I fancy *anyone's* chances.'

SCOTT

The air felt different after the most recent downpour; thinner, somehow. Less threatening. Scott wondered if that meant the worst of the rain was over, for today, at least. Not that he felt any safer being out here; the sight of the mudslide had reminded him of the sheer power of nature, the lethal amorality of the wilderness.

Next to him, Mira whimpered, the two of them trailing at the back of the group as Scott helped her walk. 'Are you still finding it hard to breathe, Mira?' he asked. She nodded weakly. *Shit*. They really needed to get her to a hospital; she might need some oxygen treatment or something.

Scott still wasn't sure they'd all done the right thing, making her walk back. But it seemed like a safer option than the group splitting up. *Poor Mira.* What a thing to happen – the worst possible luck, and to someone who was already frail, recovering from cancer and chemo. Thank God Naya had been there and able to resuscitate her – without her, Mira would most likely be dead. But now that she was through the worst, there wasn't much more they could do for her, not until they got back to the house.

Naya's first-aid kit was little more than useless now: plasters, a bandage and gauzes, some tiny scissors, a few alcohol wipes. It wasn't as if she could carry around a canister of oxygen in case of an emergency like this, or a drugstore selection of medication.

Scott thought back to the glimpse of the amphetamine he'd seen Ben carrying. He'd recognized the brand name – there'd been some talk about it on the news and social media recently, about how there was a shortage, and people who desperately needed it were having a hard time getting a prescription. Didn't Ben have some hotshot job, though? And most likely a great health insurance plan – that would probably help.

Scott sighed; he knew far too much about health systems and prescriptions and drug shortages these days. As an only child, and with his dad long gone, the burden of care for his mum had landed squarely on his shoulders.

He saw her then: the shape of her, the smell of her. How vibrant she had been – how sharp, the way she commanded the attention of the room at her lectures on marine biology. Dementia was the cruellest illness he could imagine: the slow disappearing, the fading away, the gradual transformation of a life into a wasted, babbling shell. He couldn't bear the way the nurses at the home looked at her. As if she were just another senile old lady, just some batty patient who needed their nappy changing.

Look at her, he'd wanted to scream, desperate to shove old photos into their faces, pictures of her swimming with dolphins on the Mornington Peninsula and standing on stage to give a talk about the preservation of marine life. *This is who she is.*

'Are you OK, Scott?' said Naya. She was walking directly

in front of him and Mira, and had paused for a beat to check on them.

He snapped back to the present, looked at Naya, though still careful not to let Mira – clutching tightly now to his right arm for support – lose her balance. Naya was smiling at him. Scott felt something stir deep within his chest; the same sensation he'd had this morning after breakfast when it had been just the two of them. Naya was beautiful, but it wasn't just that; she'd looked at him so intensely – as if she were really seeing him, got him on some deep level and could accept him as he was. There was a warmth to her that seemed to spread outwards, to soften the people around her.

'All good,' he said. 'Just want to get Mira out of here safely.'

Scott looked ahead again as he trudged through the thick foliage, desperately hoping they were moving in the right direction. *God damn that bloody satellite phone* – how could they have set off from the house without checking it worked properly, or that it was fully charged? And why had Hannah left it like that for them, when it was almost drained?

They'd been so stupid, not to check. Or had someone said they'd checked it? Scott couldn't remember. Either way, somebody should have done it. He should have done it himself.

Then we wouldn't be in this mess.

He needed to come back to the moment, stop his mind from taking him somewhere else – to what he'd done or not done right, to his mum, to Justine, to a past that was long gone. He could no longer let his brain ruminate on all that, if he wanted to be happy. He tried to think of what Hannah would say now, the kind of advice she'd give in one of her 'Communing with the Present' video lessons.

Just focus on the moment.

List five things you can see, five things you can hear, five things you can touch, five things you can smell.

It helped. Hannah's teachings, the way she applied these practices to life – they had reached him in a way nothing else ever had. She had touched him; she had helped him to change. Yes, he still had his struggles; he knew his brain seemed to work differently from other people's, no matter how hard he tried – he was just wired that way, and there wasn't much he could do about it. All the work he'd done on himself hadn't meant he'd been able to save his marriage, after all.

But still, he was in a better place now because of Hannah. She'd helped him learn how to accept himself, despite his flaws; to forgive himself for the myriad ways in which he'd fucked up. She'd taught him how to be compassionate towards himself, even when he'd unwittingly pushed other people away. He only hoped that, when he met her in person, he'd be able to tell her just how much she'd done for him.

'Mind your step there,' he told Mira, helping her stay on her feet while dodging a fallen branch that lay at perfect tripping height. It was a minefield out here now they were hiking off the main track – trip hazards all over the place, not helped by how slippery the ground was. The last thing they needed was another accident before they made it back.

He watched her step carefully over the branch, sighed with relief that she'd navigated another potential disaster.

But now something else was slithering through his brain.

A creeping sense that they were trespassing somehow. That the rainforest didn't want them there, not off the main track, pushing through the undergrowth like this; that they weren't welcome this deep into the jungle.

Scott tutted at himself. *You superstitious old weirdo*. Everything was fine; he was safe in Hannah's stretch of land; they all were. They'd been terrified by the mudslide, the sheer power of it, and by Mira's brush with death. Not helped by the fact, of course, that Hannah wasn't with them. No wonder everything felt surreal.

He'd reassured himself, for a moment. But as they walked on, the feeling intensified. A thousand tiny needles prickling his backbone. And then a sudden realization:

We're going the wrong way.

Scott didn't know how he knew it; he just did. Everything was screaming at him that they were moving deeper into the rainforest now, rather than out of it; becoming more and more entwined in the guts of the place, rather than making progress towards the pavilion. They should have joined up to the main track by now, surely, but there was no sign of it.

And yet, the further they went in the same direction, the harder it was getting for him to mention it. Noticing his own lack of courage appalled him – he should have said it sooner, way sooner – he should have said it before they even left the waterfall. But Carly, leading the group this way, had seemed so confident, and they were all exhausted, caked in mud and desperate to get out of there – he didn't have much of a choice but to go along with it.

He was always like this: keeping quiet, not speaking up, not wanting to cause a fuss. Assuming other people knew better than him, even when they didn't – they couldn't. He was good at navigating, good with directions, had been his whole life –

they clicked somehow in his brain, and it was as though he could create a map that he could see in front of his eyes, even if he'd only been somewhere once. It's why he was so good at his job: finding his way across even the park's most remote trails; noticing any areas where the native plants needed some extra attention.

But no one would have believed him if he'd said all that. Carly was the experienced one, the one who'd spent time in a jungle before. Scott worked in the desert parks around Melbourne, and the region's vast stretches of arid, barren bush-land were hardly a match for the dense, lush wilderness here. Who was he, someone who'd never set foot in a rainforest in his life, to push his opinion over hers? And imagine if he got it wrong, and they got lost, and all blamed it on him? The thought was horrifying.

But then again . . . it couldn't do any harm, could it? Just to raise the idea, so it was on everyone's radar. If they didn't want to listen, then fine – at least he'd have said his piece. He took a deep breath. 'Hey, guys?' he called to the others ahead of him. 'Just stop a second. Sorry, Mira – why don't you lean against this tree for a minute, take a breather.'

'Yes – what is it?' asked Naya.

'Um, have any of you seen anything you remember yet, from our walk here? Any trees or familiar landmarks?' There was silence.

'I think so, yeah,' Carly eventually called from the front of the group. 'There was a fallen tree earlier, I definitely remember seeing that on the way here.'

She sounded crystal clear; totally sure of herself. Not a waver in her voice. Much more confident than Scott felt.

'OK, then. As long as you remember,' he said. 'It's just – I'd have thought we'd have joined the main track again by now. Maybe we have, and I didn't notice, but it's just . . . this path seems different to me? Kind of, thinner? Sort of, not really a path, more like we're pushing through rainforest in a vaguely straight line.' He was rambling; his words fell deathly flat.

'No,' said Naya. 'I'm sure the track here was the same – we've been hiking on these narrow trails most of the day, I'd say.'

See? It's OK. They're right, I'm wrong. Scott tried to calm himself; he'd misremembered it. He must have done. 'Sorry, yeah. Sure you're right,' he muttered.

They walked on, Mira still clutching his arm. Scott's stomach rumbled; he wondered if anyone else was hungry yet. He looked at the sun, still bright but starting to dip lower now in the sky. It must be late afternoon – maybe around four o'clock. They'd set off from Hannah's place around eleven that morning, so they would have arrived at the waterfall a little after noon. Even with the mudslide and giving time for Mira to recover, they'd only been at the waterfall for a couple of hours, at the most.

That meant they'd been walking back for close to two hours now. *Shouldn't we be out of the rainforest already? Or at least, shouldn't we have seen some of the trees I marked when we set off earlier?* With a creeping certainty now, Scott knew it: they'd gone the wrong way. If they didn't change track soon, they could end up seriously lost.

'Listen, everyone, I really think we've gone wrong some-where. Hopefully, it's no biggie, we just need to look at the map, take stock of where we are—'

Carly came to an abrupt halt. 'Look, Scott, I know you're trying to help,' she interrupted. 'But I'm telling you, this is the way we came. I remember it.'

Scott turned his eyes towards the ground before he said what came out next: 'So then, why haven't we seen any of the marked trees?' He thought he'd been talking normally, but his voice emerged as a whisper.

'Sorry?' said Naya. 'I didn't hear you.'

Scott cleared his throat, tried again: 'I said, why haven't we seen any of the trees I sprayed with white paint? I was marking them every twenty metres or so, to make sure we'd find our way back.'

There was a beat of silence, and then: 'Oh, *mon Dieu*,' said Naya, crouching to the ground. She barked a short laugh. 'Scott's right. We've gone wrong somewhere. We've been walking in the wrong direction for ages, haven't we? Well, I'm ready for a break anyway. Can we stop here for a bit and have a rest and a snack?'

'For fuck's sake,' Ben said. 'Gone wrong? This is all we need.'

'But . . . we can't have,' said Carly, looking crestfallen. 'I could have sworn . . .' She sighed. 'OK, maybe it's a good idea to have a break and get our energy back up. I mean, I hope you're wrong, Scott, but in case I've messed up, I'm – I'm really sorry, everyone.' Scott took in her flushed face; she was clearly embarrassed – he offered her a sympathetic smile.

'Do you . . . think . . . are we . . . lost?' breathed Mira.

'No, no, I'm sure we're not *lost*,' said Naya. 'Hannah's property isn't that big, is it? What, a few hundred acres – you can't go missing in that, can you?'

Scott blurted it out before he could stop himself: 'The rainforest isn't like other land, though. The density of the trees, the foliage . . . you can get lost in a pretty small area. Much smaller than this . . .' He tailed off as he caught the look of alarm crossing Mira's face.

'Scott's exaggerating,' said Carly, walking towards him and Mira, reaching an arm out to rest on Mira's shoulder. He frowned; why did she keep dismissing him like this? *I'm not an idiot.*

'Mira, look at me,' Carly was saying. 'We're not going to get lost. We just need to—'

'Hey, shush for a minute – can you hear that?' said Naya.

The group went quiet; Scott tuned in, listened. He heard the same blend of sounds he'd heard every time he was in the forest: trills, calls, squeaks and birdsong.

'Hear what?' asked Carly.

'No, I don't hear anything different than usual,' said Ben. 'What is it?'

'I'm not sure. Maybe I was imagining it. But I heard a different kind of . . . humming.' The group fell silent again.

'Oh, yes, actually,' said Mira. 'I think I do – like a . . . swarm of insects . . . somewhere nearby?'

And then, maybe it was a change in the direction of the breeze, or his ears just tuned in all of a sudden, but Scott caught wind of it too: coming from through the forest a little way off the track to their left. It was the sound of flies, but with an unusual quality to it, as though hundreds – even thousands – of buzzing insects were gathering in the same place.

'I hear it too now. I wonder what it is,' he said. 'Do you think it's one of those plants that attracts swarms of insects? It might be quite unusual.'

'And can you see that – above the trees there?' said Naya. 'Looks like a group of birds – are they . . . they look like vultures, don't you think?'

'Oh God, do you think they're all swarming around a dead animal or something?' said Ben, wrinkling his nose.

Carly grimaced. 'I have no idea what it is, but I really don't want to find out. Can we keep moving, please?'

'I'm going to check it out,' said Naya. 'An animal might be injured or dying – we can't just let it suffer.'

'I don't know,' said Mira. 'Shouldn't we just let nature take its course?'

'Exactly,' muttered Ben. 'What can you even do for a dying animal?'

Naya looked at him as though he'd just landed from another planet.

'We can put it out of its pain and misery,' she said. Then she turned and began to step away from the track towards the dense foliage.

Scott watched her in surprise. *She really is a dark horse, isn't she?* He was shocked she had the stomach for whatever might be over there – Ben was right, of course, that it could be a rotting carcass.

'Naya, hold on a minute – you don't even know how far away it is,' he called. 'You might wander too far from the track—'

'No, I won't. Listen, it's coming from just here, the other side of these branches – I'll be back in a sec. Ben, give me the knife, so I can cut through the bush here.'

'Oh, for fuck's sake,' said Ben, under his breath but loud enough that Scott heard him. 'I'm coming too, I'll use the knife – hold on.'

Scott was torn: he didn't want to lose track of the path – even if it wasn't taking them back to the house, it was, at least, a travelled route. But, like Naya, he was curious about the source of the buzzing, and he didn't want to somehow lose her and Ben if they wandered too far off. He made the call. 'Mira, stay here with Carly – we'll be right back,' he said, gently walking her over to Carly. 'Wait for me,' he called, pushing into the trees.

'Guys, hang on – this might not be the best idea!' Carly's voice was already disappearing behind them. 'Can't you just come back?'

As he shoved his way through the bushes, Scott thought Carly might be right: the growth here was thick and dense. He saw Ben ahead, slashing with the knife, trying to chop his way through the vines and branches in front of them – as sharp as it was, this would still be difficult work. 'Guys, hold up,' he said. 'Let me go first – I can clear the way for us.'

'Ah, yes, actually – if you don't mind. It's hard to push through some of this.'

Shoving his way past the two of them, taking the knife from Ben as he passed, Scott pressed forward, slashing at giant leaves and thick vines, twisting branches out of their way. With every step he took, he stopped to listen out for the buzzing noise, checking they were moving in the right direction. It was getting louder now, and the vultures were almost directly overhead – they must be close.

'Ugh, do you smell that?' said Naya from close to his shoulder.

Scott sniffed the air; and then it hit him too. Something acrid – pungent. Something rotting. He stopped in his tracks.

'OK, definitely a dead animal, then – it's got to be more than just injured to give off that smell,' said Scott. 'Maybe we don't actually need to see it, if it's already—'

But as the words came out of his mouth, Scott realized it was too late. The buzzing was overwhelming now; there was no turning back. They'd happened upon whatever creature was producing the throng of insects, and the stink. He stumbled to a stop; Naya almost slammed into the back of him, would have done if he hadn't thrust an arm behind him to stop her – to hold her back from what was lying on the ground in front of him. He looked down at his feet, took it in.

A combination of shock, terror and bile rose in Scott's throat. And then a panic – an urgency – *don't let the others see*. He turned around, blocked Ben and Naya's path; realized, too late, that they'd seen what he'd seen – they'd caught sight of what was on the ground. The scream that erupted a millisecond later from Naya's mouth was one of the most painful sounds Scott had ever heard: terror, horror, revulsion.

'Oh my God, oh my God – what the fuck!' Ben yelled. He crouched down to the floor, clamped his hands around his mouth. There were tears streaming down his face.

Scott squatted next to the thing on the ground in front of them. They'd been wrong: it wasn't an animal. Or at least, not the kind they'd been imagining. He wanted to protect them from it – he wanted to stop them from seeing it. They shouldn't have to look at this – at her. This would hurt them; it would scar them for life.

'Don't go any closer – Ben, Naya, please. Let's go – turn around, and get out of here,' he said.

'It's – is that – oh my God,' said Naya, stumbling over her

words, turning around to retch into the ground. She'd almost said what he'd been thinking, but he'd fallen short: he couldn't find the words.

Because how could he say it?

How could he say that the dead thing in front of them was human?

NAYA

Naya's eyes could not take in what she was seeing – they couldn't allow it. Nothing about it made sense; her brain refused to process the sight in front of her. She urged her mind to focus on the person lying on the jungle floor. Her natural instincts to feel for a pulse, to check if they were breathing – to try to save a life, using her training and experience to guide her – were as extinct as the human being on the ground. She doubted it would take a nursing qualification – not even so much as a two-day workplace first aid course – to deduce from the pallor of the corpse's skin, the bloating that had started to take place, the way the rainforest's creatures had already begun to pick at her flesh, that it was far too late for any of that.

She'd seen corpses before, of course she had. It was part of her job. It was a day-to-day occurrence, especially when she'd been working in geriatric care. Elderly people died all the time. It was sad – but it was natural. Sometimes people had terrible, grim deaths – diseases that strangled the life from their bodies over decades, or gradually shrank their brains to nothing. But often, these patients died surrounded by family, loved ones holding their hands, whispering last goodbyes, words of care and love.

Never – not once – had she witnessed anything that came close to this.

The dead woman was lying face upwards to the sky. Swarming above her head was a vast cloud of flying insects, and higher up, towards the top of some of the lush green trees, circling above their prey, were the vultures – impossibly large, their distinctive hook-shaped beaks hanging open as they surveyed the scene below.

Naya shuddered, before her attention was dragged away from the body. Someone was talking – one of them had managed to produce something more than the guttural sounds of shock and horror that had punctuated the past thirty seconds. It took her a moment to place it but then she realized it was Ben. His voice wobbled as it floated to her ears, as if it were coming from underwater.

'Fuck – Naya, Scott, is that . . . it looks like . . . is that blood around her head? Do you guys see that?'

Naya's eyes travelled slowly upwards, horror and dread making even the smallest movement feel like she was wading through treacle. She focused her stare on the woman's head; she needed to look, unbearable as it was. A large, sticky-looking pool of red had oozed out from under her scalp, attracting even more buzzing insects.

'I see it,' said Naya, her skin crawling with fresh horror. It looked as though this wound was the cause of this poor woman's death. But how did it happen? A terrible accident, perhaps? *Or something more deliberate?*

Naya's eyes continued searching the scene, too transfixed to turn away, as much as the image horrified her. Covering the rain-soaked corpse was a smattering of damp, mulchy leaves, a few tangled vines and some slightly larger branches, all with fat droplets of rain stagnating in their grooves and trenches. More leaves and smaller branches, twigs, chunks of wood, lay to one side of her body, many of them trailing in the same direction – as though the wind from last night's storm had blown them away and left them scattered around her.

But the vines and branches still on top of the body – the way they were layered on her chest and limbs, over her face – it looked as though it could have been deliberate. Naya wondered if there was any possible scenario where they could have appeared by themselves. Maybe this was the work of the rainforest's creatures – but would even the most intelligent of mammals be capable of this? Or maybe – Naya sensed herself grasping at each possibility more desperately – she had placed them over herself before she died? The alternative – that this was someone's attempts at hiding her, at covering their tracks – or perhaps at giving her a kind of natural burial out here under the watchful eyes of a thousand different species – was too brutal to contemplate.

Naya's eyes moved up the length of the body. She couldn't make out much of the woman's face; so much of it was obscured by leaves and flies and the insects that had started to crawl over it. But she could see – underneath an extra thick concentration of the swarming bugs – something that snagged in her mind, beneath the dark red matted leaves at the top of her head.

Her hair.

She squinted; something to do with it had caught her eye, had jarred inside of her. She stared again at the tendrils splaying out from underneath the woman's body. Then it landed. *I know that hair.* She'd seen it so many times before. Long, blonde braids, tied with tiny, brightly coloured elastic bands.

Oh my God, no. It can't be . . . It is, isn't it?

Please, please, don't let this be her . . . It's impossible . . .

Naya didn't want to do it; she was cowering, retching just at the thought. But she had to know for sure – she had to confirm her suspicion, for all their sakes. She took a deep, shuddering breath, then moved towards the woman's face, leaned over, was about to use the sleeve of her jacket to brush some of the debris away from it, when a yell from Scott behind her made her halt in her tracks.

'Naya, stop! Don't touch anything,' he shouted. 'I know we're not sure what's happened to her exactly, but this could be a crime scene – police might need to investigate it, right? I don't think we should get our fingerprints anywhere, or disturb anything, or move anything around.'

She reeled backwards. He was right, of course. *What on earth was I thinking, trying to touch the body?* She knew better than that. It was the shock of what she'd just realized, the lack of sense it all made; it had thrown her. But in any case, she didn't need to brush the matted clumps of hair away from the face. Now she was closer, she could see enough of the woman's face to confirm exactly who she was looking at.

A new wave of horror, and of confusion, racked her body and emerged from her throat as a choking sob.

It's her. It's Hannah. This was the very woman who was supposed to be stuck on the other side of the peninsula in a beach town called Golfito, waiting for a boat ride home. Unmistakably her, in fact, now that she knew what she was looking at – even through the leaves, she could make out the glint of her nose ring, the shape of her sharp cheekbones, the curve of her slightly upturned nose. There was a small gap in the mulchy earth that surrounded her eyes, and she could even make out their colour: sky blue, half-open, staring unfocused at the canopy of trees above them.

She heard a stifled sob behind her, then a gasp. Scott's and Ben's eyes were as transfixed on the area around Hannah's head as her own. She wondered if they'd just had their suspicions confirmed too, in the same instant – or if they'd already known it was Hannah – maybe they'd realized it as soon as they saw her. Maybe Naya had too; she just didn't want to admit it. They'd all seen enough of her selfies online, watched her videos. They all knew exactly what she looked like.

She was about to voice it, to ask them if they'd seen what she had – when a surge of doubt rushed through her.

It can't be Hannah – how is this even possible?

She felt herself bargaining for a different reality, a different explanation. That the dead woman she was looking at was someone else – it had to be. A random stranger, perhaps, a tourist who bore a remarkable resemblance to the influencer – someone who'd come to explore here, lost their way in the rainforest – then had a terrible accident.

But Naya couldn't lie to herself. It was Hannah; there could be no doubt. Her brain just couldn't process yet how it could be possible – or what it could mean.

'It's her, isn't it?' said Scott, his voice cracking. 'It's Hannah.'

Before Naya could respond, a loud rustling of leaves and branches from behind startled her; she glanced towards the sound and saw Carly emerge through the foliage, helping Mira along with her.

'You've been ages! What did you find? What was making all that buzzing?' she said. And then she looked at the ground, and her voice tailed off into a terrible silence, before she leaned forward, bent her head to the floor and vomited.

'Oh, no, no, no,' said Mira, her voice weak. 'Is that – oh my God, are they dead?'

Naya searched the others' faces, each one etched with grief, fear, shock and confusion.

'Guys – it's – I don't know how, it doesn't make any sense, but yes, this woman is dead and – and . . .' Her words caught in her throat; she forced them out. 'I think it's Hannah.' *More than that*, she thought. She was *sure* it was Hannah.

'What? Hannah? No. That's impossible – it can't be her . . .' Mira's eyes moved over Hannah's body; her gaze landed on her face, and then her hands flew to her mouth and tears began to stream down her cheeks. Naya looked at Carly, still bent close to the ground, but looking upwards now. Her face had drained of all colour, and she was breathing so fast, Naya suspected she was in the throes of a full-blown panic attack.

'Try to breathe, Carly,' said Naya, moving towards her, placing one hand on her shoulder. 'In and out to the count of three.'

'But . . . this makes no sense,' cried Ben, making his way up to standing now, shaking his head. 'Hannah's in that beach town – what was it called? Golfito? She sent us that selfie of her there this morning! How could she have got back here, out into the middle of the rainforest and ended up . . . ended up . . .' He broke off, left the sentence hanging in the cloying, rotten air.

The humidity and the last whispers of the day's rain seemed to have thickened the atmosphere, making it feel oppressive in the small clearing; suffocating. The smell of death and decay in the overgrown space mingled with the damp leaves; the mixture cloyed in her nostrils. Naya had the creeping, uneasy sense of being watched by the jungle: a thousand beady eyes fixed on her from through the leaves in the trees above them.

'Ben's right,' said Carly, through her rapid breaths. 'It can't be Hannah. It's not even an option. There's no way she could have got back here and into the rainforest this fast, let alone have ended up dead – it was only a few hours ago that she sent those messages. It must be . . . it must be someone else – a woman who looks like her, maybe?'

The desperation in Carly's voice moved Naya to a fresh round of tears.

No one wants to admit it. Come on, Naya.

'I'm sorry, but there's no doubt. It's Hannah,' she sobbed, her voice thick with tears and bile, nausea fighting its way up her throat again, threatening to erupt. She forced it back down. 'It's her, and it looks as if . . .' She teetered on the edge but stopped herself from saying the next part, the part that made this discovery all the more terrifying.

Before Naya could finish her sentence, Scott snapped upright, started to swat at the swarm of insects attacking Hannah's flesh.

'Get away from her!' He was waving his arms frantically in the air now, attempting to shoo away the flock of vultures that was still hovering high above them. The creatures were bold; they hadn't been turned away by the group's presence, their voices, their loud outpourings of grief. But at least they'd managed to stave them off – for now. Naya had no doubt they'd swoop down and enjoy their spoils the minute the five of them walked away.

'We need to call the police,' he said, turning back to the group when the bulk of the creatures had moved elsewhere, his voice shaking but resolute. He looked at Mira and Carly. 'There's a wound to the back of her head – and her body is all covered up. I think – I think that maybe someone did this to her.'

'Hang on a second. Are you . . .' said Mira. 'Are you suggesting someone might have killed her? That Hannah was *murdered*?'

'No . . . no, we can't be sure that something . . . something like that happened to her,' said Ben, stumbling over his words. 'Obviously, the injury to her head, that must be how she died, but . . . did she have an accident out here, fall somehow? Hit her head on a rock as she landed?' He choked out the last few words, then dissolved into quiet sobs.

Mira nodded. 'Rainforests are dangerous places – just look at what happened to me earlier. Or you can trip over a vine that you never saw, or the base of a tree . . . especially off the main track like this.' But even as she said it, she was frowning, as if trying to make sense of something that logically wouldn't fit together.

'That's true,' said Scott. 'It could have been an accident, I guess. It's just . . . see, how she's got those leaves and twigs all over her? I don't understand how she could have done that to herself.'

At that, Mira stumbled slightly; Naya moved to catch her before she could fall. *Hold on, Mira. We don't want to lose you too.*

'We need to get help – Mira can barely walk, and the police need to come out here and take Hannah away,' said Scott. His face had crumpled around the edges, a pallor replacing his usual tan. 'The staff – Paola and Luisa – do you think they might have called for help yet? We should have been back by now, maybe they've raised the alarm.' He looked desperate as he said it, clinging to hope.

'Yes, maybe they have,' said Naya. She wanted to reassure him, even if she didn't entirely believe it. 'And if they haven't yet, then they will do soon. They'll come and find us themselves, or send a search party for us. Of course they will.'

'I don't know,' said Ben dully. He'd stopped crying now, and his eyes were blank, vacant. 'They might just think we spent longer at the waterfall or something. I can't imagine they're panicking yet.'

Scott buried his face in his hands. 'Oh God, I feel sick.' He took a long, shuddering breath. 'We need to get going, then – back to our phones – to Paola . . . to Hannah's house . . . fucking hell, *Hannah*.' He broke off, made a gasping sound.

Naya forced herself to turn and look him square in the face; tears were pooling under his chin now, the grief etched into the lines of his cheeks; he looked heartbroken and he wasn't trying to hide his pain.

She wanted to reach out to him, pull him towards her, for him to let her rock him and sway him in her arms like a child, like she did with her own children. She wanted to make the pain of the world go away. For him, for her. For both of them. But she couldn't; she couldn't do it for her children, as much as she wanted to, as much as she'd tried. She couldn't change the world – she couldn't make it better. And she couldn't do it for Scott either.

She could hold him for hours, for days, and Hannah would still be dead, lying here, most likely murdered, left to rot in the wet heat of the jungle. Nothing would be different; the world would still be tilted on its axis for him. Just like it was for the rest of them.

Mira, still leaning on Naya, was shaking her head now, taking short, sharp breaths, but trying to speak. Her next words emerged in a stilted burst. 'I still can't understand how she could have got here so quickly. How this could have happened since this morning. It doesn't make sense. The timing, I mean. Something is very wrong here, with all of this.'

Ben shook his head slowly. 'I guess it's not impossible,' he said quietly. 'She could have got a boat back right after she sent us the video, then if she came straight out into the jungle to look for us and then this happened to her . . .' He turned to look at Hannah again, then covered his eyes with his hands.

Naya swallowed. She had to say something now, but how could she? A part of her wished she didn't know what she knew, because of how much more impossible it made everything. Post-mortem care was something she had to do from time to time, in her role as a nurse. It was rare for her to have to deal with a body other than straight after death. But she knew that rigor mortis set in within a few hours of someone dying and lasted for several more, maybe even a full twenty-four hours.

Hannah's body had already passed that point: based on Naya's quick assessment of her body, her face – what she could see of it – her muscles were no longer stiff; they were becoming flaccid. Her facial muscles had begun to relax; her arms were loose; her fingers were unclenched.

And yes, while the searing temperature and the rainfall and

the humidity of the jungle could speed up the process, there was physically no way that Hannah could have died, her body gone into rigor mortis and then come out the other side in the few hours since they'd got those messages from her – it just wasn't possible. Naya's mind had been putting it together since the second they saw her body.

She looked at Ben, at all of them, and shook her head. 'That's the thing,' she said. 'To me, it looks—'

She couldn't say it. Even if they'd worked it out themselves, saying it out loud would make it too real. And the truth was unbearable:

To me, it looks as if she's been dead, and left here, for as long as twenty-four hours.

Because if that was true, it could mean only one thing: one inescapable, horrifying truth that Naya needed to face, that they would all need to.

It would mean that their time here so far had been built around a lie. A clever but terrible lie.

And it would mean that perhaps none of them were safe out here at all.

SCOTT

Oh my God, Hannah. Poor, poor Hannah.

Scott blinked, squeezed his eyes closed, trying to stem the flow. He shouldn't have bothered; his tears wouldn't be held back. His body seemed to keep moving of its own accord, bending at the middle until he was doubled over, head resting almost against his legs, arms wrapped around his stomach, sobbing, then lurching back upwards again to take great, gulping breaths. He felt small, about half of his usual size – hunched over, shrunk with heartbreak. He must look insane; he felt it, that was for sure.

But he didn't care how he looked; he wasn't the only one bowled over by the shock. For the past few moments, the sound of the group's grief had been as loud as the calls and cries of the rainforest. They were all in the grip of this; he was not alone.

'That's the thing.' Naya's voice drifted to his ears, the fear in it making him turn away from Hannah's body for a moment and look towards her. Flecks of dried mud were still splayed down the side of her face, her neck, her arms. Her hair had escaped its tie and tight curls were now flying in all directions, some framing her cheeks, some sticking upright. She would look ferocious – if it weren't for the complicated mixture of terror and bafflement etched into her expression. 'To me, it looks—'

Abruptly, she stopped talking. Scott's eyes moved from Naya's face back to Hannah's body in an absurd, repetitive motion. He couldn't place why, but he felt afraid of whatever had been on the tip of Naya's tongue just then; he had a sense that whatever she was about to say would send him freefalling even further into the abyss he'd already tumbled into.

Come on, Naya, just say it. He needed to know; they all did.

'Well – Naya, what? You were going to say something – it looks like what?' Carly said.

Naya pursed her lips; shook her head slightly. She seemed desperate not to have to talk. She shifted her weight, one foot to the other, pushed one of the escaped curls away from her face. But then, finally, she said it: 'It looks like she's been dead for around a day.'

Dead for an entire day?

But there's no way . . . she can't have been.

The group stood in silence as the impossibility of Naya's words sank in.

'But she *hasn't* been dead for a day – nothing close to it,' said Ben, voicing Scott's thoughts. 'We literally just heard from her this morning – a few hours ago! Five, six hours, right? I mean, she messaged us, she sent us a picture, we saw her face, for God's sake – and she was most definitely alive then!'

'Exactly,' said Carly, her already pale cheeks now ashen. 'She was alive and well a few hours ago, and miles away. Either

116

this is *not* actually Hannah, or she somehow got out here really quickly, and whatever happened to her – it must have happened in the past couple of hours . . .'

She stopped talking, swayed on the spot, reached a hand out to Scott's shoulders from where he was crouching in front of her to steady herself. He gripped onto her. *Please don't faint – that's the last thing we need.* But she seemed to calm down, took a breath, then carried on. 'What about . . . could it be the climate out here – the humidity, making it look like she's been – ah, gone – longer than she has? That can happen, right?'

Naya shrugged, her mouth a tight line. 'I suppose so – but that would be very unusual, for the decomposition of a corpse to be that rapid . . .'

Rapid decomposition. A corpse.

This was all wrong. They were talking about a person – about *Hannah*, for God's sake. Hannah, the real flesh and blood human being that he'd admired for so long. The woman who had helped him so much; who was an inspiration for millions of people all around the world.

How can this be real? That the same woman was lying dead on the floor of the rainforest. Either she'd had a terrible accident, or worse – unthinkably worse – someone had killed her, and left her here to rot. Who would do something so evil – and why?

Scott felt hot, acidic bile rise to the back of his throat. The air around them was rancid. He needed to move now; he was desperate to get away from the stench and the awful, relentless buzzing. But they couldn't just leave her here, could they? How would they even make sure the police could find her?

Imagine if they don't. Would she just slowly decompose

117

out here, devoured by insects and vultures, until her bones sank into the mulchy earth of the rainforest?

This is unbearable.

He didn't mean to speak – he wasn't ready to, really – but the words surged out anyway. '*None* of this makes any bloody sense. If someone killed her, why? Why the *fuck* would anyone want to hurt Hannah?' The effort of those few words left him winded, almost gasping for breath – it felt like when he'd finished a half marathon back home last year, raising money for Dementia Support. The difference then was that he could control it – he could slow his breathing down. Now that felt impossible.

'We have to find out who did this to her,' said Ben, his voice shaking. 'You know, Costa Rica isn't as safe as it used to be. I've heard some things recently. Drug cartels, gangs, shootings, stuff like that.' He moved a trembling hand to his forehead now, wiped away the line of sweat that had settled above his brow. 'The number of homicides happening here because of cocaine gangs has gone wild recently . . . it's been all over the news back home these past few months. What if . . . could she have gotten mixed up in something like that?'

Impossible. Hannah involved in drugs? Never.

Ben was still talking. 'Especially all the way out here, this far from her house . . . maybe she wandered somewhere she shouldn't have – got into some kind of territory she shouldn't have been in?'

'That's a good point,' agreed Naya. 'Ending up in such a remote area, I mean. What would she have been doing off the main track, all the way out here in this tiny clearing – not even near a proper trail?'

'But isn't this all Hannah's land? She owns these few hundred acres, right?' asked Scott.

'Maybe she got lost, then,' said Ben. 'Walked to a part of her rainforest she didn't know so well.'

This is ridiculous. 'Lost, in her own property?' said Scott. 'She made her own map of the place! I'm sorry – I just don't buy it. And this is really clutching at straws – speculating about her being involved in drugs . . . it doesn't sit right with me, not at all.'

'Jesus, I don't know then,' said Ben, the emotion thick in his throat. 'I'm just trying to come up with some kind of explanation for something so . . . inexplicable!'

Scott rubbed his face with his palms. 'I know, I know,' he said, softening. 'I'm sorry – I'm in shock, I guess. The truth is, we don't know what happened to her, or how. Which is why we have to get back and phone the police.'

Ben nodded, as if to say, *I get it*; Scott knew he understood. They were all in shock.

As he watched, Ben bent down next to Hannah's body, started to reach forward for a moment, looking as if he were going to lay a hand on her. Scott was about to call out to him, remind him not to touch anything, to leave things exactly as they were for the police to investigate – but there was no need. Abruptly, Ben seemed to change his mind, stuffed his hand away in his pocket.

There was a long silence, before Naya cleared her throat and started to speak.

'Look, I know we all want to work out what happened to Hannah, how she got here – how she ended up like this . . .' Her voice caught in her throat. 'And there will be time for all of those questions. But right now, it's well into the afternoon, it'll be getting dark soon – we're shocked and exhausted and running out of water and Mira's still recovering. We need to get out of here and call for help. That's the best thing we can do for her now.'

She broke off, and dissolved into silent tears. Scott reached an arm out; he wanted to touch her, to hold her – for them to give each other some comfort. But he wasn't sure if she'd even want that right now; he moved his arm back to his side. Naya was right, of course. They had to keep going; they couldn't stay here. But Scott could feel himself resisting; wanting to protest, to tell them they just needed to stay a few more minutes. He didn't feel ready to leave Hannah yet; he didn't think he could do it.

He wasn't sure he could face hours more trekking through the rainforest either. Especially if they didn't know where they were going.

'Listen, everyone,' he said. 'We need to get really clear on our strategy for navigating our way back. Let's—'

'I'm sorry,' Carly interrupted him, shaking her head. She looked stricken. 'I'm so sorry, everyone. I should never have taken charge – I was so stubborn, insisting I knew the way.' She broke off with a sob. 'But I've just got us all more lost, and led us to something so . . . so awful.'

'It's not your fault,' said Ben. 'And besides, it's better that we've found her, isn't it? Imagine if we hadn't – she could have been lying here for days – weeks, even.'

'I know,' said Carly sadly. 'It's just – I'm always like that, thinking I have to be the one in control. We should have listened to you, Scott, when you said you thought we were going the wrong way.'

Yes, you should have. But it wasn't all on her – he should have tried harder to convince them. Perhaps now was the time for him to take charge. 'It's OK – don't beat yourself up,' he said. 'We just have to keep trying to make our way back now, before it gets dark. Like I was about to say, let's look at the map again – Carly, can you hand it over? Let's see if we can get any idea of where we are.'

They studied the map for a moment; Scott thought the best course of action was to head back to the path where they'd first heard the buzzing noise. From there, he had an idea of how to use the sun as a guide to point them in the direction of The Hideaway.

He confirmed the first part of his plan with the others, folded the map, put it in his back pocket, felt a few dull stirrings of hope; he could give the route a half-decent shot. He looked back at Hannah, felt a hot squeeze around his heart at the sight of her lifeless body. She was still there; still motionless. The insects and vultures had returned to circling her – even more gathering now that the group had stepped away. His instinct was to pick her up, carry her with him out of the jungle and bring her back home. The idea of leaving her here, to rot, be pecked at – it wounded him; it felt utterly inhumane.

As if looking for strength from something heavenward, Scott glanced up at the sky; then he squinted. Everything above and around them looked hazy – for a second, he wondered if the shock of finding Hannah had affected his vision somehow. But then he saw the haze moving slightly, and realized that now the rain had eased off, the damp and the humidity seemed to have come together to create a fine mist that was gathering around the tops of the trees. It made everything look mystical, otherworldly.

It was also going to make it harder to see their way back through the jungle.

Taking Hannah with us is impossible.

It could be a long hike back, and he had to preserve some of his energy – Mira needed help to walk; it was only right to save his remaining strength for the living.

Not for the dead.

He felt eyes on him then; he turned to see Carly staring at him.

'I know it's awful, but we have to leave Hannah here,' she said, as if reading his thoughts. 'There's nothing we can do for her now.' She swallowed. 'We've got to think about ourselves – especially this late in the day, and without a working phone. We really don't want to end up stuck out here overnight.'

'Yes, and Scott, you can mark some trees as we go again – to help the police find Hannah once we've called them,' said Naya.

Scott nodded, amazed by Naya's confidence, her calmness, in the face of the tragedy they'd just witnessed. *How is she keeping it all together like this?* Perhaps it came from being a nurse – or a parent of young children; and autistic too. That must take some patience, some tolerance. Perhaps her poise came from all of those things.

Maybe if me and Justine had worked out, if I'd become a dad – maybe I'd be calmer, more confident too. The thought brought with it a fresh wave of grief, a new round of tears.

He gave Naya a small nod of agreement, and they began to move, Scott tailing behind under the pretence of digging the white spray paint out of his bag, but in truth, needing to take one last look at Hannah's broken body on the ground.

He forced his eyes away from her, focused on the path in front of him. He watched the others thin into a line as they went; Ben had taken the knife back from Scott now, and was at the front, using it to cut through vines and thick leaves. Scott caught up with him to help with the navigation – behind him, Naya was supporting Mira, and Carly walked at the rear.

He followed Ben, his mind in overdrive as he walked. Not only was this a horror beyond his wildest imaginings, but nothing about it made sense. A cold, creeping feeling had started to form; a doubt, a suspicion, and it was slowly making its way from his brain to trickle down his body vertebra by vertebra.

He had the awful sense that something larger could be at play here.

Because if they'd received messages from Hannah that morning, when she'd clearly already been dead for a while – then, had this all been some kind of set-up? By someone pretending to be Hannah, to fool them into believing she was alive and well this morning when they'd left for the waterfall?

But who would do something like that?

Another thought occurred to him then, and with it he felt a hot rush of panic rise up in his chest, making him breathless. What if it was one of the people he was here with – one of the people he was in the middle of a rainforest with at this very minute?

What if one of them is a murderer?

He dismissed the thought as quickly as it came. It was impossible – the timings wouldn't work. They'd all arrived here yesterday evening, around the same time, hadn't they? About six o'clock. And Naya seemed to think that Hannah was already dead by then.

He blew out a breath. *Steady on, mate. You're getting way ahead of yourself.* There was no reason to think it was one of his companions; that was way too much of a stretch. They were all here, like him, because they *loved* Hannah.

Weren't they?

Scott stumbled on a small rock, almost went crashing forward; he caught himself on the trunk of a palm tree. Away from the cleared paths, the vegetation was dense; they couldn't see more than a metre or two in front of them. The trees on either side had grown so close that their leaves and vines had fused together at hundreds of junctures, creating a thick, sprawling green carpet; a barrier.

It feels like the jungle is trying to keep us trapped here.

This wasn't a track; it wasn't a pathway. This was pure, untouched jungle. Every direction looked the same. Whoever had left Hannah in this patch of land knew it would be damn unlikely she'd ever be found.

No one belonged here, this deep in the wilderness.

The rainforest doesn't want us here.

And maybe that's why Hannah has ended up dead.

CARLY

Carly's foot caught on a branch; she almost leapt out of her skin, only just stopping herself from tumbling head first onto the ground.

Hold it together. Come on.

It was understandable she could barely walk straight: the day had been a catalogue of horrors. Carly had rarely experienced anything like it in her life, nor could she imagine ever living through something like this again.

To have first watched Mira nearly die in one of the most appalling ways imaginable, suffocating, crushed to death under a pile of mud – and then to discover the dead and mutilated body of the very person who should have been there with them.

This is all my fault. I took us this way back from the waterfall.

She was jumpy; on high alert – she was becoming irrational. But she had to get a grip; the last thing she needed was to start falling apart now, unravelling at the seams. Even though she was no longer the one navigating, her survival depended on her holding things together; on helping keep the others calm too.

Her scrambled thoughts – racing, too fast to grab hold of – were telling her horrible truths.

Or were they lies? How was she supposed to know what was even real any more?

If only they hadn't followed my lead.

If only we'd taken a different path.

If only none of us had come here at all . . .

It was too late for any of that now. She was here, and so were four other people who, after not even a full day, she felt connected to – and responsible for. She cared about them: Mira and her quiet determination to be alive; Naya and the way she seemed able to handle crises so effortlessly; Scott and his gentle awkwardness. Even Ben, who she suspected now, underneath the smooth, handsome exterior, was someone vulnerable; someone with extra challenges to deal with, based on the pills she'd seen at the waterfall. Perhaps he *was* an addict, just like her first instincts about him had told her. The drugs could be legit, but his reaction – the way he'd grabbed them back, looking shame-faced – gave her cause for suspicion.

Carly shifted her attention back to the group ahead of her. They stepped out of the thickest of the foliage onto the narrow pathway they'd been following before they'd veered off to investigate the source of the buzzing. Bile rose in her throat again; she swallowed it back down.

'Let's stop here a sec and check the map again before we carry on,' called Scott from further ahead.

The group formed a circle around him as he dug the folded-up scrap of paper from his back pocket, unfolding it and tracing his finger across its surface. She was relieved he was in charge of the navigation now; she'd made enough of a mess of things already.

Scott glanced skyward. 'I've been checking the direction the sun's been moving in for the past few minutes. It's heading that way – see?' He pointed to the right. 'That means that direction is west. And this way' – he gestured ahead – 'is south. We know The Hideaway is at the southernmost point of Hannah's land – see, here on the map? So, I reckon we just need to go in this direction – south – and we'll get back to it.'

Carly hovered at Scott's shoulder, checked the map, nodded. 'Sounds like a good plan. Let's move.'

Ben turned back towards the track, still holding the knife in his grasp, ready to start hacking at the foliage again as he went, when Naya's voice, wobbling but firm, reached Carly's ears.

'Actually, everyone, before we get going again, should we stop and check how much food and water we've all got left? It might take us a while to get back, and I don't know about all of you, but I'm pretty much out of my stock. Perhaps we can pool all our resources, share things out?'

Carly considered this for a moment. She was desperate to keep moving, to get as far away from the middle of the rainforest as possible. But a tally of their snacks and drinks wouldn't take long, and it might help keep the others calm.

'OK, let's do it – but let's make it quick,' said Carly, leaning down to open her rucksack, starting to rifle through it.

Naya, Scott and Ben mirrored her: pulling out dregs of nut packets, a cereal bar, a squashed banana, water bottles that were now mostly empty.

'Wow,' said Carly, looking at the sad selection when they'd all finished. 'Is this really all we've got?'

'Well, I wasn't expecting we'd still be out here by now,' said Ben. 'I thought Paola's snacks would tide us over.'

'Me too,' said Naya.

Carly thought back to when she'd packed her bag that morning: she'd felt uneasy about what they were doing – starting the retreat without Hannah – but she'd had no idea, not the vaguest notion, of what lay in store for them. It seemed like a lifetime ago, like a different world. Truth be told, since arriving here yesterday, she already felt like a different person altogether.

'Mira, how about you?' said Ben. 'Do you have anything left?'

'I've got nothing,' she said. 'Feel free to take a look in my bag . . .' She pulled it down from her shoulders, held it out.

'Don't worry, there's no need,' said Scott. 'We're going to keep walking and get back soon, well before we run out – I'm sure of it.'

They set off again. They walked for another fifteen, perhaps twenty minutes. The sun had started to dip lower in the sky; it was almost invisible now behind the shroud of trees and branches. The temperature had dropped slightly too, but the thick humidity still clung in the air; it tasted damp, smelled mildewy.

And we're still no closer to getting out of the rainforest.

'It's going to get dark soon,' said Naya from behind her, voicing Carly's own thoughts. 'What are we going to do if we can't find our way back before night falls?'

Think, think. Carly wanted to find a way to reassure her – people needed a voice of calm at a time like this. Her brain raced through the options, gathered her thoughts.

'Listen,' she said. 'We'll get back there – even if we don't make it tonight . . .' *Shit*. She hadn't meant to say that out loud.

'Hang on a minute,' said Ben. 'What do you mean, if we *don't make it tonight*? Do you think we're going to be stuck out here until tomorrow?'

Carly's heart began to pound. She shouldn't have shared her fear out loud – but they couldn't avoid it: it was getting dark. No matter how good Scott's navigation skills were, they had no chance in the pitch black with only a couple of small torches to guide them. She knew what the jungle was like at night – she'd been in one before.

The memory of her last time in a rainforest startled her like a splash of cold water to her face. She'd never been up for doing the plant medicine, but the group circles, the open sharing had brought Carly and her fellow travellers insights that she'd never before have believed possible. The way she fell in love with the people she was there with, felt an intimacy, a depth of connection with them that she'd never known before, or since.

And, of course, Robyn.

Carly saw her face for a second; felt a sharp jolt in her chest. She'd never been heartbroken before Robyn, not really. She'd not known what it was like to love someone, and then have to watch them change; to drift away slowly, leaving nothing but empty longing and painful memories.

Come on, not now. Pull yourself together, Carly. She knew this wasn't the time for reminiscing, for becoming overwhelmed by her sadness.

To her relief, Scott took charge again. 'Let's just take another quick look at the map.' Scott dug the map from his bag, unfolded it for the group; they all stared at it. 'Look, we're making progress – we must be on this path now, the one heading towards that stream – the big one.' He ran his tongue over dry lips. 'That means we're going in the right direction.'

'Exactly,' agreed Carly. 'And remember, Hannah's rainforest

isn't that big – we just need to keep moving and we'll be out of here in no time.'

'I don't know, man,' said Ben, shaking his head. 'The thing with this jungle is, everything looks the same – in every direction. It's hard to know which way is up and which way is down – especially when it's starting to get dark.'

'I know that, for God's sake, I—' Carly snapped. She stopped herself, shook her head apologetically; she wasn't being fair. 'Sorry,' she said. 'I didn't mean to have a go at you – I just don't want everyone to get more freaked out than they already are.'

'OK,' said Naya. She turned to Scott. 'I can see you're good with navigation, but seriously, how much further do you think it is? How much longer will it take? I just want to go home.' She rubbed her eyes, sniffed; she looked exhausted, and afraid.

Carly wanted to say something that would reassure her; that would help keep the group together. That was more important than telling her the truth, at least for now. They needed to believe they were making progress, if they were to keep on going.

'I can't say for sure,' Scott replied. 'But I think we'll be back at the house in the next hour or so,' he said.

Naya nodded; there was relief in her eyes. 'OK, let's go – Scott, keep leading the way.'

They walked on. But with every step forward now, Carly sensed their hope was fading. There was no mistaking it: the light was beginning to dim above the canopy of trees. In minutes they'd have to rely on their torches to guide their way back. And navigating through dense jungle in the dark – even with torches – was something not even the most experienced of wilderness survivors would attempt in a hurry. One wrong step and you'd have a snapped ankle or a broken arm to contend with – or worse.

Soon, the five of them could see no further than a few feet in front of them. All of them were hot and thirsty, and the shock of what they'd discovered earlier was written on every-one's faces. They were traumatized and tired, Mira especially exhausted and struggling for breath.

It's time to give up.

They couldn't keep walking; not in the dark. It was too dangerous, and in just a few minutes it would become even more so – they couldn't see what they were stepping on, they couldn't make out the undulations of the earth beneath them, the rise and fall of the ground, the jutting of rocks and branches and vines that could so easily prove lethal.

She took a deep breath, stood still and turned to face the group.

'Hey, everyone, hold up,' she said.

'What is it?' said Scott. Even in the near dark, Carly could see the wariness on his face. *He knows we're not getting back there tonight.*

'I'm just thinking – and don't freak out, it's not that big a deal – but because it's dark now and we've still got a way to go, we might be best to wait it out until it gets light – our torches can only light small patches of the ground in front of us. And even with them, it will be way too treacherous trying to walk in the jungle at night.'

She looked around the group and realized that in the brief time since they'd stopped walking, Mira was already squatting on the ground, resting.

'And we're all bloody knackered too, aren't we?' Carly went

on. 'We've been through so much today. Let's find a spot where there's a bit of space to set up camp, and rest until dawn. Then we'll get ourselves back to safety as soon as it's light.'

'You have got to be kidding,' said Ben, mouth agape. 'There's no fucking way I'm staying out here all night. If someone did that to Hannah, they could still be out here somewhere. They might come after us next! Besides, we don't have camping gear – no tents, no bedrolls, not even a sleeping sack. And what about the animals this far inside the jungle – who knows what kinds of predators might attack us?' He ran both hands through his hair, slicking a damp blond lock back from his forehead.

'Look, I know it's not ideal, but I'm sure we can find a way to feel safe,' Carly said. 'One of us can stay awake and keep a lookout – we can take it in turns to get some rest. We can try and get comfy – we've got our jackets, some towels, a few spare tops to sleep on, and then those snacks and a bit of water left between us, haven't we?'

'I do need to rest for a bit,' said Mira. 'I'm not sure I can keep going much longer.'

'I have to admit,' said Scott, 'even though we've been making progress, I was starting to wonder the same thing. It's not safe to be trying to walk around the jungle in the dark. Carly's right – we need to stop.'

'Oh God,' said Naya, her voice cracking. 'I'm sorry, everyone, I know it's what we need to do but – I'm just so desperate to get back. I want to go home, and I – I can't stop thinking about Hannah, and if she really was murdered, and the killer is still out here – well, we're not safe in this rainforest at all, let alone overnight.'

Her voice tailed off into quiet sobs. In the light of her torch, Carly saw Naya reach out an arm and stretch it around Mira's shoulders. She felt a wave of compassion for them both, of pity, so strong that she nearly stumbled on the spot.

'I know we've all had a terrible shock – we're all tired and upset and scared,' she said. 'But it's too dangerous to keep walking now. Far more dangerous than the risk of someone – or something – attacking us. Let's find a spot to rest up for a few hours – then we'll be on our way again as soon as it gets light.'

She looked around the others' faces, gave them her warmest, most soothing smile. 'We've just got to make it through the night,' she said.

NAYA

The pink and white stick was burning a hole in Naya's back-pack.

As she sat propping up Mira in the small clearing they'd found, watching Scott and Ben clearing vines from the jungle floor in the near darkness, and Carly attempting to create a more comfortable surface to sleep on with a stack of large, soft leaves, Naya knew she couldn't put it off any longer. The shock of the mudslide; of finding Hannah: the close-up, visceral reality of death; the panic about not getting back that evening; all of it had exacerbated her nausea, and the feeling of deep, bone-aching exhaustion she'd carried with her since before she left France.

And now, an extra sense of vulnerability: the risk of danger out here, the fear of running out of food and water. Dozens of questions darted around her brain – the uncertainty of it all was too much to bear.

At least there was one thing she might be able to get a clear answer about. She fished the pregnancy test from her bag, along with some tissues, shoved the test in her back pocket and stood up.

'I'll be back in a minute,' she said, waving the tissues at the group.

'Shall I come with you?' said Scott. 'It might not be safe to go off alone, especially now that it's dark.' He seemed to catch himself suddenly. 'I mean, I won't look or anything . . . I'll turn around the other way.'

Naya suppressed a smile. 'Ah, thank you, but I won't go far. Just through the trees here, see? And I've got one of the torches you suggested we bring.' She dug it out, switched the torch on and held it up to show them, its yellow glare giving the dim silhouettes of the trees a jarring, artificial glow.

Naya sensed, rather than saw, Scott's eyebrows draw closer together. 'OK, just make sure you stay close enough that we can hear you if you get in any trouble, right?'

She nodded, reached an arm towards him, grazed his elbow lightly. 'Of course.'

Then Naya edged forward, parted the foliage in front of her, her flashlight guiding her to a large enough space between the trees, ten feet or so from the others, for her to comfortably – or near enough – squat on the jungle floor. She reached a hand behind her, retrieved the rectangular stick from her pocket, pulled off the cap, then put it back on again.

Would it even be accurate now, at this time of day? The tests picked up the hormone more easily in the morning. She could wait until then to try.

On the other hand, she was dehydrated so the concentration of her pee would be stronger than normal. And if she was as far along as she suspected, in all likelihood the test would work just as well, or not, at any time of the day.

Come on, Naya. It's better to know. Thirty seconds, and you'll know.

She inhaled, pulled down her shorts and held the stick between her legs. It had been years since she'd had to do this; she'd forgotten the trick of getting her aim right, and it was being made trickier by her cramped position and the darkness around her – but within a few seconds, she could see the tip of the stick darkening. That must be enough.

She rested the test carefully on the ground next to her, wiped herself with a tissue and pulled up her shorts. Sitting down on the mulchy earth, she picked the test back up and turned her torch onto the strip in its centre.

One line for negative. Two lines for positive.

The light of the torch wobbling in her shaking hand, Naya held her breath as the first line showed up; the test had worked, then. A few more seconds and she'd know, either way.

The second line appeared almost immediately. Not a faint line; a strong, blazing stripe, just like it had been with Marcus and Elodie.

She closed her eyes, wrapped her arms around her head; held back a sob.

How could I have done this? The latest in a catalogue of careless, thoughtless actions. Making mistakes at work – arriving at the wrong time for her shift, twice in a row. Forgetting appointments at her children's school. Miscalculating her cycle, not believing it was worth taking emergency contraception after her ill-judged one-night stand. Organization had always been Naya's strong suit, but it had been starting to feel like everything was slipping away from her these past months.

She did a quick calculation: she was probably about six

weeks pregnant – maybe seven. She racked her brains to try to remember when her last period had been, but they'd been so out of whack over the past year. Her best friend Suzanne thought it was down to stress; Naya had convinced herself she was going into early perimenopause. She wasn't sure that theory was up to much now.

So here she was, lost in a remote jungle with a potential killer on the loose – and pregnant after a regrettable one-night stand that she didn't bother using protection for, so convinced was she that she couldn't get pregnant. Already with two young kids at home, dependent on her for their every move. How the hell would she cope with a baby?

I want to go home. She picked the test up again, stared at it. Just to be sure. There was no mistaking it: she was pregnant. What the hell was she going to do? Her life was spilling over the edges already without adding pregnancy sickness and sleepless nights into the mix, another child to worry about and care for.

And *love.*

Did she even have any love left to spare?

You have options. The thought flashed through her mind, unabashed. She didn't have to go through with this, to have this baby, to go through all this alone, again. She could make another choice.

A branch snapped behind her.

'Naya? Are you all right?'

She whipped her head around, held her torch up in the direction of the voice, tried to stuff the pregnancy test back in her pocket.

Mira was standing over her, torch turned towards the

ground, a look of deep concern etched across her delicate features.

Merde. She'd been so absorbed by her thoughts, she'd not heard Mira approaching through the foliage. How had she not seen the glow from her torch?

'I'm fine,' said Naya, wiping the back of her hand across her eyes. 'I was just taking a moment alone – after everything today, I just needed to . . .' She tailed off, noticing Mira's eyes flicking towards the pocket of her shorts where she'd just shoved the pregnancy test. She looked down, realizing that half of it was still hanging out of her pocket.

'I'm sorry I disturbed you,' said Mira. 'You'd been gone for a while, and I was worried you'd hurt yourself or something was wrong, so I followed your track through here. Is that . . .' Her voice turned soft. 'Is that a pregnancy test?'

So, Mira had seen it. Was there any point in hiding what she'd been doing, then – and its outcome?

In normal circumstances, back home in her everyday life, Naya wouldn't have wanted to mention anything so early on. She didn't know how she felt about it yet, or what she was going to do; and what might Mira think of her, if she knew how it had happened, how irresponsible she'd been?

But here . . . here, with everything so terribly broken, so *wrong*. Her usual ideas no longer seemed to apply. And she felt she could trust Mira – she had shown such vulnerability with them all today, been so honest about her cancer and her recovery. Of all the people who could have stumbled across her here, surely Mira was the one she'd want to talk about this with the most.

She pulled it back out of her pocket, held it up towards Mira, said simply: 'Yes.'

Mira turned her torch in the direction of Naya's outstretched hand, stared at it for a moment.

'Oh,' she said. 'And the two lines – does that mean positive? Sorry if that's silly to ask, I've never taken one myself.'

Naya nodded. Fresh tears welled behind her eyes; she willed herself to *just hold it together, please*. She didn't want to fall apart; especially not now she knew there was a life beginning to take shape inside of her.

She had to marvel at the irony: she'd come here partly as an escape from the toll motherhood was taking on her, an attempt to remember who she had been before she had her children and given herself over to them.

But even here, thousands of miles from home, motherhood had followed her.

'Yes,' she said, not meeting Mira's eyes. 'I'm pregnant.'

There was silence for a moment. Naya listened to the evening chorus of the rainforest, waited for Mira to say something. Finally, Mira moved towards her, put a hand on her shoulder, lowered herself down onto her knees next to her, and picked up her hand.

'*Mazel tov*,' she murmured, and then: 'Though perhaps you don't feel like celebrating?'

Naya laughed sadly. 'I'm not sure I do. This wasn't something I . . .' She let her words hang.

'I understand,' said Mira. 'It sounds like you have enough on your plate.'

Naya's stomach growled. 'My plate!' she exclaimed. 'I think my belly heard you.'

'Poor choice of words,' said Mira. The two women looked at each other for a moment, then dissolved into giggles. Within seconds, tears were pouring down their faces. It wasn't even that funny, thought Naya, but a moment of hysteria was helping to release something.

Gradually their laughter died away.

'I never wanted to have children,' said Mira quietly. 'I just knew motherhood wouldn't suit me – I wouldn't have had the energy or the patience for it. It's one of the reasons I married Ezra – he was happy to devote himself to his work and studies as a rabbi, rather than have a family.'

Naya thought for a moment. 'And do you ever regret it? Not having kids?' The question came out more bluntly than she'd intended; clumsy. It sounded like a judgement, and Naya was the last person to judge anyone else for their life choices, given the moments of regret she'd had about her own. 'I'm sorry, that's not what I meant, I—'

'No, it's fine,' said Mira, touching Naya lightly on the arm. 'I didn't take offence. Trust me, my extended family have made much worse comments than that. And to answer your question – yes, sometimes I do regret it, in a way. I think about the road I didn't travel, about what I've missed out on. Especially when I see my brother and sister with their beautiful children, and how much joy they bring them. But . . .' Mira paused for a moment. 'I still know it was the right decision for me.'

She squeezed Naya's hand. 'And what about you? Do you ever regret your decisions?'

Naya raised her eyebrows. Now, *that* was a question.

She'd had thoughts, in her hardest, loneliest moments – thoughts that she wasn't proud of, and that she'd never shared with anyone. About how she wasn't cut out to be a mother of autistic children; that she was failing them, that they'd be better off with someone else.

But they were temporary notions, fleeting ideas that came in the quiet hours of the night, that she secreted away in her heart. And then they passed, and she came back to herself, and she knew with her entire being that her children were exactly who they were meant to be, and that she was exactly the mother that they were supposed to have. She wouldn't change the way her life had gone so far – well, except for one thing.

And that felt like a truth she could share with Mira.

She shook her head. 'The only thing I regret is who I chose to be their father,' she said sadly.

'Ah, I see.' Mira nodded. 'We can't always help who we fall in love with, I suppose.'

Naya sniffled, squeezed Mira's hand in her own. There was a long silence; then finally, Mira sighed. 'Oh God, how long have we been here? The others will be wondering what's happened to us. Do you feel ready to go back?' She gave Naya a knowing smile. 'Scott will be getting worried about you.'

Scott.

Hearing his name, a warmth rose in Naya's chest – followed almost instantly by a rush of something else: sadness; loss. Her growing attraction towards him was problematic enough – they lived on the other side of the world from each other, for starters, and her status as a single mother of two autistic children was enough to put off men who lived even on the same street. But now? Pregnant too? Surely this would be a death knell for any potential future romance.

It wasn't just her nerves about seeing Scott, though; the idea of having to see any of the others felt exhausting. There was sure to be more hushed, panicked discussion about Hannah, and their safety out here overnight. She was fraught enough; she didn't think she could stand it. And yet she could hardly hide out here in a corner of a dark rainforest with nothing but a pregnancy test and her tiny, growing embryo for company.

'You're right,' she said, trying to keep her voice from wavering. 'Let's head back to the group and try to get some rest.'

Using the tree behind her to help herself up, she stood and supported Mira to do the same, then the pair made their way back through the foliage towards the sound of the others' voices.

When they emerged into the clearing, Scott jumped straight to his feet.

'Are you all right?' he asked. 'You've been gone for ages – and Mira, you should have told us you were going to find Naya.'

'We're fine,' said Mira, a firm edge to her voice. 'Naya was just helping me go to the toilet – I'm still pretty unsteady on my feet.'

Naya smiled at Mira gratefully. She didn't know how safe she was out in this rainforest tonight, but at least her secret was – for now, anyway.

BEN

If Ben thought he'd suffered from insomnia before, he was wrong. He'd never tried to get to sleep the night after stumbling across a dead body – *Hannah's* dead body.

Every time he closed his eyes, he saw her: Hannah's broken form, motionless, crawling with insects, blood seeping from her head. Lying there, soon to be devoured by the creatures of the jungle. Behind his shut lids, the images grew more and more hideous – nightmarish visions of her body surrounded by vultures; flocks of them picking her flesh clean until there was nothing left of her except pale bones.

The visions made him want to cry out, or sob, or vomit. In the end, the only escape from them was to force his eyes to stay open, try to adjust to the deep gloom of the damp forest around him. He tried to focus on his breathing, to force his body to relax, but he could barely keep still, he was so damn uncomfortable. The stack of branches covered over with his lightweight jacket in place of a mattress kept digging into his spine; the rucksack under his head as a pillow was too solid and bumpy to relax into. He had no blanket, nothing to cover himself with – nothing to protect him from the thousands of insects that were no doubt waiting to crawl all over his limbs, his hair, his face.

The clouds and mist had all but disappeared now, showing glimpses of a star-studded expanse and a moon hanging high in the small sections of sky Ben was able to make out through the dense canopy. The lack of cloud cover was good on one hand, as it meant another storm and heavy rainfall was unlikely while they were out here exposed all night. But on the flipside, the lack of insulation meant the temperature seemed to have dropped by at least fifteen degrees since it got dark. And while it wasn't exactly cold, there was enough of a chill in the air for Ben to wish he had at least a thin layer protecting him.

He knew he wasn't the only one lying there tortured by thoughts, uncomfortable and wide awake. He could feel eyes on him, but he didn't know whose – whether it was the stares of one of his companions, or one of the jungle's nocturnal creatures, sizing him up. He could hear Scott rustling around in the dark close to him too, and a little further away, there were fraught whispers coming from where Naya and Mira were lying down to rest.

His mind drifted to his companions, and everything they'd said this evening. They'd talked over and over the events of the day as they'd set up camp before dusk. The questions, murmured by all of them in dazed, anxious voices. The terror they all felt; the confusion.

'Could someone really have done that to Hannah?' Mira had kept asking, again and again. 'But who – and why?'

'I don't know – it's impossible. It makes me think it must have been a terrible accident, instead. I just can't imagine anyone wanting to hurt her,' Naya had said. 'Hannah seemed so . . . I can't think of any reason she'd have an enemy, you know? Her whole purpose in life is – I mean *was* – to try and help people, to do good. It makes no sense.'

'And what about those messages from her?' Ben had wondered. 'How could she have sent us those selfies from Golfito this morning, if she was already dead?'

'Well, she couldn't have – she just couldn't have,' Mira had mused. 'Someone must have faked them somehow – or perhaps Hannah even took them another time herself. Or . . . or . . .' She'd faltered then, probably realized she was unable to come up with another viable explanation for something that was so nonsensical.

'Well, there's at least one thing we can be sure of,' Scott had said.

'Oh? What's that?' Carly had asked.

'I was thinking about it and, if someone really *did* murder her, it can't have been any of us. We weren't here when she . . . you know, when Naya thinks it happened, were we? None of us were even in the area – we were making our way here.'

There'd been a silence while the group digested this. Ben swallowed. 'Hang on, man. Does that mean you even considered that as a possibility? Did you seriously think any of us could have killed Hannah?' he'd said.

'Yeah – are you saying you suspected one of us, Scott?' said Carly, an edge to her voice. This line of thought had clearly rattled her – as it had rattled him too.

'Nah, I'm not saying that. Not saying I thought it was any of you – of course not. I just mean, it's good that we can put that possibility from our minds. And the police can too.'

Naya had cleared her throat. 'I don't know . . . we were

still the ones to find her – we were still on our way to the retreat around the time she died. From the perspective of the police, that's going to make all of us seem suspicious . . .'

Something whooshed by now, uncomfortably close to Ben's ear – a bat, most likely; through the moonlight his eyes had caught a bunch of them swooping through the trees, identifying them through their fluttering, erratic movements and sharp, chaotic turns. It brought him back to the present, lying there alone, awake in the dark.

He thought the same thing now, though: that it was impossible to imagine any of the group here could have killed Hannah. And he still had the nagging suspicion that the real cause of this might lie elsewhere; that Hannah might have managed to get herself tangled up in something she wasn't meant to. All those news articles he'd read about supposedly innocent tourists getting caught up in drug gangs and cocaine cartels were still floating around in his head. It was most likely that Hannah had gotten herself involved in something out here in the Costa Rican wilderness that she shouldn't have. But he had to know; one way or another, he had to find out: *who did this to her?*

Ben imagined these same, inevitable questions running through the minds of the police when they got here. As well as Hannah's friends and family, of course, and her followers. They'd be desperate to find the culprit. Then, surely, those questions would start to take on a shape, a focus. They'd zoom in on the people who'd been in contact with Hannah close to the time she died – wouldn't they?

A flash of light to his right-hand side, a few feet away, caught his attention, and he pushed himself up to sitting.

Underneath the beam of her torch, he could see Carly, her face eerily hollowed out and bony white under its gaze. She hadn't even tried to lie down in the hours they'd been here, by the looks of things; she was just sitting on the trunk of a fallen tree, moving her flashlight around the space. She looked like she was keeping watch for – Ben wasn't sure. *Something.* Just like him, Carly was too scared to sleep – to even close her eyes.

Ben squirmed, shifted on the spot, then: 'Ouch,' he said, as something sharp dug into the base of his spine, sending a wave of hot pain through his back. *For fuck's sake.* He was getting nowhere with this. He might as well get up, have some company instead of being stuck alone with his awful thoughts.

'Hey, Carly?' he whispered.

It took her a few beats to respond, then finally, 'Yeah?' he heard back. Her voice sounded thick with something: sleep, or maybe tears, he couldn't be sure.

'How are you holding up?' he said.

'I'm . . . not sure I am, really,' she said.

'Yeah, me neither. I can't sleep – I keep thinking over and over about . . . and besides, I can't get comfortable enough on the ground. Do you want to take my spot over here? Try and get some rest?'

Another pause, then: 'I don't know. Shouldn't one of us stay on the lookout? You know, for any predators – animal ones, I mean.'

Or human, thought Ben.

'I can do that,' he said. 'Give me your flashlight and I'll take over for a while, so you can get some rest.'

There was a crunch of footsteps and then Carly was next to him. 'Are you sure?' she said, the beam from her flashlight bouncing again off the grooves and hollows of her face. 'I wouldn't mind lying down for a bit.'

'Totally sure, you can take my spot,' said Ben, pointing to the pathetic nest behind him. 'Just let me grab my bag.'

He reached for his rucksack, then fumbled his way to the lookout point where Carly had been sitting. He sat down, stared at his bag.

Just a small one.

After everything I've been through . . . finding Hannah . . . the shock.

I can't do this any more without a hit.

Instantly he recoiled at the voice inside his head – he wasn't still that dependent, surely? He didn't need them that much – not now? Not after the last stint in rehab, when he'd really, truly, thought he didn't need them in the same way; that he could take them or leave them.

No. It wasn't withdrawal or cravings that was messing with his head. It was all *this*. Hannah's death, getting lost in the jungle, the whole disaster of coming here.

He should never have got on that plane. He should be at home in his apartment right now, catching up on work emails, the dog snoring at his feet. He could have avoided ever being part of this, ever having to see the horrors of the day.

He turned back to his bag, checked again to make sure no one was awake, watching him. Because it wasn't only the remnants of what was inside his pill packet that he needed to protect now.

There was something else in there too; something he was keeping a tightly held secret from his companions.

Just for now; just until he knew what to do with it.

Ben thought back to the moment he'd first seen it. When he'd pushed through the trees and taken in the horror in front of him; when, after a moment, he'd realized what – and *who* – he was seeing, his body had responded without his brain's command: he had moved towards her, fallen to his knees, let his hands sink to the earth near her head.

He was at once repulsed by her body, and at the same time compelled to move closer to her; as if to confirm this was really, truly her – the same Hannah whose voice could both energize and soothe at the same time; whose facial expressions could tell a hundred different stories at once. That woman, who was so vibrant, so full of life – how could that be the same person that was now inhabiting this lifeless, bloated corpse?

And then, as his eyes moved over her, they had latched on to something else, something he'd not expected to see. It was poking out the top of one of her unfurled hands, but buried almost underneath it – as though she were both trying to tuck it away and make sure it would be found.

A photo.

Four inches by six, printed on shiny paper. He'd almost said it out loud, that he'd seen it. He was so close to doing that, to telling them, wondering out loud whose picture it was, and why Hannah was holding it when she died. But at the last second he decided against it. Quickly, with no more than a brief glance at the stranger in the photograph, he shoved it into the side pocket of his rucksack, not knowing exactly why. But if he could work out who it was, perhaps it would help to incriminate the right person – and shift suspicion away from anyone else who'd happened to be there, who might be seen – wrongly – as a suspect.

Ben looked across at the others: all four of them seemed to be resting now – or at least, they were all lying on the ground, turned away from him. *Perhaps now is a good time to take a look at it?* If he kept the flashlight on, but turned his back to the others, he could focus the beam on the photo without them noticing.

He glanced behind him again, waved the flashlight across the faces of his companions; yes, they all had their eyes closed. He turned back to his bag, rooted around in the side pocket, and felt his fingers touch the edges of the picture. He pulled it out, turning the flashlight onto it as steadily as he could with trembling hands. He paused, the roar of blood in his ears nearly drowning out the rainforest's nocturnal cries, and stared at it.

The woman in the picture was unfamiliar to him; he didn't recognize her face, and he was sure he'd remember seeing her, if he had. She was cute: tan skin, choppy, bobbed hair and bright blue eyes looking up under heavy lids; brows raised teasingly, as if to say, *Get over here*. She was smiling broadly, showing neat rows of teeth, and Ben could just tell she had one of those deep, throaty laughs that always made his heart thump a little faster. She seemed to be in a bedroom; Ben could see the shape of a pillow behind her, but nothing much else. There were deep grooves criss-crossing the centre of the photo, as if it had been folded up and carried around; tucked in a pocket, or a wallet maybe. But no other clues as to who she was. Was this woman in the picture Hannah's killer? Or might she know who was? Ben wanted to will the photo to talk back to him; to ask this person all the questions turning over and over in his mind.

He flipped the photo over, scanned its back for any letters

or dates – anything that might give him a hint as to who this woman was, or why Hannah died holding her picture. He found nothing; just a blank white surface.

He sighed, folded the picture carefully back up and tucked it in his bag. He should tell the others about it – he should show it to them, see if they could shed any light on it. It wasn't that he didn't trust them exactly, though he doubted he was the only one holding things back. He just needed to find a good moment, that was all. In the morning, when they all got up, he'd tell them about it.

Until then, just for tonight, he'd keep it to himself; a secret he could grip close to his chest.

It wasn't the only secret he was keeping, of course. But there was no way in hell he could let the other one slip.

He needed to be far away from Costa Rica before anyone here found that one out.

MIRA

Mira opened her eyes and the memories of the day before flooded her brain in a sickening rush.

First, the mudslide, the desperation of almost suffocating, being buried under piles of earth. Then the sheer, devastating horror of finding Hannah – of grasping that someone could have done that to her, plus the confusion over the timings. Then the sinking realization that they were lost; that they weren't going to make it out of the rainforest before nightfall.

Confronted with this onslaught of thoughts, she felt strangely numb. That was the only way to describe it. As if she were now frozen in time and space, unable to feel anything except the sharp, stabbing pain around her ribs – and a cold ache in her chest that told her something awful had happened. She'd felt this coldness before, more than once. The day the doctors had first given her the diagnosis. Then having to tell Ezra; the dread written across his face.

And again, when they'd told her that unless she continued with more and more rounds of invasive, painful treatment, then she'd likely never recover.

A sob rose up in her chest. She shouldn't have come here;

it was so stupid. What had she done? What had she been *thinking*?

Lying on the application form, pretending to be in the best of health. And worse perhaps, lying in the video to Hannah, and even now letting the others think she was better: basing her whole story about why she wanted to come here on a series of mistruths.

The truth was different: the truth was that her cancer was not gone; it had never been gone. To her family's despair and her husband's fury, she had simply refused to undergo more treatment, seemingly content to let the cancer grow and mutate inside her body until she was nothing but tumours.

She'd just wanted to experience something of life, one last adventure. So it had seemed worth it, lying to come here, if it could give her that. But she hadn't thought about the impact of her lies on everyone else. She hadn't realized how much she'd be slowing them down, how much she would need their support – yes, even without the mudslide, even if Hannah were here and alive and everything was going exactly to plan. Even then, she'd have struggled, she'd have needed them to help her the whole way; she'd never have managed it alone.

And now they were lost out here, and Hannah was dead, and she was slowing them down. She could see now that telling her lies had been a reckless thing to do; it was selfish. Her husband had told her that, over and over. And he was right. How could she justify it now? Especially if her dishonesty led to any of them coming to harm – *more* harm.

To make matters worse, she couldn't ignore the signs her body was giving her now, more furiously.

The pain – the awful, tender throbbing that had first alerted her that something was wrong, deep in her body. It was a different kind of pain from anything else she'd ever experienced; it was unique, and that meant she knew exactly what it was. The cancer was still spreading. The tumours that the chemo had started to make a dent in were too deeply rooted for her body to shake off – at least, not without more treatment. Real, proper medical treatment, not trying to grasp one last life-affirming experience in the middle of a rainforest.

Another stab of pain hit her, deep in her spine. A vision of the cancerous cells multiplying inside her body flashed into her mind: she imagined them pushing through her skeleton with a vengeance, on a mission to destroy her. She stifled a sob. Just when she'd decided she wanted to embrace life, she'd left it too late.

And yesterday she'd witnessed something else that was causing her to revisit the crushing weight of grief; that life was over long before it should be: Hannah was dead. The woman who had shone a light into the darkest of places, who seemed to only want to help people. And it looked like some evil person had done this to her on purpose; that maybe they had orchestrated all of this, like the plot of some awful horror film.

She swallowed; the sensation painful in her dry throat. *Water*. How long had it been since she'd drunk anything? The humidity here meant that – even in the relative cool of the early morning – she was constantly sweating. She must have lost a half-litre of water from her body overnight just lying on the ground. She was about to reach out for whatever was left in her water bottle, but then she remembered the people she was out here with. Most of all, she remembered Naya, and what she'd told her last night.

She needs this more than me. I should save it for her.

Mira put the bottle back down, moved to stand up – but was hit by a rush of vertigo and slumped back to the ground. Perhaps she shouldn't be trying to move yet – she was more exhausted than she thought.

'Hey,' said Ben. Mira looked up. Ben was standing, gathering his things, stuffing them in his backpack. He was pale, with dark grey circles settling underneath his eyes. He looked like he'd been awake all night. 'How are you holding up?'

Mira opened her mouth to speak. But instead, she felt her hands start shaking again, fresh tears forming behind her eyelids. She said nothing in the end; only managed to shake her head.

'Yeah,' said Ben. 'Me too. Well, the only small piece of good news is, it's getting light now, so we can get the hell out of here. And the staff back at Hannah's place – they must have sounded the alarm by now, seeing as we didn't make it back last night. There'll be a search and rescue team out looking for us already – there has to be.'

Mira turned to look at the other three still huddled on the ground, jackets and towels wrapped around them. Even though there'd been no more rain overnight and the sun was already shining, the morning air was still cool. She let her gaze linger on Naya's face; one of her hands was cupped underneath her cheek like a pillow. Her mouth had turned down slightly at the edges. Her brow was furrowed, her lids flickering gently. Mira observed her like this for a moment until, as if feeling her watching, Naya stirred slightly.

'Ouch,' Mira hissed as a jolt of pain erupted from between her ribs. Her voice woke the other two. Carly sat up first, rubbing her eyes. They were swollen and bloodshot, with large purple rings underneath. Next to Carly, Naya sat up slowly, gingerly, taking deep breaths as she moved. Mira wondered if she was trying to quell her nausea.

'Morning, guys,' Ben said. 'Are we all OK?'

'I think so,' said Scott weakly.

'Just about,' said Carly, with a sad twist of her mouth. 'Let's get up and going soon, shall we?'

'Hey,' Scott said. 'I think we should definitely use the sun to help us navigate today. I know we tried it yesterday, but if we take it more slowly and concentrate on keeping it in view, it should help us.'

Carly, squatting now to put her stuff in her bag, looked thoughtful. 'It's a good idea – but the jungle is so thick, we can barely see the sun through the canopy.'

Mira looked upward, squinted through the foliage, caught only a slim flash of the rising sun beyond the tall trees. Carly was right: it was hard to make it out clearly. But perhaps they could see enough to at least attempt it.

She decided to try to stand up again, to see if she could get a better view of the sky that way. Slowly she moved her legs in front of her, had just started to stretch upwards when a sharp stab of pain jabbed her between the eyebrows. She clutched a hand to her forehead, wobbled on her feet and reached towards a nearby tree to steady herself. The pain subsided.

'Are you OK, Mira?' said Scott, rushing towards her.

She nodded weakly. 'Just a headache, I think.'

'Let's find you something to eat – you need some calories to get you through the hike back . . . are there any snacks left in your bag from yesterday?' asked Naya.

Mira shook her head. 'I'm sorry, I've got nothing left.'

'Not at all,' said Naya. 'Totally understandable you didn't bring much – we only thought we'd be out for a few hours. OK, let me see then,' she said, as she started to rifle through her bag, pulling out her first-aid kit, an empty water bottle, a head scarf and then, finally, a protein bar and a squashed looking banana that Mira vaguely remembered seeing yesterday when they'd been examining all their supplies.

'Here – take it,' she said, shoving the banana into Mira's hand.

'Are you sure?' said Mira. 'You should eat something too – especially now we know you're—' She stopped, but not before a flash of something – concern? curiosity? – ran across Scott's face.

'I'll just take the protein bar – you have the banana,' Naya said, unwrapping it.

'Is there enough to share with everyone?' said Ben. 'Though I guess some of us need it more than others . . .'

Mira saw Naya pause, the bar halfway to her lips. She put it down – her cheeks had flushed a little; Mira wasn't sure whether she looked annoyed or embarrassed.

'I don't think we agreed what to do with the food yesterday, did we?' said Naya. 'But yes, I'm sorry – of course, we should share it out. Here, take half of this,' she said, snapping the bar in two and handing it over.

Ben reached out to take it, then seemed to change his mind. 'Don't worry,' he muttered. 'I'm not hungry anyway.'

Scott rubbed at the spot between his eyebrows; Mira wondered if a headache was starting to form for him too, the likely consequence of the mix of exhaustion, dehydration and the cloying humidity.

'It's all right,' he said. 'We'll be OK without food and water if we get going now – we should be back at the house in a couple of hours.'

'Exactly,' said Carly. Then quietly, 'To be honest, I don't know how you can eat at the moment. I've got no appetite.'

'Agreed. Let's get going, then. The sooner we start walking, the sooner we'll get out of here,' said Ben. 'Carly, if you don't think we can use the sun to find our way, shall we take a look at the map? And how about the satellite phone – can we try and give it one more go again before we set off? It might have gotten itself just a spark of extra charge by now, right?'

'I doubt it'll work, but knock yourself out,' said Carly, digging the phone from her bag. She handed it to Ben.

'And here's the map,' said Scott, walking over to Ben so they could study it together. 'Look, I reckon we're about here now – see, this area, about halfway between the waterfall and the house – a bit closer to the stream? Mira, Carly, Naya – does this look right to you?'

They all peered at the map, then looked up at the sun. 'I can't be totally sure, but I think so,' said Carly.

'I'll mark the trees again as we go, to make sure we're not going around in circles,' said Scott.

'This thing is still dead,' said Ben crossly, waving the satellite phone at them and then shoving it in his backpack. 'Let's get going, then. Everyone ready?'

Mira nodded, then turned wearily to do up her bag, pausing for a moment at ground level to survey the area around her in case she'd dropped anything. Eyes roaming the earth, she caught a flash of colour that stood out from the browns and greens of the forest floor. Something shiny, metallic. She lost it, then searched the ground again, and there it was.

A small silver package.

She frowned, crouched to pick up a stick and nudged it out of the earth; stared at it. Even half-buried under the leaves, with soil and dirt now encrusted across its face, there was no doubting what she'd found: a cereal bar. A kind of snack bar that definitely wasn't in the collection they'd pooled together yesterday.

Someone had been keeping extra food to themselves, then. Not the worst thing in the world – understandable, maybe, under the circumstances. But still, a bit selfish, and sneaky with it.

Should I say anything? Mira was genuinely stumped. She didn't want to make too much of a fuss over it – in the grand scheme of things, it was only a snack, and if she drew attention to it, it might cause an argument. What they needed now was to all stick together – it was their best hope of getting back to safety, as fast as they could.

'Are you all right, Mira?' Naya's soft voice caught her off guard. Mira knees creaked; she felt suddenly even weaker, too weak to walk. She blew the air out from her cheeks then, slow and steady, made her way up to standing. Before she could think about it too hard, she started to stuff the bar in the pocket of her trousers – but, too late, she caught Naya's eyes tracking the movement.

'What's that?' she said, pointing at her pocket. 'Did you forget something?'

Mira felt heat flood to her cheeks. *No, no.* Was she going to think it was hers, now? That she'd dropped it there, and now she was trying to hide it? She decided to come clean; it was her only option now anyway.

'Ah – it's, well, I'm not sure. I just found it. On the ground, there.' She pulled the bar back out of her pocket, held it in Naya's direction. Naya stared at it for a moment.

'What's that?' said Ben.

'It's a snack bar,' said Naya. She reached out, took it from Mira's hand, then turned to show it to the others. 'A Costa Rican one. I don't remember anyone having one like this – I thought we'd run out of stuff, to be honest.'

'Me too. So what were you doing with it?' said Carly, turning on Mira, eyes flashing.

They think it was me hiding food, eating it in secret.

'Oh, no – it's not mine,' said Mira. 'I just found it – right here.' She pointed to the patch of earth where she'd picked it up, lamely waited for someone to speak. Then she looked around at the others' faces: all the same picture of mild confusion, with flickers of irritation.

Except for Scott's. Scott's expression was different.

He wore a look of guilt; of panic.

As Mira watched, Scott began to shake his head. He moved it slowly at first, then more and more quickly, frantically.

'Scott?' said Naya. 'Are you OK? Is there something you want to say?'

His face flushed purple. 'It's not what you think . . . I just . . . I was trying to . . .' he said.

And then, as Mira watched, rooted to the spot, Scott started to move backwards, bumping into branches and vines, brushing against the enormous leaves, eyes darting wildly from side to side.

'I . . . I . . .' Scott stuttered. 'I can't do this. I'm so sorry—'

And with one more step backwards, as his body started to disappear into the lush green foliage, Mira caught sight of him turn and begin to stumble, alone, into the dense rainforest.

NAYA

'Scott – stop! Don't leave – it's not safe for you to be alone. Whatever it is, let's talk about it, we can deal with it . . .' Naya called out after him as he backed through the thick vines.

It was too late; Scott had disappeared into the foliage frighteningly fast. Now Naya wasn't sure whether to risk trying to follow him and ending up lost – even *more* lost – herself.

She turned back to the others, shaking her head. She could feel the heat rising through her body, another wave of nausea taking hold. *Not now, baby – please. Give your maman a break.* The stifling humidity, the growing heat of today's sun, the terror and trauma of yesterday – it was all joining forces with her hormones to force thick, hot bile to rise up in her throat. She swallowed it back down, took a breath.

'*Bordel de merde*, why would he run off like that?' she said. 'Of all the times to disappear . . . Even if he's got some extra food he's been hiding, it's hardly the worst thing in the world – not after everything we've just been through!' She looked at the group, saw the confusion registered in their faces, mirroring her own.

'That was a bloody stupid move,' said Carly, shaking her

head. 'He'll never find the way back out of the jungle by himself. And besides, this is the time to stick together. The rainforest is a dangerous place at the best of times, but after what happened to Hannah – well, there's good reason to think there are more lethal things out here than just bloody snakes and spiders.'

Carly was right: it was insane, what Scott had just done – even more so when they needed him, with his expertise in the wilderness, to help them navigate out of there.

They needed him – *she* needed him.

Naya gave a grunt of frustration, flung her backpack over her shoulders, turned on her heel and started to walk in the direction of where Scott had just vanished into the jungle. 'I'm going after him,' she said.

'No, Naya, hold on,' said Ben. 'Just wait a second – let's think this through.' He paused, cleared his throat; it sounded dry, scratchy. They were all nearly out of water, and after the amount of fluid they'd all lost, sweating their way through the sticky, humid jungle, they needed to drink something – and soon.

She peered at him: the surface of his skin was greyish, dull and clammy; his lips were dry, with small cracks appearing at their edges. The area below his eyes was sunken, hollowed out. The signs of dehydration were settling into his face. Hers would start to look the same soon, given the humidity of the air and the effort of pushing through dense jungle in the oppressive heat. *We've got to get back soon.* Perhaps there was a water source they could find on the way, if they got desperate – or could they collect some rainwater somehow? She resolved to keep an eye out.

'Running away like that by himself, when he must realize

how dangerous it is to be wandering around alone,' Ben was saying. 'It kinda feels like the behaviour of a person with something to hide, don't you think? And I mean, more than just sneaking extra snacks in his bag and hiding them from us.' He paused, then added: 'Maybe there's something else he doesn't want us to find out.'

'I know what you mean – it does looks suspicious,' Carly agreed. 'And did you hear what he said just before he turned and ran?'

'Yeah,' said Mira, her face grim. 'He did say he was sorry. But surely he just meant he was sorry he'd kept some extra food without telling us. I can't imagine there being anything more to it than that . . .'

She tailed off, and Naya looked at her closely. She was on edge, like they all were, but she looked crestfallen; lost, just like she had ever since the mudslide; or was it since they'd found Hannah's body? She looked as though she wanted to give up. There was something disconcerting about seeing someone with Mira's quiet strength, someone who had survived everything she had, looking so completely beaten.

'Look, you're probably right,' said Carly. 'I can't picture him having anything to hide – but all I'll say is this: if there's one thing I've learned in my job, it's that people often aren't who they seem to be on the surface.' She waved away a fly buzzing near her face. 'I can't tell you the number of times I've seen clients for therapy who would swear blind they were victims of some kind, the ones to feel sorry for, the good ones – they'd suck me in completely and only in the end I'd realize . . .' She paused; swallowed. 'Well, I'd realize I was wrong,' she said softly.

Naya paused, let this sink in. She'd considered the fact that any of them could be hiding something – she barely knew them, after all. But even if some of them were keeping secrets, holding things back – there was simply *no way* Scott would be capable of something sinister. She was getting to know him; she had a sense of him. Everything about him – his energy, the way he spoke – was gentle. She felt like she could trust him.

But I'm just basing my trust of Scott on intuition, warned a voice inside Naya's head. And her intuition had been wrong before, more than once. Perhaps it was wrong again now; Naya's relationship history was living proof that she shouldn't trust herself. Mathieu had made out that he'd be the perfect partner, the model father. She'd trusted him, and she'd fallen for it – over and over again, even after she'd caught him in lie after lie. He was just so good at it; he still was. And worse than that, even after all his deceptions, she'd *still slept with him*.

A moment – rather, an entire night – of madness, when he'd actually shown up for the children, done what he'd said he was going to do and more. He always knew how to get to her; the kinds of things she wanted from him. The kinds of things she wanted him to say, too.

How wrong; how stupid. How could the desire for a quick fuck have been enough to pull her back towards him – and now with these consequences? Was she really that easy to get into bed, that desperate to feel someone's touch? She'd been so young when they'd met and married, barely twenty-four when she'd first got pregnant. Now, at thirty-three, she already felt washed up; an invisible, exhausted mother. Of course she'd fallen for his whispered compliments, his empty sweet talk.

Naya sighed, rubbed at the spot between her eyes – then moved her other hand instinctively to her stomach, as if to say, *Don't worry, I'll protect you.*

'Sorry, Carly, but there's no way we could have got Scott that wrong,' Mira was saying. 'And anyway, it doesn't feel right, leaving him out there on his own – we're much safer as a group, aren't we? We need to stick together, like you said.'

At the mention of Scott being out there alone, an image flashed through Naya's mind: turning to look back at the school playground when she'd dropped Marcus off at school the morning before she left, standing to watch a few minutes longer than usual, with no work to rush off to, only packing to do at home.

Seeing him standing there by himself, dragging his schoolbag along the concrete ground, watching other children form playful huddles; all of them brushing past him, not so much as looking at him. Her heart ached for him that moment outside the school gates; it ached for him again now – and, she realized, it was aching for Scott too, not able to articulate what he wanted to say, and now alone, afraid, in a hostile place.

'I'm with Mira,' Naya blurted out. 'She's right – of course we can't leave him out here. He's exhausted, in shock, starting to get dehydrated like the rest of us – he could die out here without water and proper rest. We can't let that happen, no matter what he might have done – which, in all likelihood, is nothing more than keeping a couple of snacks to himself.' She paused, glanced at the others. 'I'm going after him now before he can get too far away from us.'

'Hang on,' said Ben. His jaw was tense, his eyebrows furrowed, creating a deep crease along the centre of his forehead.

He looked like he was wrestling with something, as though there was something more he wanted to say, but couldn't quite spit out. He opened his mouth, then closed it again, repeating this a few times, goldfish-like, before finally saying: 'Before we go after him – there's something I need to show you all. It'll only take a second, then we'll go after him. I should have told you before now, but . . .'

Naya watched as he unzipped a section of his backpack and took out a small piece of paper; no – not paper, she realized. It was a photograph. Why did Ben need to show this to everyone, now of all times?

Ben swallowed. 'I found this on Hannah's dead body,' he said.

There was a stunned silence. *He . . . what?*

Ben held the picture up; the rest of them stared at the woman in it, took in her pretty, smiling face.

Naya frowned. 'But who is she?' she said.

Ben shrugged. 'No idea. I was hoping one of you might know.'

Naya looked at Carly and Mira. They were both staring at the picture, wide-eyed. No one spoke.

'Well, I've never seen her before in my life,' said Naya.

'Me neither,' said Carly.

Mira shook her head vigorously. 'Where did you find it exactly?' she said.

'It was in one of her hands, all crumpled up,' said Ben.

Naya considered this for a moment. 'Perhaps it's someone close to her – doesn't she have a sister?' she said. 'There's a slight resemblance in their faces – maybe it's her?'

Ben looked stricken for a moment. 'I mean, I don't see that

exactly, but you're probably right that it's someone she is . . . I mean, *was* close to.' He wiped a droplet of something – sweat, or was it tears? – from the side of his right eye. 'It's just strange, is all.'

And that's not the only thing that's strange.

'Hang on, Ben – I don't get it. Why didn't you just show us the photo at the time, when you found it?' Naya asked. 'Why keep it a secret and only tell us about it now? And you've tampered with possible evidence – what if there were finger-prints on there, or something the police could have used to find out what happened to her?'

Ben shifted on the spot. 'I know . . . I'm sorry, I don't know what I was thinking. I felt like maybe it could help – if the police can't find her body or something, the photo might help incriminate the person who killed Hannah, you know? But then I thought, if—' He broke off abruptly and Naya wondered what he'd been about to say.

'Listen, guys, can we discuss this later?' said Mira, her voice betraying a note of irritation, Naya thought. 'I really think we need to start looking for Scott, before he gets too far away from us.'

'You're right – and I'm sorry for doing this now,' said Ben, sighing. 'I just didn't want to keep it a secret any more, I guess. Let's start walking, then – he went this way, right? Carly – hand me the knife, I'll lead the way.'

Looking uncomfortable, Carly gave Ben a curt nod and passed him the knife. Grasping it in front of him, Ben started to cut a path through the leaves in the direction Scott had run, Naya close at his heels, Carly and Mira behind them. It was still early in the morning and the sun had only started to peek over the trees in the past few minutes; visible through the foliage were patches of a blue, cloudless sky. *No rain today, then, at least.*

'Hey,' said Ben, pointing to some flattened leaves, a few thin branches that had been snapped and fallen to the ground. These hints – left for them, helpfully, by the dense jungle, where a human body would have to mark its surroundings when passing through – were enough for them to pursue. 'See here?' Ben called behind his shoulder to the others. 'Look at the bend in these branches and vines – he must have pushed his way through here.'

'This could be a bad idea,' came Carly's voice, from the tail of the line. 'Ben, are you sure we'll be able to find our way back after this? We don't want to end up going around in circles . . .'

'I'm sure we'll find the way,' Ben reassured her. 'If Scott's leaving a trail behind him, then we will too. We'll be able to follow it when we find him.'

'*If* we find him,' Carly muttered.

Naya stopped dead, turned to face Carly, met her gaze. 'We are *going* to find him.'

She kept the rest of the thought to herself: *Or at least, I am – and nothing is going to stop me.*

SCOTT

With each step forward, Scott was slowing down; even his bulky arms were no match for the thick jungle, and already he had tripped, stumbled on vines and branches, the huge leaves surrounding him clouding his view, making it tough to see where he was stepping. Without the others and the knife to help cut through the dense foliage, and trying to go at a pace, he was gathering cuts and scratches with almost every movement. Every minute or so, he was letting out a yell, stopping in his tracks, and then pushing himself on, making it a little further through the trees. But he forced himself to carry on, making the slowest and most painful progress he could imagine.

As he walked, harsh thoughts battered at him, rattling around his brain. *What are you doing, you idiot?* He was always making stupid decisions; doing things like this on impulse, not thinking things through properly. And he could never come up with the right thing to say, especially under pressure, with people looking at him, waiting for him to speak, expecting an answer.

It was like when Justine had first told him that she wasn't happy with him; and then again when she'd told him she was leaving. That she couldn't cope any longer with the loneliness she felt being married to Scott. He remembered how baffled he'd been; how dumbstruck. How the words he needed to express how he felt about her, the words that would help him fight for her, completely eluded him.

He loved her so deeply – *could she really not see that? Not feel it?* He just didn't always say the right thing – or anything at all. Sometimes he didn't know how to react in the ways she wanted him to. And he was useless with his phone, which used to drive her insane; sometimes he'd forget to message when he was away with work for a couple of days, even though she'd asked him to stay in touch. It wasn't that he didn't think about her – he just couldn't keep track of the days sometimes, couldn't keep everything in his head. But that didn't mean he didn't love her. He'd have done anything for her.

He just didn't know how to tell her that. And he didn't know how to tell the others – Naya, especially – what he'd done either.

A large bird – something colourful, a macaw, maybe – flew out of one of the nearby trees, shaking the branches, startling him out of his thoughts. With the shock came a jolt of adrenaline, and a new realization: he knew loads about nature, about the wilderness. He could identify most of the birds out here just by their colours. Wildlife was literally what he lived and breathed for his day job – OK, the bush he was used to wasn't exactly the jungle, but still, working as a ranger in Yarra Ranges National Park meant he'd been on his fair share of hikes in remote places. He'd had to find his way back enough times, when he and his team had been out monitoring conditions in the furthest reaches of the sites.

He could get himself out of here – even without a map to guide him, he could probably manage it. He could just disappear now, quietly slip away, out of the rainforest, back to the house, and away home. He could get away from them all without ever having to explain himself.

But then I'd never see Naya again.

He'd known Naya less than two days, and already the thought of disappearing on her – leaving her to make all kinds of assumptions about what he might have done – was unbearable; it made his chest ache. No, it wasn't an option.

What should I do then?

He needed to stop, think for a minute. As if the rainforest had heard him, at that moment he stumbled into a small clearing dominated by an enormous tree – vast, with huge, sprawling roots a metre thick. This was one of the kapok trees he'd read about, one of Costa Rica's wonders – he recognized it by its shape and breadth.

It was as good a place to take a pause as any. He checked the tree for spiders and ants; finding it clear, he set his bag down. Only then, when he'd scanned in every direction to make sure, and seen no trace of the others – he couldn't hear them calling for him any more; couldn't even be sure which direction they were in – only then did he allow himself to take a breath.

He sat down, leaned back, pushed his body into the huge, hefty bulk of the tree's trunk, then began to turn the options over in his mind.

He could go back to the others, try to explain himself. Would they even believe him, though? Would they understand why he'd done it?

They'd think he was lying – or crazy.

Bloody hell.

Scott rested his head in his palms, covered his eyes. It was too late for any of this ruminating now anyway. He'd fled, and they were all bound to be thinking the worst about him – who could blame them, under the circumstances? He thought of Naya – lovely, kind Naya – assuming he was a liar, a fake; perhaps a *murderer*, even.

I've been so stupid.

It was all of them seeing the snack bar, and Naya in particular, that had done it. The realization he was about to be found out – all right, he hadn't done the worst thing in the world, keeping some food to himself, and he'd had good intentions for doing it. But it was the way he'd handled it – the running off, looking so guilty, and now his fear of the sorts of suspicions it might have aroused in them: that he was dishonest, that he was capable of being that selfish, of keeping secrets.

Which, of course, he was. He just hadn't meant it to come out like that; he hadn't meant to *behave* like that, in such a bizarre way. It was just that everything had come together in one horrible, perfect storm: the trauma of the previous day; the shock of finding poor Hannah dead, murdered. Of realizing they weren't making it back to the house that night. By bolting like that, though, he'd only made himself look guilty – *more* guilty. More suspicious. And what on earth was he thinking, blurting out that he was *sorry* as he backed away?

Yes, he'd lied about the food, he'd hidden that from them. But everything else that had happened – everything that had gone wrong, the storm, the mudslide, Hannah – none of those things were his fault.

Lulled by the heat, the rhythmic, pulsating hum of the

cicadas, and his dry-mouthed exhaustion, Scott's eyelids began to droop. He forced them open again. *Come on, now, focus.* This wasn't the time for a nap; there were pressing issues at stake. He attempted to swallow; his throat was parched, his lips arid. Perhaps he could just have a sip of water. Enough to sustain him, so he could keep going long enough to get out of this large but non-insurmountable patch of jungle.

How much stuff did he have with him exactly? Scott turned to his backpack, opened the zip to the main compartment, started pulling things out – grabbing at whatever he could lay his hands on. His fingers emerged with two packet of nuts, another cereal bar and some dried fruit. He laid them all on top of the bag, covered them with his hands to avoid attracting the insects that would no doubt begin swarming once they caught the sweet scent.

At the sight of the rest of his secret stash, a flash of guilt slapped Scott across the face. How stupid he'd been to let a snack bar fall out of his bag like that, where he was sleeping – when he thought he'd been so careful.

Oh God, what have I done? He should have stayed with the group. Even if they'd given him a hard time over the food, even if they'd suspected he was hiding something else – running off like that was the worst possible thing he could have done.

He should try to find them again – he could trace his path back to the clearing where they'd slept easily enough. He hadn't made it far. Yes, he'd do that. Find them and explain. Hope that they'd understand, that they'd forgive him.

He'd just got to his feet when he heard it.

Their voices coming through the thicket straight ahead of him. Rooted to the spot, he listened as the sound became louder, the bushes started to bend and shift with the shape of bodies and arms and then, finally, faces.

'Scott – here you are! Guys, I can see him – he's through here, look.'

They had found him.

NAYA

Naya couldn't tell if Scott looked pleased or horrified to see the four of them as they shouldered their way through the dense undergrowth towards him. Perhaps it was a mixture of both; a mix of everything. Maybe none of them knew what to feel out here any more, or how to feel it.

'Are you OK?' she whispered, glancing behind her. She wasn't sure why she didn't want the others to hear; she just knew she wanted this to stay between them. She wanted Scott to know she understood who he was; that she wasn't suspicious of him. And that if he'd been hiding food for himself – or if whatever he had to say sorry for was something worse than that, even – well, none of that meant he deserved to dehydrate or stumble to his death alone in the wilderness.

Naya watched as Scott's expression turned from panic to something that looked like embarrassment – and then to pure relief. He closed his eyelids briefly, moved his head in the slightest bob, then sniffed, and looked at her.

'I don't know. Not really,' he croaked. 'Are you?'

Naya was about as far away from being OK as it was possible to be. She shook her head. 'No, not OK at all.'

Scott nodded, looked at the ground. 'I'm sorry for running off like that,' he said. 'It's not what you think – with the food, I mean.'

Naya shrugged. 'OK. Why did you do it, then?'

She saw Scott glance behind her. Hearing an intake of breath at her shoulder, she looked back at the other three standing there. She turned back to Scott before she could register their expressions too deeply; she didn't want to know if they were angry with him, or suspicious. She couldn't pinpoint why exactly, but she just knew she couldn't bear it.

Scott looked at the four of them, his eyes landing, and fixing eventually, on Naya's.

'I just didn't know how to tell you,' he said. 'With everything that's happened . . . everything we've been through. I was only trying to help – I just . . . I panicked.'

'We're all shocked, we're all not thinking straight – I can understand you panicking,' said Mira, from behind Naya, her voice soft.

'But why did you say sorry, then?' asked Ben. 'What do you have to be sorry for?'

Scott stared at the ground, scuffed at the root of a tree with his shoe. 'I did something . . . something stupid, I guess. I thought it was the right thing to do, but . . .'

Naya felt a dull lurch in her guts. Whatever Scott had done, she wasn't sure he should be telling them – she wasn't sure she wanted to know. What if she'd misjudged him? What if he was capable of doing something terrible – something she'd never imagined he could do? She tried to communicate that as she stared at him, willing him not to say anything.

It didn't work.

'I don't know what I was thinking,' he said. 'But I, I . . .' He paused for a moment, reached an arm towards a vine to steady himself; looked as though he was steeling himself for something. 'You're right, I was keeping some extra food aside.'

He was . . . but why? Naya tried to understand what she was hearing – and why it had led to him fleeing on his own into the wilderness. Keeping food to himself was a selfish thing to do, and running away was potentially dangerous to himself – but it was hardly murder.

'Yesterday, I pretended I didn't have any food left, but I did, because I was scared we'd be stuck out here today too, and I didn't think I could trust you all to ration it out properly.' His words erupted in a furious rush; Naya had to take a moment to translate and process what he'd said.

He took a deep breath, then carried on: 'So I thought it'd be a good idea if I could keep some aside – conserve it, before we ran out of everything – that's what you're supposed to do, you know, if you're trapped somewhere away from food and water, spread it out rather than eat and drink it all in one go.' He paused for breath again. 'But I was never planning to keep it all to myself, I swear. I was trying to ration it for all of us – especially for those of us who might need it the most.'

Of course. Naya's relief washed over her like a warm bath. She could believe that of him, far more than she could believe he had anything sinister to hide.

Ben exhaled angrily behind her. 'Can we see it, then – the food you've been *rationing* for us?' His tone was pure cynicism. Naya glared at him.

'Yeah,' said Scott. 'Here – take a look.' He opened his

rucksack, pulled out a handful of snacks, a half-full water bottle, offered them towards the group. 'See?'

There was a moment's silence, then: 'Fine,' Ben huffed. 'So why didn't you just tell us that, instead of disappearing on your own?' His eyes were still narrowed, one finger jabbed out in Scott's direction. *How dare he? When his own behaviour – keeping that photo secret from them all, for hours – was hardly beyond suspicion?* She felt an immediate rush of sympathy for Scott; a protectiveness. She didn't want him to have to explain himself.

'I don't know – I don't know how to describe it. I just . . . panicked,' Scott said. 'I get like that sometimes . . . like I can't find the right words – my brain kind of shuts down. And then my legs just started kind of moving by themselves, and then it was too late and I'd gone.' His hands moved to his face, rubbed his eyes with long fingers. 'I know it must sound stupid.'

Naya shifted on the spot, uncomfortable. He'd said enough now, surely. This pressure on him was too much – she didn't want him to crumble.

'It doesn't sound stupid at all – I understand. We all do,' she said firmly, eyes fixed on Scott. 'And it was really thoughtful of you to be keeping food to one side like that. Now listen, everyone, I think we need to focus on what's most urgent at the moment.' She glanced around the group. 'Right now, there's only one thing we all need to be thinking about, together. And that's getting out of the rainforest and back to safety.'

Scott caught Naya's eyes; he smiled at her gratefully.

'Fine,' said Ben. 'I'll go ahead and lead the way.'

Naya fell into line in front of Scott as they made their way back to the clearing where they'd set up camp last night. Ben, leading the group, with Carly and Mira close behind, was following the same track he'd pushed through a few minutes earlier. It didn't take them long to make their way back to the clearing; after that, Scott instructed Ben to keep walking in the direction they'd decided on that morning – before he'd done his disappearing act. Ben was content to stay in the lead, wielding the knife in front of him.

Naya let her pace slow a little, so that she and Scott were a few metres back from the others. She wanted to be near him; she wanted to talk to him, and only him, at least for a few moments, out of the others' earshot. The pure physical bulk of him, combined with his gentle, slightly awkward way of communicating, worked together somehow to make her feel safe with him. She trusted him, certainly more than Ben, but perhaps more than Carly too – even Mira.

She still wasn't entirely sure whether this draw to him was friendship or something more – or whether there'd be any hope of the *something more* anyway, knowing now that she was pregnant again. But it was warm and peaceful, being around him – not the fireworks she had with Mathieu, the chaos of never knowing if or when or how he'd show up for her. This was different; quieter. And she liked it.

'Hey, Scott.' She slowed her pace, glanced back at him. 'Can we chat?'

He smiled in a way that lit up his whole face. 'I'd like that,' he said, moving into step with her. Then more quietly, he added: 'How are you doing?'

Naya grimaced; shook her head. 'I don't know. Shocked and scared and tired. I can't stop thinking about Hannah. I'm worried about Mira and how she's going to make it back. I totally panicked when you ran off like that – I'm so glad we found you.' She paused; she wanted to fill Scott in on what Ben had shown them and the nagging feeling of mistrust that his secrecy had left her with. 'And there's something else . . .' Scott raised his eyebrows. Naya lowered her voice to a whisper: 'Just after you'd run off earlier, Ben showed us a photo.'

Scott frowned. 'What do you mean – what photo?'

Naya sighed. 'He said he found it on Hannah's body, and he didn't know who the picture was of.' She described the woman in the photo with as much detail as she could remember, watched as Scott's eyes widened.

'Does she sound familiar to you at all?'

Scott looked thoughtful. 'No, I don't think so. But I don't get it – why didn't he tell us about the photo straight away? Why wait until this morning?'

'Exactly. I can't understand why he hid it from us. Unless—' She faltered for a second.

'Unless there are other things he's not telling us,' Scott finished.

As he said it, a bird of prey shrieked wildly overhead and Naya startled, nearly stumbled over. He took hold of her arm to steady her. 'I'm OK – thanks,' she said. 'Yeah, exactly. But I can't imagine Ben lying to us about something bigger, like . . .' She swallowed. 'Like what happened to Hannah – can you?'

Scott's eyes widened; he shook his head. 'No, of course not. But then, I can't imagine anyone doing that. I mean, what kind of person would hurt someone like Hannah? Or pretend to be her in those messages – send those photos of her, know what she'd say, sound exactly like her, to throw us all off track?'

Naya let his words settle. Something in them had jarred, nudged something in her brain.

Sound exactly like Hannah.

Naya hadn't thought of it like that before. But it was true. If someone else sent those messages, they'd have to know her pretty well, wouldn't they? The kinds of things she'd say, how she'd have planned the retreat, the lay of the land here, where to find the maps and the satellite phone . . . Yes, you could get a good sense of Hannah's personality from her hundreds of TikTok videos and Instagram reels – but what if it was more than that?

What if – and at the thought, Naya's stomach dropped – what if one of the people here *knew much more about Hannah and this retreat than they'd been letting on*?

And what if that same person had come here with a specific plan in mind – a plan to kill Hannah?

Surely there was only one person, out of the five of them, who'd been acting strangely; who'd been behaving as though they had something to hide; who didn't quite seem to fit in here; whose reasons for being here seemed less plausible.

The hairs on her arms prickled and stood upright despite the clammy heat. She had the overwhelming urge to turn and bolt from the rest of them, to fend for herself out here alone. Her expression must have given her away.

'What is it?' said Scott. 'What's wrong?'

Naya's eyes darted from Scott's face to glance at the others in front of her: Carly helping Mira to keep walking, and Ben still in the lead. Then she found her resolve, trusting that feeling inside her that told her she could rely on Scott, and she said, quietly enough that the others couldn't hear: 'I don't know –

it's just a thought. It probably doesn't even make sense, but now I can't shake it out of my head.'

'OK,' said Scott. 'Do you want to share it with me?'

She chewed on the side of her lip. 'It's going to sound crazy, I think,' she said.

He gave her a wide smile. 'I promise I won't think you're crazy. Try me.'

Naya blew the air out of her cheeks. 'What if one of us – one of the five of us, I mean – knew Hannah *before*?' she said softly. She stopped herself from revealing the rest of her thought: that the most likely suspect, in her mind at least, was Ben. As soon as she'd said it, though, she realized how ridiculous her words sounded. She covered her hand with her mouth and shook her head. 'I know it doesn't make sense.'

Scott frowned. 'Knew Hannah before? Why would you think that?'

Before she could tell him her reasoning, they saw Mira ahead of them, holding Carly's arm, stumble and almost fall to the ground, before she caught her, steadied her. Holding on to her tightly, she turned to face the others.

'Guys, we need to stop for a minute. Mira needs a breather.'

Merde. They'd only been walking for ten minutes, if that. Hopefully, they'd make it quick. She nodded, helped Mira to get comfortable on her rucksack and spent a moment wafting a huge leaf back and forth in front of her face in an attempt to cool her down. She looked terrible: pale and clammy. Naya did a quick check of her pulse; it was rapid, well over one hundred beats per minute even after a few moments at rest. *Too fast*.

Naya stood up, gestured to Ben, Scott and Carly. 'We should try and keep going. Do you think we might be able to take it in turns carrying Mira, just for short stints? Perhaps Ben, Scott, you could hoist her onto your backs for a few moments each? I'm worried about her body giving out altogether.'

Scott frowned. 'I guess we could try – Ben, what do you think? We can keep swapping.'

Ben nodded. 'Sure,' he said. 'I can take first shift, if you like. Here, you take the knife.' Scott took it from his outstretched hand, and Ben walked to Mira's side, spoke gently into her ear.

'Before we go, I need to talk to you both.' Carly had appeared next to Naya and Scott, and her whisper was urgent, loaded.

'What is it?' asked Naya.

Before she'd even asked, though, she thought she could guess what Carly wanted to say. Her pupils were large and black; they darted behind Naya and Scott, then back to their faces again. 'I know you said to walk in this direction, and I don't want to take over again – I know that didn't exactly work out last time . . .' She paused, took a deep breath in and out, swallowed. 'But I'm worried we're still lost – I'm not sure we're going the right way.'

Naya inhaled deeply; felt the rainforest – the world – around her shift and tilt from side to side. 'Scott?' she whispered.

He wouldn't meet her eyes. 'I . . . I don't know,' he muttered.

No, please, no. A new stab of despair lodged deep in her belly. Because wasn't Carly most likely right? That even though they'd been using the sun to help guide them, and following the map as best they could, they still didn't seem to be making progress. They'd not even come across any of the trees Scott had marked yesterday, as impossible as that seemed. Perhaps they were simply walking around in circles. Everything looked exactly the same in the jungle; it was impossible to tell whether they were simply treading the same ground.

What if it took them the whole day, another night even, to get out of here? That was possible, unless they were lucky in their choice of direction.

And luck didn't seem to be something they'd had much of on this trip.

'What are our chances of making it back there today?' Naya asked.

'I think we can manage it,' said Scott, determination now in his voice. 'What if we—'

But Carly interrupted him: 'I've been thinking.' She raked her fingers through the ends of her hair; Naya saw it had got tangled and knotty. She hadn't noticed before – she'd not been close enough, perhaps – but purplish-grey circles had formed underneath eyes that were bloodshot. She looked like a different person to the one Naya had met less than two days ago: a shell, an empty casing of herself. Naya imagined she must look exactly the same.

'What if we separate now?' Carly suggested. 'It might make more sense, you know – we could cover more ground that way?'

Naya frowned. 'But . . . aren't we safer all being together?'

'Well, maybe, but the most dangerous thing now is for us not to find our way back, isn't it? I could go with Ben and Mira, and you two could . . .'

Carly gestured towards them, but as she moved, she swayed on the spot, righted herself, then clasped a hand to her forehead.

Scott held an arm out, propped her up. 'Carly, are you OK? What happened?'

She leaned against him. Her eyes darted around the trees

behind him for a moment, then landed back on his face. 'I don't know,' she said weakly. 'I got so dizzy, all of a sudden. I don't feel too good, to be honest.' She pushed forward slightly, sending Scott stumbling backwards towards a lush-leaved tree with bright purple flowers.

'You need something to drink,' he said. 'And some food too – you didn't eat anything when we got up today, did you? Let me find something for you – I've still got a few things left.'

Scott opened his rucksack; Naya watched as he started to root around inside it for something to offer Carly. But he mustn't have been able to find what he was looking for; he crouched down on the ground, started pulling everything out of his bag, carefully at first and then frantically.

Naya reached a hand out to help calm him; but she wasn't thinking, she wasn't careful enough with her touch, because he startled – and as he did, his foot slid across the rainforest floor towards a small, dark hole at the foot of the tree.

'Scott – be careful – move your foot!' Naya yelled.

But he was distracted; he hadn't seen the brown, yellow and black snake he'd woken from its slumber at the edge of its lair – camouflaged so perfectly amongst the leaves and bark.

And Naya could only scream in terror as it uncoiled its body, hissed, drew back its head and lunged towards him with open jaws.

BEN

Ben whirled around at the sound of Naya's roar.

'What the hell just happened?'

'Move!' Scott yelled. 'That's a fer-de-lance – they're fucking lethal.'

Ben's eyes darted towards the ground, where a large, muscular snake with diamond-shaped patterns across its back was slithering, mercifully, back towards the bottom of the tree, disappearing between its roots.

'Scott, are you OK?' said Naya, grabbing his arm. 'It didn't bite you, did it?'

'No, I'm all right,' said Scott, breathless. 'Just spooked. Naya, you saw it just in time, thank fuck. But we've got to be more careful – a single bite from one of those is enough to kill you in minutes.'

'Oh my God,' said Naya. 'I thought there weren't many dangerous snakes in Costa Rica. Why would Hannah have planned the whole trip out here if there were lethal things waiting . . .' She tailed off, blanched; realizing what she'd just said.

'But Hannah didn't plan for us to be out here, like this,' murmured Mira.

'In her defence, I think dangerous snakes like the fer-de-lance are pretty rare out here,' said Carly. 'We were unlucky to come across one.'

A thought occurred to Ben then – one he'd had a bunch of times over the past couple of days since they got here, but never put words to. He turned to Carly. 'Remind me how you know so much about all this stuff? You know, jungle survival and snakes and all?' he said.

Carly frowned. 'I spent some time in the rainforest a few years back – didn't I mention that before?'

Ben shrugged. 'I guess so. Maybe.'

'It wasn't here in Costa Rica, though – it was in the Amazon. Very different kind of rainforest – wilder, more dangerous in a lot of ways,' she said. Her eyes seemed to lose focus for a moment, as if she'd gone somewhere else. 'It was where I met my ex too, so it's got special memories for me, I suppose.'

Then Ben remembered something else. 'Didn't Hannah spend some time in the Amazon? I'm sure I heard her talking about it on a video once.'

Carly looked at him; there was something wary in her eyes. Something suspicious, even. 'Did she? I don't remember that.'

'Yeah, I saw that video,' said Naya. 'She said she went there recently, though. Not years ago, like Carly.'

Ben swallowed down the lump that was building in his throat. 'I must be getting it wrong then.'

His skin felt like it was crawling suddenly, as if that damn snake was gliding across his body, its rough, dry scales skimming the surface of his skin. He shuddered, despite the hot clamminess of the air.

It was the tension within the group; he could feel it, something starting to grow, to take shape in their fear and shock. Suspicions; paranoia.

He'd felt it first towards Scott when he'd bolted off, and now he felt it towards Carly – irrationally, by the sounds of it.

He tried to shake off the feeling; he was probably over-reacting – and understandably, given everything they'd been through. Carly hadn't given him any reason to believe she was lying about anything. None of them had, except Scott, but what he'd explained to them seemed to stack up.

'Please, can we just keep going?' said Naya. 'With lethal snakes out here on top of everything else, we really need to find our way back to civilization . . . and the longer we're wandering around in this rainforest, the longer it's going to take the authorities to get out here and find Hannah.'

Her voice came out with a wobble – and then Ben saw it. He saw her look at him, and in her eyes was the same wariness and apprehension he'd seen in Carly's. She couldn't hide her distrust.

That was it. He had to say something.

'Yes, we can keep walking,' he said. 'But before we set off again – don't y'all think it would be good to clear the air?'

Naya was the first to turn to face him, a frown creasing her brow. 'What do you mean, *clear the air*?'

'Well, things just feel a little frosty between us now, right? It seems like we don't trust each other any more. I just think we should talk about it.'

Mira shook her head, but she still looked afraid. 'I've never said I don't trust anyone – I don't think that at all,' she said. 'None of us said that.'

Scott sighed, put down his backpack. 'But we all feel it, don't we?' he said. 'I know what Ben's saying. I've had . . .

thoughts about some of the people here. I can't be the only one. Let's at least be honest about that.'

'All right then. Let's get it all out in the open,' agreed Carly. 'Because, well – how much do we all know about each other, really? We only met a couple of days ago. We've got no idea who each other really is – what anyone here is really capable of.'

There it is. The truth.

They were doubting each other – and Ben had the feeling that most of those misgivings were aimed towards him.

'Hang on a minute,' said Mira. 'I want to know who killed Hannah as much as anyone. But there's no way any of us could have done it – the timings don't add up, do they? We all got here at the same time – and we've all been together every minute since then.'

'That's true,' said Naya. But she didn't sound convinced.

Mira kept going: 'And besides, there are other people who were here at the right time. People who knew Hannah, who were here when she died. There's Paola and Luisa, even Isabel and Thiago who were all at the house. And that's without even considering it was a complete stranger, someone we've never even met – like those drug gangs Ben mentioned earlier? That seems a likelier scenario to me.'

No one spoke for a moment. Carly looked thoughtful, then said: 'You know what, it does seem more logical for it to have been someone else. It makes more sense than the idea of any of us doing this, anyway.'

'Unless . . .' said Naya. She swallowed, looked at the ground, kicked against a rock with her shoe. Then her words came out in a rush. 'Unless one of us lied about what time they got here – and someone was here earlier.' She looked up then.

Did she just look at me when she said that?

He needed to defend himself. 'Is there something you want to say to me, Naya? Are you accusing me of . . . of what, exactly?' demanded Ben.

'Hang on a minute,' said Naya. 'I'm not accusing *anyone* of *anything* – I'm just saying, it's possible that one of us turned up here earlier, isn't it?' She was looking right at him that time as she said it, Ben was sure.

He'd had about enough of this.

'And who do you think that might be?' he said. 'Because if you ask me, there's only one of us who's been acting weird – and that's the person who ran off by himself into the middle of the jungle earlier today.' He glared at Scott, who seemed to crumple into himself at the words.

'No, everyone – you can't think . . .' he said weakly. 'I know it was stupid, running off like that – but I've told you why, haven't I?'

'Scott, stop. You don't have to explain yourself again,' said Naya. 'Ben is just trying to stir up trouble, maybe to take the attention off *himself.*'

His blood pounded in his ears. 'What the fuck is that supposed to mean?'

'Come on, Ben, Naya – this isn't helping,' said Carly, moving to stand in front of him.

A rush of thoughts sprinted into Ben's brain. 'No, I'm sorry – hold up a second, Scott,' he said. 'Didn't you say you'd hitched a lift to Hannah's place from Playa Blanca? That's the nearest village, right? What were you even doing so close to here – and how long had you been there?' He felt bad saying it, disloyal somehow, but it was true. If they were stacking up evidence against everyone, they should at least make it fair.

Before Scott could reply, Ben rushed on: 'And Naya, you got here later than everyone else – how do we know you weren't just coming back from the middle of the rainforest?'

'*Bordel de merde*, Ben, that is ridiculous!' said Naya. 'How dare you try to—'

'That's enough, both of you. We need to think about this rationally,' interrupted Mira; even weak and exhausted, there was a quiet power to her voice. 'There'd be one way to settle it for certain.' She looked around the group. 'By getting back to the house, finding our phones. They'll all have our location history logged on there, as well as our flight details, our email conversations with Hannah – that'll show exactly where we've all been and whether we're here in good faith, right? I know mine will show I've got nothing to hide.'

'Mine neither,' said Naya and Scott in unison.

'Nor mine,' said Carly.

Ben swallowed.

Jesus. What the fuck was he going to do if they all looked at his phone?

'Well, it's a good idea, but it's not much use to us here, is it?' he said. 'Look at where we are. It's late morning already, and it doesn't feel like we're any closer to getting back there than we were yesterday.'

'I know it feels like that now,' said Scott, 'but we're making progress. We'll be back before long.'

Ben needed to think fast. 'This idea is nowhere near as foolproof as you're all making out – any of us could just wipe our recent locations,' he said desperately, hoping this would be enough to put them off the plan.

There was silence; he risked a glance at Carly, who was nibbling at her lower lip. 'Yeah. That's a good point, to be fair,' she said eventually. 'But still – it's probably the best idea we've got, isn't it?'

Naya nodded. 'I agree – it's better than nothing. And we can make it fair – we all show each other our phones at the same time, or something. We don't want anyone to feel that we're – ah – picking on them, or cornering them unfairly.'

Again, Ben caught Naya looking at him, but it was quick; subtle. He turned his head so she wouldn't catch the panic in his eyes.

'Fine,' said Ben. 'As soon as we get back to the house, we'll all show each other our phones so we can prove there's nothing to hide.'

The others nodded, satisfied.

Ben waited for them to check the map and the sun one more time and start walking again.

He hovered behind them, under the pretence of doing up a shoelace.

And then, when they all had their backs to him, he turned around and bolted through a gap in the trees as fast as his exhausted, grief-stricken body could carry him.

MIRA

What on earth is going on?

Ben had just turned and hot-footed it away from all of them, right when they were trying to make a plan that would give them some clarity on whether everyone was being honest. It made no sense. Why would he do that?

Unless . . .

'Ben, don't you dare run off,' Naya was yelling after him, turning on her heel, about to start chasing in the direction of the gap in the trees he'd disappeared into – before, abruptly, she stopped herself.

'Don't you want to go after him?' said Scott.

'I was going to, but I've changed my mind,' said Naya, her voice still hushed. 'I think we should let him go. He's clearly got an awful lot to hide. He could even be the one who killed Hannah.'

Mira stared at her. Was she serious? Ben – a murderer?

'There's been something off about him since the start – first the pills, and now he's run off when we were discussing evidence on our phones, and he didn't tell us about the photo he found on Hannah,' Naya explained. 'And remember that conversation when we first arrived, between him and Paola?'

Mira frowned. 'What was that?' she said. 'I didn't hear a conversation – and I didn't know about any pills . . .'

'It was when we got here,' said Scott quietly. 'I thought it was strange – Paola asked to see our passports, but only mine and Ben's. When she was looking at his, they had kind of an argument, I guess? He was saying something like, it wasn't his fault she didn't have the right information.'

Mira's eyes widened.

'And when you were recovering, after the mudslide,' said Naya, 'Ben was looking for some painkillers for you, and he pulled out something else. A kind of amphetamine, but one you can get prescribed. Those drugs are highly addictive, and they can alter your mood. He's probably been taking them on and off since we've been here.'

'But, so what if he's taking some prescription meds? That still doesn't make him a—' Mira shook her head. 'I just can't imagine him turning up here uninvited, let alone being the person who killed Hannah,' she said. 'And think about it – how would anyone who wasn't invited know how to get here? Hannah was pretty cagey about where this place is on her socials, wasn't she?' She paused. 'I always thought that was a bit strange, to be honest, that she didn't want people to know where her retreat was.'

Naya nodded. 'Yeah, I noticed that too. She never said exactly where this place is, not until we got those last emails. But if . . . if someone knew her already – someone she was close to, maybe – she might have told them the location, and . . .' She sighed. 'And there's something else, but—'

'What is it?' said Carly. 'Now's not the time to be keeping thoughts to ourselves – whatever it is, just say it.'

'Fine. You might all think I'm crazy, but do you remember when Hannah talked in that video a couple of months ago about her ex, who she broke up with because he lied to her?'

Mira frowned. She had a vague memory of Hannah saying something about a break-up, but the details were foggy.

'I remember that,' said Scott, so softly Mira had to strain her ears to hear him. 'She said . . . she said he worked in some hotshot tech job, didn't she? And that she'd had to break up with him because he kept—'

'He kept choosing his addiction over her,' interrupted Naya firmly.

'Oh my God,' said Carly. 'It sounds exactly like Ben – it has to be him.'

'It certainly sounds like him,' said Naya. 'And what if, while they were together, she told him where this place was – he could even have visited her here, while she was building it, couldn't he?'

Scott's face darkened. 'Right,' he said. 'I hadn't thought of that.'

Mira shook her head sadly. She didn't like the thought of Ben – of any of them – running off alone and scared in the jungle. But perhaps Naya was right. Maybe it was better this way? If he had hurt Hannah, wasn't it safer to let him go – let him get lost out there?

'Well, if you ask me, the fact that he ran off just as we were talking about checking everyone's phones when we got back – that settles it,' Carly said. 'He has something to hide, there's no doubt about it, and we're probably better off now he's gone.'

Mira rubbed at her eyes; ran her parched tongue over dry, cracked lips. Just the movement of her arms and fingers caused ripples of pain to spread through her. Everything in her body hurt. The thought nudged at the edge of her awareness: *I won't last much longer out here. And the others will be able to see it too.*

They had to keep walking. 'We need to find our way back, as quick as we can – without Ben,' Naya was saying.

'I agree,' said Carly. 'Getting out of the rainforest . . . calling the authorities to come and find Hannah, taking Mira to a hospital – even just getting ourselves water and something to eat – all of that is much more important than going after Ben.' She paused for breath. 'The police can find him and figure out what to do with him, right?'

Naya nodded; she looked relieved they were all in agreement. 'Who knows if we were even safe out here with him around? Maybe Hannah wasn't . . .' Her voice caught in her throat; she wiped at the side of her eye. 'Come on – let's go.'

Mira felt a new resolve; a new energy. She pushed Scott's arm away as he reached out to support her, and gave her head a firm shake. She could do this; she wouldn't exhaust him more than he already was.

They began to walk, following Scott's lead this time – thank God he'd taken the knife back from Ben – but they could only have been walking for a few minutes when she felt a new rush of dizziness, a sweeping light-headedness, and she stumbled. Carly, behind her, reached out an arm to catch her before she fell bottom-first onto the damp vines and leaves beneath their feet.

'Mira, hold on there, love,' Carly said, trying her best to prop her upwards, to stop her from crashing to the ground; but she seemed to have lost some of her usual strength, and

Mira could feel herself slipping from her grasp. 'Scott, Naya – help me, I can't hold her!' Scott hurried next to her, helped to prop Mira up.

'We need to find her somewhere to sit down.' Carly's voice was faint in her ears. 'She has to rest for a bit.'

'I'm not sure we can afford to stop and let her rest,' came Naya's urgent whisper. 'If we don't get out of here in the next few hours, we're all going to dehydrate. We'll start getting lethargic, our brains will stop functioning at their usual speed . . .'

Mira looked around to see Carly sigh, rub at the spot between her eyebrows. 'I know,' she muttered back. 'But there's no way she can walk like this. Let's at least give her a minute, then maybe together we can try and help her walk again – Scott, could you try and carry Mira again for a while?'

Scott nodded, and he and Carly helped to ease Mira into a sitting position on the ground as gently as they could, while Naya laid down her jacket beneath her. Carly found her water bottle, unscrewed its lid and lifted it to Mira's lips, let the last couple of sad drops fall onto her tongue.

Mira looked up at the three of them; saw Naya's face screwed up in concentration.

'What is it?' Mira asked.

Naya shrugged. 'I was just thinking . . . we need some other way of making contact with rescuers . . . if only that satellite phone was working, or we could make a smoke signal with fire – anything,' she said.

'The satellite phone . . . hang on a minute,' said Scott. The last dregs of colour seemed to have drained from his face. 'Who was the last person to use it?'

Slivers of ice travelled from the top of Mira's neck down to the base of her spine.

'It was me – wasn't it?' Carly said. 'We just tried it again this morning . . .' But her words hung in the air. 'Oh my God,' she said softly. 'I gave it to Ben. He shoved it in his bag, didn't he?'

'Yeah, I thought so,' said Scott.

Carly's expression was flat. 'I shouldn't have let him do that.'

'Guys, does it even matter?' said Naya. 'He can't use it anyway, can he? The phone is dead. Who cares if he's taken it with him? And at least we have the knife now – he didn't run off with that as well.'

'Yeah, I know – but sorry, that's not the point,' said Scott. He paused, looked at the others, one by one. 'Carly, the fact that he asked you to give the phone to him earlier – did we even need to try it again today? He knew it wasn't working – why did he even do that?'

'Are you saying . . . you think he planned it?' said Mira, trying to keep the wobble out of her voice.

'He must have done,' said Carly, her mouth set in a tight line. 'And I think it can only mean one thing, to be honest. Ben must have been planning something like this all along.' She swallowed, gathered her strength with a deep breath before she spoke again. 'Naya, I think you're right. He might have killed Hannah.'

Mira waited for the others to speak; but in the pause, there was a sound – a new one, unfamiliar, so different to the calls and cries of the rainforest, the beats of nature, that her ears couldn't quite fathom it.

Chug chug chug.

Chug chug chug.

This noise was rhythmic, mechanical.

And it was coming from above them – above the trees, even. It was coming from the sky.

Chug chug chug.

Chug chug chug.

It was getting louder; the sound was coming closer.

'Do you hear that?' said Naya, pointing wildly towards the sky through a gap in the trees. 'I think it's . . . oh my God, look! They're here to rescue us!'

Mira's gaze followed the direction of Naya's finger.

And then, as she watched in mute shock, Naya, Scott and Carly all began screaming and waving, up towards the light, the break in the thick canopy, where a red and white helicopter had appeared, hovering above them, directly within their line of sight.

BEN

Ben felt bad for turning and bolting away from the others like that. Bad – and now scared.

He didn't have the navigation skills of Carly or Scott, and he no longer had the knife to help quicken his progress; his best hope was to work his way along the path of the sun in the same direction – south, he was sure that was where the lodge had been in relation to the rainforest – and pray for the best.

Shit. Perhaps he should have stayed, confessed to everything, tried to explain himself.

No, it was too late for that. *They'd never have believed me. They've all already turned against me.*

Ben wasn't sure if it was the shock of Hannah's death, the fear of being lost alone in this place, the relentless heat or the onset of dehydration – but he felt like he was starting to lose his grip on reality. He was sweating from every pore after that run through the forest, the wet slick on his body exacerbated by the thick, damp air.

Worse still was that the rainforest was beginning to play games with him; it was playing tricks on his brain. Every tree that he passed, every rock his feet stumbled over; it was like they were calling out to him, whispering his name, mocking him.

And now the vines and branches he was shoving through seemed to stick to every part of his body, to move after him, clinging onto his shoulders, his arms – as if the rainforest was coming alive now, and it was tormenting him. It was talking to him; telling him it knew his secrets. Sprawling tendrils wrapped around his wrists; every time he broke free of one, he felt another take its place.

It was like the jungle could see into the core of him – and Ben was afraid this place would find him sorely lacking.

You shouldn't have come here, Ben.

You're ours now.

You will never leave here.

Nothing looked familiar, and yet everything did. He couldn't tell whether he'd seen this exact fallen trunk, this very same patch of clearing, this one goddamn branch, for the hundredth time – or whether he'd never seen them before in his life. Everything looked exactly, dizzyingly, the *same*.

Face it. You're totally fucking lost.

He was an idiot; he had fucked up on so many levels. Setting aside the way he'd run off from the rest of the group – leaving behind the only person with a *map* – it was a mistake to even have come here in the first place.

What had he been thinking, honestly? Had he really needed to see Hannah, to talk to her, to get his damn *closure* that much? Because of Hannah, his life had been half in ruins when he got on that plane at Austin. But in coming here, all he'd succeeded in doing was destroying it even more – or possibly, he thought, with a lurch to his guts – finishing it, ending up as dead as Hannah on the jungle floor, dehydrated and exhausted and consumed by the creatures of the forest.

He closed his eyes as an image of her body flashed in front of them, felt his body shudder despite the relentless humidity. He wished he hadn't looked so closely at her face – her empty expression, her slack, gaping mouth, her flesh already being devoured by the jungle's creatures. She had been decaying, rotting, wasting away. And the thing he couldn't stop thinking about was how – in life, like the very last time he'd seen her – she was the most vibrant, animated, the most *alive* person he'd ever known.

It was nearly a year ago that he'd first met her.

He'd just started back on the programme, enforced for the second time by his manager after colleagues had commented on Ben's agitated, hyped-up demeanour – he'd only been in rehab for two days. He remembered that, because he'd been counting them down, *Sunday, Monday,* desperate to tick each date off of his calendar so he could get back to his life – and his Adderall, of course. People didn't get it, but ADHD meds, for someone without ADHD, well – it affected him like speed. Except, these drugs were *legal*. Easy to get hold of without a prescription, if you knew the right people.

And Ben did – if there was one thing that growing up in a white trash trailer park just outside of Austin was good for, it was *knowing the right people*. He'd been smarter than most of the guys he grew up with, though – their drug of choice was almost always meth, and half of them were in jail now or, at the very least, still living in the same trailers they grew up in. Not like Ben, with his smart condo and his white-collar job and his crisp shirts. He had made it – well, *almost* made it, he corrected himself, with the familiar surge of anger in his chest.

He had remembered *that* day, because it was the day Hannah arrived, and he'd never be able to forget how he'd felt when he met her. As much as he might want to, especially now. There'd been a sort of quiet buzz about the place that morning; whispers of a new arrival, a celebrity – some kind of *influencer*.

Ben had scoffed at the rumours – famous people in rehab was hardly a revelation, they'd been in and out of the place pretty much non-stop since he'd got there. The last time he'd been in, he'd been in group therapy with an A-list actress who was known as much for her wholesome, healthy lifestyle as her on-screen performances. She'd finally been forced to clean herself up when her partner found her passed out in a pool of blood, after she'd run out of veins in her arm and injected a needle into an artery on her thigh instead.

It no longer surprised him how good people were at hiding their true selves – in fact, not much shocked him at all. So, when he met Hannah – when she took her seat across from him in the daily ten o'clock Narcotics Anonymous meeting – the feeling was unfamiliar. He was surprised by her – by how different she was from what he'd expected.

But more than that: he was spellbound.

He'd never heard of her before – online spiritual communities weren't exactly his thing – but immediately he wanted to know everything about her. He wanted to be entrusted with her secrets. It was powerful, this desire to know her – possess her, almost. She was gorgeous in that hippy, sun-kissed way, all lithe and supple, showing off gleaming bronzed legs as she sat tucked into the chair opposite him in her tight-fitting shorts.

His attraction to her was about so much more than the way she looked, though. There was an ease about her, a charm. She made everyone feel like they were special; like they were loved. Like she *saw* them.

He remembered the first thing she'd said to him, after the meeting was over. She came straight up to him, grabbed him by the hands and stared deep into his eyes, the blue of her irises dazzling him.

'It was so good to hear you, Ben,' she'd said softly, her gaze moving between his eyes and his mouth. 'I felt every word of what you shared – I felt it *in here*.' She'd taken his hands, then, and placed both of them close to her heart, above her left breast. And the heat that had spread throughout his chest, flooded his limbs and flushed his cheeks and yes, turned him on, got him hard and made him ache for her – it was stronger than any high he'd ever known.

Ben was snagged from his memories by a whirring, chopping sound – something motorized, something at odds with the relentless screams of the jungle's creatures.

It took him a moment to locate the source – there was nothing in front of him or behind him. It was only when he looked up at the sky that he saw it. And when he did, his heart slammed against his ribs and battered at his chest like an animal in a cage.

Fuck yeah. It's a chopper. The staff back at Hannah's place must have sent out a search party for them. *Thank God.*

He needed to get its attention. 'Hey there!' he screamed,

waving his arms frantically, jumping up and down as he did. 'I'm down here! Help – HELP ME!'

The helicopter – a small one, probably only a few seats – was circling overhead. It was looking for something.

Has it come to rescue us?

He ran towards where it was hovering above, stumbling blindly through the thick vines, tripping once, twice, landing on his face on the wet ground. He hauled himself up again, wiped the mulch from his eyes, spat wet leaves from his mouth, started running again, looking up as he went, feet pounding the sodden earth as fast as he could go.

No, no, no. The chopper, which had been looping up there so close to him a moment ago, was moving away. Whoever was flying it hadn't seen him.

Why can't they see me?

He let out a roar of rage and frustration. Of course they couldn't see him – he could barely see himself in the near dark of the forest's canopy. It would be impossible to make out anyone or anything from way up there, except, maybe, a fire or an area of flattened trees . . .

He paused, pondered for a moment. Were either of those things worth a try, in case it came back, or another one passed overhead? Could he try to start a fire – or fell some trees, somehow, to make himself more visible? *No, no, don't be so freaking dumb.* He had no matches, no lighter – quitting smoking recently was another bad choice to add to the list, he thought wryly – and certainly nothing to chop down a giant tree with. Besides, setting a fire in a rainforest was about as sure a way to cause his own death as getting stuck here for ever.

What do I have, then? Was there anything in his possession that could help him?

Ben stopped pushing through the trees, stopping at a small gap in the foliage, where he crouched to the ground and started pulling things out of his rucksack. He was poorly equipped for this trip – practically, emotionally; *in every way, let's face it* – but perhaps he'd missed something? His hands grabbed hold of whatever they could find: a magazine, some lip balm, his empty water bottle. They struck something slim, cylindrical and smooth.

My vape.

Ben plucked the e-cigarette out of his bag, lifted the tip to his lips, inhaled. Nothing came out; instead, the little blue light at the other end flashed at him: no charge left. Damn – now that he'd thought of the idea, he could really do with the hit of nicotine at the back of his throat.

Hang on a minute. This might be something he'd actually prepared for. Ben turned back to his bag, sifted through the inside, this time with purpose. He was looking for something: his portable charger – the battery pack worked with his phone, his tablet, his vape – pretty much anything, as long as he had the right cable. And he knew he did, because he'd packed a small pouch full of them, one of the perks of working for a tech company – whipping from meeting to meeting, briefcase in one hand and a Starbucks in the other, needing a fully charged phone wherever he went.

Digging the right cable out of the zip-up pouch, he plugged his vape into the charger and perched on a tree trunk – sweeping it, first, for snakes and spiders – and waited for its light to turn green. It wouldn't take long.

As he waited, he carried on turning over his dwindling options in his mind. *What else, what else?* There had to be something else he could make use of. A way out of this mess. Staring at the charger in his hand, a flash of something shot through his mind, but it was fast, too fast – it had gone as quick as it came.

What was that; what was it? Something to do with the charger. How it worked on anything. How he had a cable for pretty much any kind of tech – any tablets, any phones . . .

'Oh my God,' he said aloud, as the realization hit him.

The satellite phone. He'd been the last one to try to turn it on, hadn't he? They'd tried again only a couple of hours ago – and then he'd shoved it back in his bag.

That meant it was still in there now. He dug inside the bag again, one of the side pockets this time, rifled through it until his hands closed over the phone's solid, hefty bulk.

Shit. A flash of guilt ran through him; he'd run away from the others and left them, still lost out here, without the only possible means of contact – and all along, he'd had a potential way of charging it up, making it work again.

But if I can get it working and call for help – then I can get everyone out of here.

He would be the one to come to their rescue; they'd understand then that he'd not meant any of them harm. That his reason for being here – for doing everything he'd done – was nothing to do with them.

Ben stood up, whipped the vape off the end of the charging cable, examined the satellite phone's charging port, let out a *whoop* of delight. It needed a cable with a USB connector – and he had one of those.

He found the right connector, plugged one end into his charging pack, the other into the phone. There was a knot of excitement in his stomach, a growing sense of hope.

This was going to fix everything.

He shrugged back into his backpack, took a deep breath, checked out the direction of the sun and started walking, one eye on the phone as he went.

Now all he had to do was wait.

NAYA

The helicopter flew past. It had missed them.

'Stop . . . wait! No!' Her voice was becoming hoarse from all her futile screaming into the sky. But she couldn't let it go yet – she couldn't face it. It was unbearable, the idea that rescue had been so close by, and yet so far out of reach.

'It's gone, Naya,' Scott called out from a few metres behind her. 'They mustn't have seen us down here . . . I can't believe it.'

Neither could she. But it was true: it hadn't spotted them, despite their screams and cries and waves. The forest must have been too dense to make them out through the canopy; the sound of the helicopter's blades too thunderous for their voices to carry over it.

She stopped her frantic pacing, reached for a nearby tree trunk, brushed some brightly coloured beetles off its surface, then leaned her back against it and sobbed. She was too hot with her anorak on – it had been providing useful protection against the sharp branches as she walked, but she needed her skin to breathe now. She peeled it off and tied it around her waist, then let her body sink to the ground. She was devastated.

To have her hopes raised and dashed like that – it was almost worse than never having hope in the first place.

Naya felt a hand on her shoulder, turned her face upwards to see Scott looking down at her, his eyes full of disappointment; of the despair she knew was mirrored in her own expression. They'd drifted away from Carly and Mira now; they were alone, with no one's eyes on them. Without saying anything, she stood up and moved into his arms, aware that the top of her head didn't even reach his shoulder. She let him hold her like this while she cried. After a long moment, she pulled back, looked up at him.

'I'm sorry,' she said. 'I've got your T-shirt all wet.'

'No worries,' he said. 'Any time.' His eyes were still on her face; she saw them move towards her mouth. She felt a stirring in her belly, lower. She tilted her face upwards.

'We shouldn't,' Naya whispered, even as everything in her body was screaming that they should. 'I – apart from everything else that makes this a bad idea, I took a test last night, and I'm—' *Why am I telling him this?*

'Naya? You're . . . what?'

'I'm pregnant,' she blurted. A flicker of shock passed across Scott's features; she opened her mouth to tell him more. 'And—'

'Ah, sorry to disturb you two.' At the sound of Carly's voice, Naya pulled back from Scott's arms, embarrassed. She hadn't even finished her sentence – and there was so much more she wanted to say. 'But we should really get going again – we've only got so much daylight left, and chasing after that bloody helicopter has taken us right off track again.'

Carly sounded breathless and a little irritated; Naya couldn't blame her – they'd left her alone with Mira, who was still struggling to walk without help. 'Of course,' she said. 'Sorry – let's keep walking.'

Scott did his calculations again, using the map and the sun as their guide. Then they set off again in the direction they'd worked out was directly south – taking them back to The Hideaway, out of the rainforest.

'Let me support Mira for a while,' Naya said, taking Mira's arm from where Carly was holding it and resting it gently around her shoulder. 'I've got a little more energy now, and you could do with a rest, I think.'

'Thanks, hun,' said Carly. 'You're right, I'm flagging now – we all are.'

'Just a bit longer now, hopefully,' said Scott. 'As long as we don't get off track again, we should be back at the lodge soon enough.'

Naya desperately hoped he was right. She was still devastated that the helicopter had missed them. But in amongst her despair, she noticed, there was something else: a quiet sigh of relief.

You're safer now.

She prodded at her thoughts, wondered where that had come from.

I feel safer without Ben.

That was it. Something in her had lightened, eased a little since Ben had left the group; since he'd turned and disappeared into the depths of the jungle. If she were honest with herself, she felt better without him there.

It was still difficult to believe that he'd murdered Hannah – killed her with a blow to the head, dragged her body into the jungle, left her there to rot under the dense canopy of trees.

She couldn't believe *anyone* could do that. But too many signs were pointing to his guilt; too many things about him were just . . . *off*.

Naya's foot caught on a fallen branch and she stumbled forward, stopping herself at the last second from landing flat on her face and taking Mira down with her. Her exhaustion, low-level nausea, the lack of water to drink – combined with the shock of everything they'd been through – it was all working together to chip away at her resilience, and, it seemed, her sense of balance. Shoving her way through the trees, attempting to half-carry, half-prop up Mira as she went – it had only been ten minutes of walking, and already she was exhausted, in desperate need of a rest.

'You all right, Naya?' said Scott. 'We can take a break for a minute, if you need – and let me walk with Mira now.'

'Ah, yes, you know, I'd appreciate that,' said Naya. 'I'm struggling a little, I have to admit.'

'I'm sorry, Naya,' Mira's face was stricken. 'I'm sorry for all of you, that you have to help me like this.' She was close to tears.

Naya moved to face Mira, held onto her shoulders as she said, 'Please, I don't want you to apologize for anything. We are all taking care of each other out here, OK?'

Mira gave her a watery smile and moved to Scott, let him take her weight. Naya took a moment to enjoy the sensation of lightness; she stretched out her hands, her arms. She had needed that; her body had started to complain, but she hadn't wanted to say anything, hadn't wanted to let Mira down.

At ease now, her energy coming back, she took the knife from Scott and moved ahead of the other three, doing her best to clear the way through trees and foliage for the others, cutting at the leaves to one side to help them pass more easily. After a few minutes, as she got into her stride, she started to walk a little further ahead from the group, checking behind her every few steps to make sure they were close by.

As she walked, she tuned into the sounds of the jungle: the rasping of tree frogs, the calls of toucans and the rhythmic hum of cicadas. For all of the horrors of the past day, there was no denying this was a magical place.

But as she listened now, she realized there was something else: a new sound, a different one. Not the chopper this time, but something else that made her chest swell with hope.

Something was moving; rushing past them.

Was it . . . had they reached a road?

Were those cars whizzing by?

Had they somehow, against all the odds, stumbled along blindly in exactly the right direction? She heard it again; louder now, and clearer.

Oh my God, we are saved.

She had to get to it. This could be it, their chance of rescue – to get Mira the medical help she needed, to call the emergency services, have the police find Hannah's body and get her out of the jungle. To help Naya and Scott and Carly get back home, without dehydrating or succumbing to heat exhaustion.

'Hey, guys, do you hear that?' Naya called out behind her. 'I can hear cars – I think we've found a road!'

She started to move more quickly now, her tiredness and thirst pushing her forward, propelling her faster, if anything, rather than holding her back.

She could hear the others calling after her, urging her to

take care, to slow down, be careful not to trip and fall, but it was as if she couldn't hear them, it was as if Naya could only run towards the source of this sound – this beautiful, hopeful roar, which was getting louder with every step she took, with every dense chunk of leaves and vines she pushed through.

But she didn't care; it didn't matter what they told her – nothing would stop her from running. Naya was fighting back sobs of joy, of excitement. Of elation. They were going to be out of here; they'd be saved. They would be free. She could get out of this place, and she'd be the one to help the others get out too.

As she bolted on, her mind whirred through a hastily made plan. She'd flag down a passing car for help, ask for a ride to the nearest police station, tell them everything – everything she knew. And they'd help her then, wouldn't they? Even though she had no phone on her now, and maybe not enough money in her bank account to pay for a new flight home – they'd be able to cover that, wouldn't they, when she explained the situation? When she told them how much she needed to get out of Costa Rica; back home, back to her babies.

Bursting forward now, the sound so close, so loud, she could see the trees starting to thin out – there was something behind them, there was an end to them. She was almost there – she'd almost made it to the road!

Carving through the last thicket of branches and vines, she burst into the open air, exhilarated, breathless, ready to start waving at cars passing by, flagging down help.

When she saw what was in front of her, the disappointment slammed into her like a breaking dam; the knife fell from her hand to the ground.

This was not a road. It was a river; a stream, rushing by. She'd mistaken the sound of the current for the sound of cars.

How could I have been so stupid?

A wave of dizziness, of nausea, of raging disappointment, swept through the length of her body. Feeling the bile start to rise at the back of her throat, she took off her backpack, crouched down, dipped her head into her hands and took the deepest breath she could manage: in through her nose, out through her mouth.

In through her nose, out through her mouth.

It was not just an attempt to feel better; this was a necessity. She could not afford to vomit now – she'd barely drunk anything since yesterday afternoon, and her body needed desperately to hold on to every drop of liquid it could.

Hold it down, hold it down.

Still feeling the earth spin, she tried to picture something solid, something grounded. The kapok tree where they'd found Scott earlier, its height, its bulk. The way it seemed to carry on growing all the way up to the sky. The feel of it, as she rested her hand on its roots. *Yes, that's it. That's good.* The image was helping.

Another image landed in her mind.

Scott.

The tall, loping shape of him. The broad slope of his shoulders. His giant hands. When she thought about him, she felt herself come back to her body, to her very centre. She smiled; the worst of the nausea had passed. She could move again. But instead she was left with howls of rage; of disappointment. Of sadness.

None of this is how it was supposed to be.

'Are you all still behind me?' she called, in the direction she thought they'd last been. There was silence. 'Carly? Scott? Mira?' she said. 'Are you still there – can you hear me?' Still nothing. She crouched to the ground, picked up the knife, shoved it in her backpack. Then, quietly at first, but gradually getting louder, she heard the snap of twigs, the crackle of branches underfoot and finally, 'Naya? Are you there?' Scott, still supporting Mira, appeared through the trees; Carly was directly behind them.

They had caught up with her – she had to tell them. 'I – I thought it was a road,' she said. She could feel hot tears of shame and disappointment springing to her eyes, spilling over, splashing down her cheeks. 'I'm sorry, everyone, for getting your hopes up – I feel so stupid now, but I was so sure of it.'

'Hey,' said Carly, moving towards her, reaching an arm out to touch her shoulder. 'It might not be a road full of cars, but this is good – you've still found us something that's going to help.' She smiled at her. 'Streams lead to rivers, and rivers lead to people – they can help us navigate our way out of here. It's a really great spot to have brought us to.'

Naya nodded, grateful for the way Carly seemed able to turn her disappointment – her failure, even – into something hopeful.

Licking her dry lips, another idea occurred to her. 'And can we drink it?' she said. 'The water here – it's fresh, coming straight from these rocks, right?' She leaned towards it, turned the palm of her hand up into a cup and started to gather some water inside it. She was about to lift her hand up to her lips, when Scott roared her name.

'Naya, stop! No, you can't bloody drink it,' he said, his

voice throbbing with anger. 'You'll make yourself sick with whatever parasites are living in the waters here.'

Please don't yell at me. Naya looked at the ground; she felt stupid now, on yet another level. *How did I not know that, with my medical training?* Clearly, she had no business being here, as woefully underprepared as she was. A sudden thought made her stomach churn: imagine if she were stuck out here with her children instead? She'd have killed them, or at least made them fatally sick by now, if they were going on her advice and intuition.

She was getting it all so wrong – *what was I even doing, thinking I'd cope somewhere like this?*

But it wasn't supposed to *be* like this, she remembered.

Hannah was supposed to be here. They were never supposed to have been wandering around the wilderness like this, lost, in shock, grieving and afraid. A sob caught in her throat, and Scott must have caught the anguish on her face, because then he was moving towards her, reaching an arm out to hold her, reassuring her.

'I'm sorry for talking to you like that. I'm not myself – not thinking straight,' he said. 'And you scared me – I thought you were about to start gulping it back, and we can't afford for you to go down as well. We can't lose you.'

He forced a smile, and Naya looked at him, then at the others, noticing again how red-faced and sweaty everyone was, the clammy heat out here never letting them catch a break. Perhaps what she'd discovered here could still help them – she could still be useful to them after leading them all astray.

'Well, let me at least try and cool us all down – we're all overheating out here. I can soak my swimming towel in the water and you can hold that to your head – that's OK to do with the water, right?'

Scott nodded.

'OK then,' said Naya, turning and moving towards the edge of the stream, the others close behind her, throwing her rucksack back over her shoulders. She made her way to the edge of the water, watched it flowing by, whipping past her feet. The air here was cooler, cleaner. The cloying, damp scent of the jungle had gone. She breathed in the freshness, closed her eyes for a moment.

And then a branch cracked right behind her and she was jumpy, so jumpy after everything they'd been through, on edge, nerves shredded, and she startled – her foot somehow slipping forward, losing its grip on the edge of the water.

Her hands flailed wildly, reaching for something – anything – desperate to cling on to something solid, not to be swept away.

But they only moved through air, and more air.

And then the cool shock of the water as her body plunged in and the rushing stream dragged her under, into its gloomy depths.

SCOTT

'Naya! No! NAYA!'

Scott didn't realize he still had the energy to roar her name, didn't know his voice could even reach that volume with his energy levels so low, his throat so hoarse and dry. But the sound erupted from his body like the wail of a banshee as he watched Naya's limbs flail in the chaotic water, her hands grabbing at something – anything – and then at nothing.

He yelled her name frantically over and over, as he watched her head emerge briefly, too briefly, from the frothing white foam that gathered on the stream's rushing surface; he saw her take a huge gulp of air – *come on, Naya, breathe!* – and then go under again. With every passing second, the current was taking her further and further down the stream, which would soon begin to bend away from them.

He would soon lose sight of her.

Breathless, panting, Scott handed Mira into Carly's arms, and started to race along the water's edge, calling out, the other two staggering behind him, crying Naya's name, knowing it was futile as his screams of panic would no doubt be drowned out by the rushing water.

For one wild moment, a second of pure insanity, he considered flinging himself into the water after her, his shaking legs almost barrelling into the raging stream. He stopped himself in time; he knew if he did that, they'd most likely *both* end up drowning – and that would do nothing to help save Naya.

What should I do then? What can I do?

Drained of energy, suddenly hit by the full force of seeing her thrashing in the clutches of the rushing water, Scott bent his head over, placed his hands on his knees, eyes still facing forward, searching the stream.

'Scott, are you OK? Did you see Naya? I lost sight of her!' He jumped at the sound of Carly's panicked voice; she was behind him – trailing a few steps further back, he caught sight of Mira slowly making her way along the water's edge. *Thank God* – he'd been running for at least a minute and could have lost them too.

Mira spoke next, her face blanched, even more horror etched into the grooves of her forehead. 'Where's Naya? Scott, did you see where she went – were you able to keep your eyes on her? Please tell me you did!'

'I don't know!' He gestured further downstream in the direction of the current, where he thought Naya had been swept to. 'It was somewhere up there . . . I can't see her any more – can you? Can anyone see her?' Carly and Mira's eyes scoured the water too, then they turned back to look at him; both their gazes empty.

Stop looking at me like that.

Don't look at me like you're giving up.

'We need to keep searching for her,' he said. 'Do you think she can climb out by herself – maybe if the current eases off a little further round the bend?' said Scott. 'It's moving fast, but it's shallow in places – and she can swim, right?'

The other two said nothing; just stared at the stream in mute shock.

'Think, Carly, Mira – did she swim at the waterfall, or was she just paddling?'

'I – I can't remember,' whispered Mira. 'I'm sorry.' She looked defeated; hopeless. Carly did too.

They can't give up. And neither can I.

Come on, come on.

'What's wrong with you both? We have to help her – and her baby!' He didn't mean to say it – the words seemed to splurge out of his mouth – and Scott felt a hot stab of guilt that he'd revealed something Naya had told him in confidence. It wasn't his secret to tell.

Scott saw a flicker of shock pass across Carly's face, then a twist at the edge of her mouth. 'Oh, fuck. I didn't know she was pregnant.'

Mira turned and met Scott's gaze; he saw straight away that she too had known about Naya's pregnancy. The look on her face was haunting: horror, grief, fear, mixed with a kind of vacant numbness. He knew that look; he understood it. He'd seen it before – and felt it himself. Total overwhelm – a person reaching their limit. And who could blame her? After everything they'd already suffered, everything they'd witnessed – to lose Naya as well. It was unbearable, he knew it was. But they couldn't fall apart now. Naya needed them.

Then Mira's expression shifted; there was a new firmness to her mouth, a steely resolve in her eyes.

'You're right,' she said. 'She's pregnant, and it's Naya, and we can't give up on her. Carly, Scott, we have to follow the stream – we can try and track her down. We're going to split up, so we can cover more ground – all right?' Scott was taken aback, but encouraged by the strength in Mira's voice.

'Scott, you're the fastest,' she continued. 'I think you should keep going, tracing the edge of the stream – you need to go as quick as you can, as far along as you can, and scour the water as you go.'

'She's right,' said Carly, nodding, her energy more frantic now too. 'Scott, you run ahead and search further downstream – I'll keep looking a bit behind you, closer to where she fell in.'

'And I'll stay here and search the edge of the water,' said Mira. 'I'm sorry, I just can't move as quickly as you two – but I can keep a lookout and shout to you both if I see anything. Go!'

Carly nodded. 'Just stay where you've said you'll stay, all right? So we can find you again. Don't wander off – it's way too easy to get lost out here.'

With that, Carly turned and began to move along the water's edge; within seconds, she was out of sight. Scott gave Mira's hand a quick squeeze, then raced further down the stream, tracking the direction Naya had been travelling, eyes searching the water with increasing desperation. The humid air kept catching at the back of his throat; within seconds, his lungs were starting to burn, rivulets of sweat running down his forehead, his neck.

Don't stop. Keep moving. You have to find her.

Breathless now, he kept running, eyes darting between the rocky shore at his feet and the frothing water, then back, over and over. Next to a large, flat rock, he paused to take some air into his lungs, wiped the sweat from his cheeks, and bellowed her name.

'Naya! NAYA!' His voice was hoarse, his throat arid; he was losing most of the remaining water in his body through his sweaty efforts. He saw nothing but the rushing stream – there was no sign of her thrashing arms and legs, her drenched hair.

He tried to swallow; winced, as a thought occurred to him: that perhaps she might no longer be thrashing in the water. A new image, one that filled him with despair, rushed into his brain: that instead he might see her floating face down, a lifeless body bashed over and over against the stones.

No. He couldn't even entertain the thought. Naya was strong; she would survive this. He forced himself to move again, stumbled on a few more metres, and then he saw it.

The water, just ahead, dividing into two separate courses.

The one furthest away – the one he'd need to be on the other bank to follow – continued its rushing path uninterrupted.

And the side closest to him, the one he could reach, plummeted downwards, a plunging, racing waterfall that would slam a human body roughly six metres down onto the circle of sharp rocks at its foot.

MIRA

Mira moved closer to the bank of water, edging slowly and carefully along the stream's edge, close to where Naya had fallen in. She whipped her head from side to side, frantic, still trying to catch a glimpse of Naya.

She scanned the frothing waters, looking for . . . for what, exactly, she wasn't sure, or didn't want to fully register. For the clothes Naya was wearing – for the shape of her jacket? For the black tendrils of her hair?

Mira swallowed back a sob, leaned closer, dangerously close to the stream. Her hand reached for a branch to hold herself steady as her eyes darted across the surface.

There – what's that?

She had caught sight of something – a shape, something dark and heavy, trapped somehow behind a rock that sat only a little way out, towards the centre of the stream.

What was it?

Could it be . . . was it Naya – was she stuck there, somehow?

'Naya!' she screamed.

I have to get to her.

She would have to make her way into the water. She'd been

a strong swimmer once: taking part in competitions in her school days, swimming twice a week all the way into her early adulthood, teaching her nieces and nephews how to doggy paddle at only a year old. Perhaps the recollection of all her time in the pool lived in her body still, a kind of muscle memory.

Clambering across the rocks, she leaned as far forward as she could, tried to see what was floating, lodged, in the middle of the stream. With a jolt of relief she realized it wasn't Naya stuck there at all: it was her bag. The straps of her rucksack must have got caught on something underneath the surface of the water.

I should try to reach it. She knew there was a proper first-aid kit in there, and God knows Naya might need that if – *when* – they found her.

Was there a way she could get to it, safely? Turning back towards the jungle, Mira looked around for a stick or a vine; something sturdy, strong enough to drag the bag with, but light enough that she could pick it up, manoeuvre it. Picking up a long, slim branch with a fork shape at the end, she sat on a rock at the edge of the stream, one hand gripping the surface beneath her, the other stretching the branch out as far as she could.

It took her three, four tries, before she was able to hook the bag onto the tip of her branch. After a moment, she managed to pull it free from the rock it was attached to, and yank it towards her. Hauling it out of the water, she sat back down roughly on the ground to catch her breath.

When she'd gathered some strength, she picked up the bag – sodden, it felt like the thing was full of rocks – and moved to a fallen tree trunk, a little way back from the water's edge. She collapsed down onto it, her energy drained now. Despite her panic over Naya, she was simply too weak to do even the most basic things out here – and little wonder. She should be getting checked over in a hospital: she might have some kind of lasting damage from the mudslide. But she was starting to worry she wouldn't ever make it to a hospital now, or out of this rainforest at all.

I should never have come here. Her mistake felt even more apparent, now that she'd found her will to live again. She realized she felt vaguely ridiculous for having taken in, even if it was on an unconscious level, Hannah's advice about shunning Western medicine. Hannah had even made a whole video about how chemotherapy was evil – that it did more harm than good. Mira had been so sick of her treatment at the time, she'd enjoyed listening to it. She hadn't thought, then, that she actually *believed* it. But perhaps a part of her did; perhaps she was holding a small sliver of hope about the possibility of an alternative route to healing.

Now, though, she'd give anything in the world for the chance to have one more round of something – anything, no matter how gruelling and brutal – that at least had an honest, evidence-based shot at extending the time she had left.

Mira took a breath and started calling out for Scott and Carly. A few minutes later, they both appeared, running from different directions at almost the exact same second. She felt a wild surge of hope that Naya might be with one of them – but her heart sank when she saw they were both alone.

Scott looked frantic. 'Mira – what is it? Did you find her? Have you seen something?'

'No – I couldn't see her – but I found her bag,' said Mira, holding the rucksack out to show the others then placing it back on the floor next to her feet, her voice so quiet now that it was almost drowned out by the rushing water. 'There's no sign of her. She's nowhere near here, anyway – maybe she got carried further down and . . . did you see anything?'

Scott was shaking so wildly, he could barely answer. 'No – I couldn't – but I followed the stream as far as I could – until it reached a fork . . . where one side dropped a long way down into a rock pool.' He turned away from them both, and sobbed into his hands. 'I couldn't see her in there, but I think, if she went that way—'

Mira gasped. *Oh, Naya, no.*

Carly shook her head. 'I'm so sorry, both of you, and I hate myself for saying this, but if she went down there, I just don't see how she'd survive it. The shock of the water, the current moving so fast, not to mention a fall onto rocks . . . I know it's too awful to imagine, but I think she . . . she might be gone.' Carly's eyes had welled up; she looked distraught as she spoke.

Mira turned to Scott, his face a picture of pain.

'No,' he said. 'We can't give up on her yet.' He stood up, rushed back towards the stream, took a moment to examine the water, then turned back to Mira and Carly. 'What if we try to find a safe place to cross the stream? Somewhere shallow – we could use those big flat rocks as stepping stones, right? Then we can trace the other fork of the stream – she could have been taken that way, couldn't she?'

Carly looked doubtful, but nodded. 'OK, let's see if there's somewhere we might be able to get across – but Mira, just stay here, won't you? You're not in a good way.'

THE HIDEAWAY

Mira didn't want to be left behind this time. 'I can come too – I've had a rest now, I'll be OK . . .'

'No, Mira, I'm sorry – you might slow us down.' Scott's words were hard to hear, but his tone was gentle. 'Don't worry,' he added. 'We'll stay close to the edge of the stream, and I'll mark the trees nearby so we can be sure to find you.'

'Good plan,' agreed Carly. 'We'll be back soon.' She stepped towards Mira, and whispered, out of Scott's earshot: 'I'm really sorry, but we can't risk spending hours looking for her, not when we all need to get out of here so desperately – you need medical help, we're getting dehydrated – we can't end up here for another night.'

Mira closed her eyes briefly, nodded. It was an awful thing to admit – to even think – but she knew Carly was right: they had to focus on who they could actually help, who they could save. The three of them still had time; they could be rescued, they could still walk out of here pretty much unscathed.

For Naya, it was probably already too late. Mira felt a rush of anger, an energizing jolt that, when it passed, left her feeling even weaker. This was all wrong; how could something so horrific have happened to Naya – and to Hannah?

The thought overwhelmed her again: she should never have come here. She was already depleted, and had only lost more of herself by being here. And for what? The belief that she should just give up on proven, scientific treatment and simply allow herself to die?

'I understand,' she said, tears pooling in her eyes. Carly touched her shoulder gently, then Mira watched as she jogged over to join Scott and the two of them walked away through the trees, heading downstream, swallowed by the foliage in the time it took for her to blink.

It couldn't have been more than ten seconds later that she heard the crack of branches falling and the low, rumbling roar of Scott's scream.

CARLY

Scott was lying flat on his back on the ground, clutching his right ankle. The scream that had erupted from his chest was loud enough to have woken every animal in the rainforest. Carly needed to move fast.

'Shit – Scott, what the hell happened? Are you OK?' she said.

'No, I'm not OK! I tripped over something – I didn't see it, but whatever it was, it came out of nowhere. I went down on my ankle – bloody hell, I've twisted it – badly.'

'Scott? Carly?' She heard Mira's voice only seconds later. 'Where are you? Are you all right? I heard a scream.'

'Mira – we're over here!' Carly shouted back. 'Scott's gone over on his ankle – it looks bad.'

A few moments later, Mira's anxious face appeared through the bushes. She walked slowly to where Scott was lying, joined Carly as she crouched down next to him. Together they tried to take a look at where he was holding onto his ankle, Carly's hand stretched out towards it.

'No, no, please don't touch it,' Scott moaned. 'It hurts like hell.'

'Oh God,' said Mira. 'What happened?'

'Ah, I'm not sure, exactly,' said Scott. 'Either a rock, or a tree trunk, underfoot – I stumbled over it, hard, and went down – I felt it twist all the way round as I went. Shit, it really hurts – I don't even know if I can walk on it right now.'

'Oh, Scott, this is the last thing we need – and while you were trying to look for Naya as well.' Mira looked stricken; her eyes were glassy, tears ready to spill. 'What are we going to do? Do you think you can move at all? Can you try to stand up, putting your weight on your other foot, maybe?'

Scott managed to sit up, then to kneel on his left knee – but in the process, he must have brushed against his ankle, and he let out another howl of pain.

'I can't,' he said weakly.

Carly stayed silent, thought for a moment. 'Maybe if you had some kind of crutch? Could we see if there's a big stick or something nearby that he can use?'

'Oh, good idea,' said Mira, as Carly turned away and started to survey the nearby trees and branches. After a moment, she plucked a branch from the tree and headed back over to Scott, holding it out to him.

'Here,' she said. 'Do you want to give this one a go?'

Scott looked up at the branch, and at the expression of hope on his face, Carly felt a deep ache of sadness – for everything that had gone wrong, and everything that might still go wrong; for Hannah and for Naya and now this. Scott was a decent guy – none of this should have happened to him. It shouldn't have happened to any of them.

'It looks about right – thanks.' Groaning as he pulled himself forward to sitting, he reached up a hand to Carly. 'Can you help me stand?'

'I'll try.' Using her as a support, Scott hauled himself up, yelling as he leaned his weight on his right-hand side.

'Quick – give me the stick,' he said, reaching for it. Carly handed it over, and Scott propped the end of it under his shoulder, resting his weight on it. It was just sturdy enough for the job.

'Thanks – you're a lifesaver,' he muttered. Carly felt her eyes flicker to the ground; a lifesaver was the last thing she felt like.

Mira was glancing around the path. 'There's nowhere decent to rest here – do you think you can make it back to the tree trunk where I was just sitting? It's only a few metres away,' she said.

'Yeah, I reckon so – it might just take us a few minutes,' said Scott, turning around and limping back through the trees, one lopsided step at a time.

'Just take it slow and steady,' said Carly.

Carly's thoughts were racing. She needed to figure out their next steps. She turned to Mira. 'Listen. Now that Scott's injured himself too, there's no way I can help both of you to walk out of here as well as keep searching for Naya. I'm sorry – but we're running out of time. I have to focus on getting you back to safety, before dehydration and heat exhaustion properly kick in . . .' She grimaced. 'Before it's too late.'

Mira's face fell. 'I know – you're right. We need you to help us find our way out of the rainforest. You're the only one of us who isn't injured or lost or . . .' She tailed off, found she hadn't the stomach to finish her sentence. 'Or missing.'

'I think we should follow the stream, like we said we'd do – but keep looking out for Naya, calling her name every minute or so as we go – we can scour the water for her the whole way,' said Carly.

Mira nodded. 'OK, that sounds good. I just need to find somewhere private before we go,' she said. 'I need . . . ah . . . well, my stomach doesn't feel very settled.'

'Of course,' said Carly. 'Stay close to the stream so you don't get lost – we'll wait for you here. You feel safe to go on your own, don't you?'

Something flashed in Mira's eyes then – determination, or fear maybe. But to her credit, she nodded and started to make her way upstream through the trees.

Carly watched her go for a moment, then turned to Scott. *He isn't there.*

Carly was alone.

Where the hell has he gone?

'Scott?' she said, whirling around, checking behind her, to the side. She spotted him then limping back towards her from a few metres away, using the stick to help him walk.

'What were you doing – were you trying to walk off?' she asked. 'Or just wandering around?'

'I thought I heard something,' he said, pointing towards the thicket of trees behind him. 'Over there. I wanted to check it out – I had this crazy thought that it could have been Naya . . .'

'Fuck's sake, Scott, what the hell were you thinking?' It came out more forcefully than she'd intended; Scott flinched and Carly raised a palm in apology.

'Sorry, I didn't mean to sound harsh. But you shouldn't be trying to go off on your own – it's not safe,' she said. 'Especially not now that you're injured. Anything could have happened to you.' She gave him her warmest, most reassuring smile. But the truth was, she was frightened too; she was quick to panic now. They were running out of time; she couldn't afford for anything else to go wrong.

'Ouch,' said Scott, reaching for his ankle again. 'Shit, it really hurts. I need to sit down. I probably shouldn't have walked on it again so soon.' He flopped onto the tree trunk.

'Let's see if I can find you something to help ease the pain,' Carly said. Naya's bag was near her feet, so she reached down and rummaged through. She dug out some tablets from the first-aid kit – they were only aspirin, they wouldn't take much of the pain away, but perhaps they would do something – and popped them out of their foil packet. With no water left, she passed Scott the pills and watched him struggle to gulp them down dry, grimacing as he swallowed.

Scott nodded. 'Thanks. Sorry for scaring you – I really did think I heard something over there.'

Carly frowned. 'What do you think you heard, exactly?'

Scott shrugged. 'I'm not sure. There were branches cracking, the trees were rustling really loudly . . . and just something in the way it was moving.' He dipped his head into his palms for a moment, then lifted his head again. 'I'm sorry, this probably isn't making any sense. It's just . . . it sounded like something bigger than a sloth, or a monkey. It sounded . . . *human.*'

Human.

Carly's heart kicked against her ribcage. She swallowed, took a breath.

'Where did the sound come from, exactly – that direction, there?' Scott's eyes followed her pointing finger; he nodded. 'Right. I'm going to check it out,' she said, standing up, then bending quickly to look Scott right in the face when she saw a look of panic flicker across it. 'I'll just go and look in the area for a bit. Make sure it's not Naya, wandering around injured or something. Will you be OK here alone for a few minutes?'

'Let me come with you, please,' said Scott, his tone urgent. 'I think I can walk with my crutch – I'll get faster as I get used to it. I might not even slow you down.'

Carly thought for a moment, then: 'I really think it's best if you don't,' she said. 'I promise, I won't be gone long. You'll be better off staying put here, resting that ankle.'

Scott groaned. 'Yeah. You're probably right. Just stay within earshot, OK? And if . . . you know, if you think it makes more sense for you to get yourself out of here and call for help – I understand. I'll only slow you down now.'

Carly whistled softly. 'Scott, come on – I'd never just leave you here.' She smiled at him, laying a gentle hand on his shoulder. Then she bent down to pick up her rucksack, swung it across her shoulder and started to walk towards the trees.

'Don't worry,' she said, looking back at Scott. 'All of this is going to be over soon.'

NAYA

This must be what it feels like when you die.

Naya was drowning, and then she was breathing again. Over and over and over. Her lungs grasped desperately for air every time she bobbed briefly above the surface of the water before submerging again in a torturous cycle.

When she first fell in, the shock of the water had almost finished her off, as her mouth gaped open and closed; she knew she had to control her breathing if she was going to have any chance of survival. Once or twice, she'd seen patients who'd taken a tumble into stretches of fast-moving water; that was enough experience to know that managing to breathe for the first minute meant the difference between life and death.

But a minute had passed now, and she was still grasping at something, any kind of way out. She'd managed to stay calm for a moment, but the peace had passed and now she was panicking.

Flailing, desperate for something to grab onto, she kicked into the rocks underneath her – and then buckled as a hot jolt of pain rushed across the top of her right leg. The front of her thigh had snagged, at violent speed, on something rough and sharp in the stream. She caught a flash of red changing the colour of the water. *Shit.*

This is it; it's all over now, surely.

Her life didn't flash before her eyes exactly, like people said happened right before you die. It was more random images, random pictures, memories. The tiny seed in her belly, about the size of a grape right now, whose life would end the very same moment hers did. Her children.

Oh God, my children.

How would Elodie and Marcus cope without her? They had her mother, at least. They would be loved; they would be cared for. But who else would understand them the way she did? Who else would fight for them, claw, tooth and nail, to get them the support they needed? Her mother was nurturing and wonderful – but did she have the energy for all those battles?

And then, triggered by the image of her little boy's face, a flash of memory: one of his fixations. A temporary obsession – he had one after another, and Naya supported and encouraged them; she knew that it was how he calmed himself and that these passions brought him so much joy – and this one had been about rivers. He'd learned the names of the biggest rivers in the world, where they started and ended, what country they were in, with encyclopaedic precision. When he discovered a new special interest, he needed to absorb it entirely, and sometimes that meant veering off on random tangents, travelling down knowledge rabbit holes. Rivers were no exception. *But my God, what a useful rabbit hole.*

He'd found something, in one of his Google searches, about what to do if you fell into the water. She could picture his eyes, fervent with excitement, as he told her: 'Did you know, you're supposed to not struggle, *maman*? You have to stay calm, and go with the water. Isn't that crazy?'

Stay calm. Go with the water.

What else, what else did he tell her? There was something about feet – *yes, that was it*: you were supposed to keep them up. *Don't try to touch the bottom, that's how you get injured.* She'd remembered that one too late. But that was the shape she needed to be in now – feet up and together, knees bent, arms out to make a kind of fin. *Back stroke – that should slow you down a bit. Wait for an eddy created by a rock, sprint in front crawl to the edge of the water and get the hell out.*

Forcing her shocked, exhausted body to comply with her instructions took every ounce of strength, but she did it: pulled her feet up and in towards her knees, stretched out her arms. Immediately, she felt her body begin to slow, just a touch, but enough to give her hope.

Next, she tried a few backstrokes. At first it was frustrating, making no difference, but gradually, as she got into a rhythm with the water, she made progress: she had managed to reduce her speed. She was moving more slowly, giving herself time to look at what was around her and see if she could use any of it to get herself out of the water.

Come on, Naya. You can do this.

And then she saw it. Stretching her neck higher out of the water, Naya caught sight of a large rock coming up on her right-hand side – large enough to grab onto, if she could just slow down enough as she got nearer. Just past the rock, the stream looked as though it forked into two distinct paths. If she could grab hold of it, though, then from there, it was only a jump or a long step onto some smaller rocks that led all the way out of the stream.

Slow and steady. Slow and steady.

As she got closer, she pushed against the water with everything she had left to slow herself as much as she could; her hands made contact with the edges of the stone, grabbed hold – her left hand kept slipping off, leaving her flailing wildly, trying to find something to catch onto. She tried again, felt a ledge, small but it was something, and grabbed at it with her fingers. Now both of her hands were holding tight; carefully, inch by inch, she lowered her legs, then curled them around the edges of the rock as tightly as she could.

Gasping, retching, she clung on, waves of nausea racking her body now that she'd come to a standstill within the dizzying motions of the currents. Once she'd caught her breath, she began to slowly pull herself around the rock, clinging on with all four limbs and shifting along its slippery edge. She could not afford to let go; could not afford to fall back into the water. She had no strength left to fight the currents again.

As she approached the other side of the rock, her feet jarred suddenly against something; and again. A solid surface. There was ground underneath her feet; the stream became abruptly shallower here, on the other side of the rock, just as she'd hoped it would. She could stand; she could walk.

Naya pushed her legs forward, stumbled out of the water, then collapsed onto the stony ground at the edge of the stream.

I've made it.

By some miracle, Naya wasn't dead. But her whole body hurt – everything, from head to toe, now starting to register the knocks, bumps and hits she'd taken. By the state of her breathing, the numbness that was creeping across her body, the way she needed to fight against a desperate urge to close her eyes, and the throbbing, stinging pain that was starting to ramp up on her mid-thigh – she knew she was not in a good way.

First things first, she needed to get out of her wet clothes. Despite the muggy warmth of the afternoon, she was soaking and cold; she'd take an age to warm up if she left these things on. She felt for her waterproof – *waterproof, what a joke, the thing is sodden* – jacket, its arms still miraculously wrapped around her waist in a firm knot, untied it and lifted up her hips to wriggle it out from beneath her. The motion took a surprising amount of energy; after she'd pulled it free, she lay back down on her back, gasping for breath, gathering her strength. The pain in her leg was screaming at her now that the shock was starting to wear off; she was afraid to look at it.

One step at a time.

Hauling the top half of her body up to sitting, she began to peel off her T-shirt; the fabric clung to her arms, resisting her every move. Once she'd managed to take it off and lain back down again to catch her breath, her hands reached instinctively towards her belly; she clasped her shaking fingers together and laid them over her stomach for a moment. She breathed.

Unzipping her shorts next, she shuffled them a little way down her hips, but the pain and thought of the nasty gash in her thigh stopped her from taking them all the way down.

One step at a time.

Forcing herself to sit up again, her whole body now shaking violently, she rubbed her arms briskly, then set about wringing as much water from her clothes as she could. The waterproof outside of her jacket had dried off now; she turned it inside out and put it on, dry side against her body. Glancing down at her right leg, she could see blood seeping through her shorts and into the ground beneath her.

Fuck, fuck, fuck. She needed to pack the wound to stop the bleeding, but wrapping a compress on top of sopping wet shorts would stop her warming up, and mean she couldn't examine the wound, or clean it. As much as it would hurt, she needed to get her legs free and take a closer look.

Steeling herself with a deep breath, she yanked the shorts down her left leg first, then, an inch at a time, started to pull the right side down, the pain intensifying as she got closer to her wound. She realized with a sickening lurch that as the tightness of her wet shorts was pushed down closer to the injury, it was forcing out more blood – she could see the spurts trickling down her thigh, her calf; pooling at her ankle, into her shoe.

She needed to wrap it tight – and fast.

Pushing through the searing pain and the increasing flow of blood, Naya wrung as much of the water from her T-shirt as she could, then pulled her shorts the rest of the way off her leg, rolled up her top and tied it around her thigh as a tourniquet. Immediately it became soaked red with blood – it was far from ideal, but it was all she had for now. She held the makeshift bandage around her thigh as tightly as she could, waiting for the bleeding to stop, or at least slow down, which it did after a few moments.

But how much blood have I lost?

And how far away from the others have I travelled?

She had lost all concept of time, of distance, when she was in the water. For all she knew, she could have been hauled downstream for hundreds of metres. Peering through the trees and foliage that led back into the jungle's dark undergrowth, she saw nothing she recognized. And she certainly couldn't see, or hear, anyone else.

'Guys? Hello – can you hear me? Is anyone there?'

Her voice was barely a whisper. She was too hoarse, throaty, from all her coughing and retching in the water, no doubt. She sounded weak – about as weak as she felt. She wished she had something to drink, and her first aid kit.

She turned to face the water, edged a tiny bit closer. Maybe her bag was floating somewhere nearby? If she had it, she could do a rough job of patching up her thigh – clean it up a bit, at least, if anything from her kit had survived. The bag it lived in was supposed to be waterproof – finding it had to be worth a shot.

But she spotted nothing; and now that she thought back, she remembered feeling the bag being tugged off her back only seconds after she'd fallen in the stream, snagged by the branch of a fallen tree, perhaps.

It was long gone, and it looked like anyone who might be able to help her was long gone too. Instead, she was trapped in a jungle, most likely with a murderer on the loose. *I'm defenceless. I'm going to die out here, alone.*

And then a new thought, a soft whisper at the edge of her consciousness, as if it was coming from somewhere outside of herself: *follow the water.*

Naya's knowledge of wilderness survival was, admittedly, not the greatest – she'd barely even watched any of those endurance reality shows on TV – but there was one thing she did know. If you got lost in a jungle – in any kind of wilderness – water would help you navigate. Isn't that what Carly had said too? And she seemed to know about surviving in the rainforest. Streams would lead to rivers, which would lead eventually to the sea – and almost always, long before that, they led to people – to villages, small towns, cities even. To civilization – to hope.

But how long would that take her – how far would she have to keep walking to reach a village, with her leg hurting so badly, with her loss of blood, the lack of water? Even resting here on the ground, there were still surges of searing hot pain rushing up and down her leg. Was there another way, a route that could return her more reliably to the Hideaway? She assessed her options: what if she tried to use the sun to navigate? They'd given that a go earlier, of course, but it hadn't got them very far – it was too hard to track its movement when the trees were so high, blocking it from view. By the edge of the stream, though, out from the interior of the jungle, she had clearer sight of it.

She looked upwards; it must be getting towards midday now, and the sun was high in the sky, straight ahead of where Naya was sitting. She watched it for a few minutes, her eyes focused on its movements in the sky. Yes; she was sure it had tracked ever so slightly to the right.

Rises in the east, sets in the west. So, to her right, that was west. Straight ahead must be south. She felt a fizz of excitement in her belly; of hope. She'd worked that out quickly enough; perhaps this was worth a try. But . . .

Putain. I have no idea how far along the river I am – or which bank I'm on.

She closed her eyes, tried to bring to mind an image of the map. How large was the stream? Was it running parallel to Hannah's house, or perpendicular to it? *Think, Naya*. Or was there, in fact, more than one body of water drawn on that map – a river, and then some smaller lines, a couple of streams perhaps – and how was she supposed to know which one this was?

No; this would be pure guesswork. Just sticking with the stream was much safer – it would lead to *something* other than pure jungle – and if it took her straight to the Hideaway, then so much the better. She would follow the water as long and as far as it would take her; that would be her way out of here.

She felt such relief at the idea of limping into a village somewhere, asking some local to borrow their phone, getting to a hospital, calling for help . . . Yet, at the thought of leaving the others behind, there was also a snag of guilt. The idea of abandoning Carly and Scott and Mira out here, potentially with a killer on the loose, didn't sit right with her. But her inner voice was screaming at her.

I have to think of myself and the baby inside me.

It's not just about me right now, remember?

Her intuition had rarely failed her before; she had to listen to it now.

Hauling herself up to standing, wincing through the hot, stabbing pain in her thigh, Naya looked down and felt a surge of relief that her waterproof jacket was long enough to reach her upper thighs.

It struck her as absurd that she should care, in her current situation, about whether or not anyone saw her in her underwear, and yet the idea of it still embarrassed her. She knew she would simply feel more comfortable with something covering her; less vulnerable somehow.

Perhaps it was the thought of Scott seeing her like this, if she stumbled across him. Something broiled in the pit of her stomach; she hated the idea of looking like such a state in his presence. She wanted him to think of her as attractive, sure, but it was more than that; she didn't want to seem weak in front of him. Like someone who needed help, or protection. She'd been through enough with men who'd acted like she could rely on them, like they wanted to commit to her, to take care of her – but she always ended up worse off because of them.

He wouldn't do that. She couldn't be certain, not yet, but Scott didn't seem like the sort of man who'd try to reel her in, make her think he was someone she could trust – and then, out of the blue, drop her, let her down, abandon her. He didn't seem like someone who'd be capable of being dishonest about who he really was or what he really wanted from her.

Unlike Mathieu, who had made her so many empty promises; told her that it would be different this time, if she'd just give him another chance. That he would change; he'd stop disappearing for hours, sometimes days at a time; he'd stop staying out drinking until four in the morning, coming home smelling of cigarette smoke and stale beer. That he'd do more to help her, spend more time with his own damn children, rather than staying in bed all weekend sleeping off his hangover.

And unlike Ben.

The thought resonated uncomfortably in her mind. She couldn't shake it, this feeling that he was another one of them: a dishonest man, a faker. Someone not to be trusted.

Ben was probably just like Mathieu, wasn't he? Another useless, disappointing guy. If she was right about who he was,

Naya would bet anything that Ben had let Hannah down, the way Mathieu had let Naya down.

With that thought came a jolt of iron-hot rage. These *men*. How dare they – how fucking *dare* they? Worming their way into women's lives, slither by slither; probably promising them goodness knows what. Then revealing their true, toxic and destructive colours, leaving nothing but pain and heartache in their wake.

Yes, she was glad Ben was gone, alone, most likely lost to the wilderness. It was no less than he deserved.

But it wasn't what *she* deserved. Naya and her children and her unborn baby deserved a good life, a happy one. She needed to live. She needed to fight for herself, and for them.

She took a deep breath, steeling herself, decided to give her voice one more try. 'Hello? Is anyone there?' She was still so hoarse, her throat so ragged and sore that her voice was little more than a half-hearted croak. The sound would barely travel into the trees – and it would have no hope of reaching anyone over the shrieks of the rainforest's animals.

There was nothing else for it. She needed to move. Being up on her feet had felt bearable so far, even on her wounded leg, but she wasn't sure how she'd cope with walking. Gingerly, setting out with her good leg, she took one step and then another.

'Ouch!' A hot knife of pain sliced through her again. She blew air out of her mouth, clasped and unclasped her fingers. The pain subsided. She could do this – she had to.

She stepped forward again; and then again. The pain throbbed and then eased. Throbbed and then eased. She kept going. She was finding her rhythm now; striding along the water's edge, pushing forward, managing somehow to put thoughts of the pain in her leg to one side, thoughts of her weakness, her hunger. Adrenaline was a magical thing, she thought. It could compel you to keep going even when you had nothing left.

Naya kept her gaze focused on the stream as she moved, but her eyes darted in and out of the trees at the edge of the water that led back into the jungle, just in case she saw one of the others there.

But there was nothing; there was no one. Just the calls of the birds in the trees and the insects in the air; all oblivious to her fear, and pain, and the cold shock of these past two days. She was alone; no one was coming to rescue her, to help her in her time of need.

So, this time, she was going to save herself.

MIRA

'Carly! Scott!'

Where the hell had they gone?

And how had she managed to lose them?

She'd only been gone a few minutes to relieve herself, and her progress was so slow that she'd hardly covered any distance – but now there was no sign of them. They wouldn't have gone off anywhere without her, surely? Not with Scott's twisted ankle and Carly so worried about them losing each other.

She stood still; waited, then called their names again. Still nothing – no reply. Only the calls of the birds, the insistent croaking of frogs.

She'd not gone far from where Scott was sitting on the tree trunk, resting his ankle, to find a spot to go to the loo. She'd found somewhere close to the water's edge that gave her some privacy, and allowed her to clean herself up afterwards. It took her no more than five minutes to trace back the path she'd just walked.

But now she was back at the same place, right where she'd just left them – she was *sure* this was it – but there was no one there. She stood on the spot, looking all around for any sign of the two of them.

Damn. She must have taken a wrong turn – but how? She'd barely gone twenty metres, and that was in almost a straight line.

In her mind she saw again an image of the water, just as she had a moment ago while down by the stream – of Naya, tumbling in where the current was at its strongest. Had she done enough to try and find her? Had she looked hard enough? Mira knew she'd searched up and down every part of the water and bank that she could see – and there was no sign of Naya other than her bag. But perhaps she should have carried on looking?

A part of Mira was clinging desperately to the hope that it was somehow a good sign, the fact they hadn't come across her – that perhaps that meant that Naya had been able to claw herself out of the water somehow. But another part – more realistic, maybe – knew the chances of that were slim.

Grief welled in her chest. Poor, poor Naya, and the tiny human growing inside of her. So young, so much ahead of her. She and her unborn baby had so much to live for.

And Mira had so much to live for too. She could barely believe now that there'd been a time she'd been ready to give up on life. Not that she'd actively wanted to die, but even that she'd just been living in a kind of passive acceptance – she couldn't make sense of it. Now that she'd got so close to losing her life – now that she'd had to find the strength and resilience to keep herself alive, keep herself moving – she couldn't imagine how she'd been ready to let life go.

She'd never give up on life again. When she got home – *if*

I get home, please God – she would claw her way back to better health, to more time with Ezra, with every fibre of her being. If that meant brutal rounds of chemo, more hospital trips, more second and third and fourth opinions – like her friends wanted, and Ezra; like all of them wanted – then so be it. An extra week, an extra day, an hour even, of life would make that pain worthwhile.

A squawking toucan just behind her brought Mira back to her surroundings; she realized she'd been turning in circles in the same spot now for several minutes, calling the others' names. There was no trace of them. Had the two of them walked off and left her behind?

It was starting to look increasingly that way.

Unless one, or both of them, have been lying to me? Was this part of a plan – to separate her from them, to leave her, weak and defenceless, in the wilderness? Were Scott or Carly hiding something bigger – could either of them have been responsible for what happened to Hannah?

But how could they? How is that even possible?

No, she was becoming paranoid. She must simply be in the wrong place. It was so easy to get lost here; everything looked the same. Mira was about to start walking again, to head back to the stream and move a little further along, try the next gap in the trees, when she saw them: the two rucksacks lying on the ground, on the other side of the tree stump.

My bag. Naya's bag. Her heart gave a little surge of hope, foolish hope, that somehow Naya had found her way back and was about to emerge from the trees right now – but of course, no, she remembered: she had put Naya's bag here after she'd dragged it from the water.

She'd left the bags right in this spot when she'd rushed off to help Scott after he'd fallen. Then she'd forgotten all about them.

That meant she was in the right place. And Scott had been sitting here only minutes ago.

So where the hell is he now?

Mira clearly wasn't going to solve the mystery of wherever the two of them had gone, but she was determined to try one last time to find Naya, and then to get out of this rainforest. Opening Naya's bag, tipping its contents – a few drops left in a water bottle, the first aid kit, nothing much else – into her own backpack, she set off again towards the stream.

She was close – so close – to getting away from the trees, had taken her first steps back towards the water, when she heard it.

A snap of branches, a crunching of leaves, only a little way behind her, off somewhere to the right.

Thank God – that must be one of the others.

She turned towards the source of the sound, tried to see who was there.

'Carly? Is that you?'

There was no reply, but the crunches carried on. They seemed to be coming from a different place now, still behind her, but to the left – whoever this was, they were moving.

Mira shook her head, tried to make sense of what she was hearing. Was she losing her mind? Had her senses fully given up on her now, after so long without water, without proper food in her failing body? Was it the damp, overbearing heat, the relentless humidity, the cacophony of jungle sounds that were so deafening – had all of it come together in one maddening maelstrom that meant she was no longer able to tell what was real and what was a figment of her traumatized mind?

She stayed glued to the spot, forcing her body not to move, trying to quiet down the booming beat of her heart, so loud now in her ears that she was sure whoever – *whatever* – was circling her could hear it too.

She was being irrational, surely? This was likely just one of the jungle's creatures – a sloth or a coati – or one of the group – Carly or Scott or even Ben, perhaps?

Or maybe it was Paola or Luisa – *yes, that could be it!* The helicopter hadn't managed to find them earlier, so perhaps they'd come themselves, on foot – or even brought the search party with them. Was help finally here?

'Hello?' she called out. 'I'm over here! Who is it – and where are you?'

Another snap, a crack of branches. Closer now. But no answer. A spike of adrenaline hit Mira behind her ribcage.

'Carly? Scott?'

If it's rescuers, or one of the others . . . why didn't they shout back when I called?

A rustle of leaves behind her – or was it in front of her? She tried to tune her ears into the sound, tracing where exactly the movement was coming from – but she couldn't home in on it properly, not with the squawks and cries of the rainforest's creatures reverberating across her eardrums like a poorly tuned orchestra.

Where are you?

Snap. Rustle.

Silence.

Her instinct to flee took over then, and she whirled around on the spot, her feet grasping for something solid on the damp, soft earth beneath her, and then she was running as best she could, wildly, straight ahead, and she was slipping and sliding on the jungle's mulchy floor, panting with every movement.

And now, she was sure of it, Mira could make out footsteps behind her – someone was pounding the ground now, pushing through leaves and vines, perhaps only metres away.

Who was it – and why were they running after her?

But those questions didn't matter right now; all that mattered was her survival. Whoever it was, Mira knew she couldn't outrun them, not for long – any second now, her body would give up and she'd collapse on the ground; it was a miracle she was able to run for this long. Her best chance was to try to outwit them – to turn sharply, keep twisting and turning, pushing through small gaps and cracks that her body was mercifully small enough for, and pray they wouldn't be able to track her down.

She stopped suddenly, hid behind a tree trunk, tried to still her shaking limbs. She waited, forced herself to hold her nerve even as she felt something crawling along the back of her neck – oh God, what was it? Was there even anything there, or was she imagining it? In her mind's eye, she saw one of the large worms she'd stepped over on the jungle floor writhing its way over her bare flesh. She resisted the urge to move, to retch. Staying still for a moment was her best shot at losing whoever was on her tail.

The footsteps and shaking branches approached, got louder. Mira shrank into the tree, tried to make her body as small as possible – her petite stature was just about the only thing she had going for her when it came to survival, but at least it was something.

They were approaching now. They were almost in front of her. Through the dense foliage, Mira could make out a human outline, but no more than that.

And then, a different noise: a grunt of frustration, of rage, coming from whoever was following her. It was guttural; not obviously male or female – inhuman, even, though she knew it was a person who'd made the sound. She could make out their silhouette through the branches of the trees.

Whoever that is, they're angry.

On instinct, Mira grabbed wildly for something – anything – she could use to defend herself if her pursuer found her. There was nothing.

Snap.

Closer now – almost in front of her.

Then all her courage failed her, and, as if they were acting on pure instinct, without her brain's command, her feet began to move again, and she was running, stumbling and slipping on the wet earth, all the while cursing herself and the people who were out in this hellscape with her; any and all of them were the enemy now, and she could trust no one. No one except herself.

BEN

Ben had never tried to charge a one hundred per cent dead phone from his portable pack before – let alone a big old brick like this. The label on the back of his charger said it was best used on devices before they went flat, and now he could see why. This thing was taking *for ever*.

As he walked, Ben kept his other eye on the sun, which he could make out high in the sky, above the tops of the trees. He had perhaps five or six hours of daylight left, but he was thirsty, and hungry, and tired – he needed to keep walking, get back to the lodge and call for help.

Glancing at the phone in his hand, waiting for it to charge, he kept thinking about who it belonged to, and what had happened to her – *Hannah is dead, Hannah is dead* – and he was hit by a wrecking ball of memories, and with them, waves of sadness.

Hannah sharing his ramen at Tadashi in the Hill Country, breathing in the fresh air outside the city.

Hannah's hot breath at the side of his neck as she danced her fingers down his spine to the small of his back, in that way that always drove him wild.

Hannah squealing excitedly as she showed him the plans for her new retreat in Costa Rica, right the way down to the decor in each of the bedrooms, because she trusted him so implicitly with every idea she had – every thought in her head.

The level of detail she'd given him about the retreat meant Ben had little trouble convincing Paola he'd been officially invited. How else could he have known about the top-secret location and itinerary? She'd not wanted to share any of it publicly, not yet at least, because she knew she had some enemies out there; people who took against her ideas, who thought what she was preaching was dangerous. People who'd sent her death threats; who hated her enough to want to track her down and cause her harm. But she'd shared it all with him.

And then – and this one thwacked him hard in the chest – Hannah breaking up with him after ten beautiful months when she found out he'd been lying to her about kicking his addiction; that he was still using, pretty much every day.

He'd messed up so badly. He'd chosen those fucking pills over his feelings for her, when it came down to it. He'd let his addiction become his *primary relationship*, just like they talked about in rehab.

And because of his all-consuming powerlessness over that very addiction, he'd lost the best thing that had ever happened to him.

Because as much as she drove him crazy, he loved Hannah. He'd never stopped, not for a second – not when she'd told him what she'd done, not when his boss had called him into that meeting room.

He might have thought that he hated her for doing it. He was livid, for sure. But he could see it now; now that he was alone, and she was dead and gone, never to be there to help him or love him or make him laugh or fuck him or drive him to the point of insanity, ever again. Any anger that he'd felt towards her – straight after she got off the phone and blocked him on every fucking channel – he felt all that only towards himself now, for the decades-long role he'd played in his own destruction.

He – with a little help from some prescription meds – had ruined his own life, and then he had kept ruining it, over and over again, doing the same old shit and expecting it to somehow be different the next time; chipping away at his happiness and his peace and his success a little more each time. He'd been doing that for years, ever since his first sniff of cocaine in college.

And, in spite of her flaws – the way she went about things that sometimes pissed him off – Hannah had been trying to help him see that. He'd come here because, on some level, he wanted to tell her he understood. That he still loved her; still wanted her. That he needed her: she was the only person who could help him.

Ben closed his eyes, replayed in his mind the last thing she'd said to him, only a few weeks ago.

'I'm sorry, Ben. I hope you know I was only thinking of what's best for both of us,' she'd said when she'd answered the phone that day.

But he'd been angry – so angry. He'd spoken to her harshly. 'What's *best* for us? Did you actually think you were trying to help me? That this would do me good? It was none of your business – how was it your place to talk to my fucking *boss*?' He'd had to stop then, the gasps of hurt erupting from his belly, his throat, so hard and loud that he could hardly breathe through them.

Hannah said nothing. After a long moment, he spoke again. 'Trish is going to give me the sack now, Hannah, you know that, right? I'll be finished – finished at work, probably finished everywhere in Austin now – thanks to *you*.'

'You got fired – for having a relapse? Shit, that's harsh – can they even do that?' He could believe Hannah's surprise. She hadn't realized – having never had a real job, having never truly lived in the real world, insulated from all this by her pseudo-spiritual social media career – what kind of impact she'd have by telling Trish that Ben needed help.

Even before she found fame online, she'd never had to work – her dad was one of Houston's oil billionaires; Hannah had grown up with more money than she'd ever be able to spend, and almost no love. She barely saw her father, and her mom was too busy running galas and charity luncheons to ever pay her much attention. She'd been brought up by a series of strict, impassive nannies – from her teens, her brand of spirituality had become her escape; her source of love.

'But . . . I thought she'd help you! I thought telling her would help with your recovery. Come on, she should at least give you a chance to get better,' Hannah had insisted. 'I guess I could reach out to my dad and ask if you can talk to his lawyer . . .'

'I don't want anything from you,' Ben said coldly. 'Ever again. Don't you fucking dare try to help me. I mean it, Hannah. And no, Trish doesn't have to give me a chance to get well – she's already given me enough of them, remember?'

Silence, then, for a moment – only the sound of the two of them breathing hard, shakily.

'Look, I get it, if you don't forgive me,' said Hannah finally. 'But at least try to understand that I was doing what I thought was right for you – and, to be honest, for me too.' She sighed. 'I mean, look at what I'm doing – think about how many people listen to what I have to say. I'm making a difference to all their lives! And if it gets out that I'm dating an *addict* . . .'

Of course. This was all about her image, her follower count. He smarted at the irony of it. *How dare she*, when she was nothing but a garden variety, run-of-the-mill addict herself!

When she spoke again, her voice was soft but resolute: 'I'm sorry, Ben, but it's over between us. We've had a great time and all, but let's face it – this isn't working.'

Ben knew the conversation should be over; he knew he needed to get off the phone, try to clean up the mess of his life. But still, after all this, he couldn't bear to let her go. He didn't want her to hang up, even then. 'This is all about your precious followers, isn't it?' He barked a laugh; it was hollow, bitter. He could taste the fury on his tongue.

'Not *all*,' said Hannah. 'But these people need me – they rely on me, remember?'

He'd heard enough. It was over between them; she'd made that clear. He didn't need to hear her messed-up reasoning now – or ever again. He'd ended the call, switched his phone off, tried to clear his head.

But those words. *These people rely on me.* The phrase had rattled inside his brain; it had kept on plaguing him in the hours and days after that last call.

Couldn't she see that he relied on her too? That he needed her more than people on the internet that she'd never even met? He'd tried to call her back later that same day, and found the dial tone dead. He'd sent her messages on Instagram, Facebook, WhatsApp; none of them went through. Hannah had blocked him, deleted him from her life, just like that. Did their relationship mean that little to her? Their history – everything they'd shared, everything he knew about her?

He couldn't let it go that easily, even if she could. And if he couldn't get through to her on his phone or his computer, there was nothing else he could do except turn up at the retreat he knew she was hosting. What other choice had she left him?

And then he'd got here – and found Hannah dead.

After they'd found her body, he'd been torn. On the one hand, he'd wanted to stick with the group – it was his best shot at getting back to safety, and helping find out who'd done this to Hannah. On the other, he was keenly aware that suspicions were more likely to fall on him than anyone else for her murder. Women were usually killed by their boyfriends, their husbands, their exes, right? Men who knew them – not random drug dealers in the jungle. He'd be the most likely suspect, and his reasons for being here would only make him seem guiltier.

A soft beep drew his attention back to the satellite phone clutched in his grasp. He stared at it, as if he were seeing it more clearly now, as if he were looking at it for the first time. A large black and grey thing, resembling one of those old school Nokia phones from the early 2000s – except it had a different brand name, one he'd never heard of. *Iridium*.

He drew a breath in sharply, as the memory of another phone came hurtling towards him. *Hannah's phone*. She'd had this hare-brained idea in rehab, not long after they'd met, when Ben was lamenting not being able to access his work emails, that they could get round the recovery centre's rules – *no phones or other handheld devices allowed, to ensure all patients focus only on their recovery* – by asking for permission to check each other's phones instead of their own.

'I'll tell the nurses that, because of my online presence, I need to at least be able to make sure there are no emergencies – and to check in with my community moderator and my virtual assistant,' she'd said.

Ben had scoffed when Hannah suggested it; he knew the staff would laugh her straight out of the room. But he hadn't realized then the extent of her ego; of her arrogance; her stubbornness. Traits that he both disliked in her and felt in awe of. The way that, when she got an idea in her mind, she wouldn't drop it until she'd exhausted every possibility to make it happen. He'd been right, of course. The duty nurse had shooed her away with a click of her tongue and Hannah had taken her seat next to him in the evening's group session, muted, shamefaced. She wasn't used to being turned down; this was a woman who'd gotten pretty much everything she'd ever wished for.

But Hannah not getting what she wanted that day – it cracked something in her, just a little, and in a good way. She'd opened up to Ben properly that evening; to the whole group. She'd told them how dishonest she felt, portraying this squeaky clean, wholesome image, all while she was struggling to make it as far as lunchtime without a half bottle of wine and a couple of joints.

'It's the pressure of it all – the stress of having to be online all the time, having to look like I know all the fucking answers – when on the inside, I'm just as screwed up as the rest of the world,' she'd said, her words blurred by her tears. 'I don't fucking know how to help anyone really, do I? And the need to use something to get away from the feelings – it's just getting worse all the time – I need to get a handle on it. I need to stop.'

It was that version of her that he'd fallen in love with – the part of her that was vulnerable, and sweet, and honest. She'd tried to get recovery right, after that – she'd thrown herself into it, got herself clean. But it was as if, after she'd beaten her addiction to drink and weed, she'd replaced it with something else. Her spirituality, always a force for good in her life, took a darker turn after she gave up the other stuff; she'd become obsessed with growing her following, gaining influence, becoming famous. And even though a part of him was scared by it, her increasing power had drawn him to her at the same time; made him feel even more special, more important, being in her inner circle.

Another rush in his chest at that thought, a tremulous wave of grief for her. He should never have come here; he knew that now. He should have respected her decision to end things with him, to cut him out of her life, if that's what she wanted. She'd have hated him turning up here like this, professing his love for her. She'd have cringed at him showing Paola their most romantic messages so he could make out that they were still together, pretending he'd turned up here to surprise her at her first live retreat. It was a gamble – he couldn't be sure exactly what Hannah might have told her staff about him and their break-up – but he'd had little choice: Paola had dismissed his initial suggestion that she had the wrong information about Hannah's guest list.

And anyway, it had paid off. His story, and the texts, had worked and Paola had believed him.

If Hannah had found out he'd done that, she'd have hated him – or worse.

She'd have pitied him.

And could I have blamed her?

It was enough, now. Once he got home, he would get his life back in order. He'd stop using the drugs – he meant it this time. He'd do it in Hannah's memory; in honour of her. He'd go to meetings every single day, he'd get a sponsor, he'd go back to fucking rehab if he had to. Whatever it took. This could no longer be his life; he was done with the suffering his addiction kept causing him.

Another beep dragged Ben's attention back to the present. The phone had enough battery now for him to be able to turn it on; he slowed to a stop, found a tree trunk to rest on. He held down the switch at the side of the phone, waited a moment for the screen to light up. A few seconds later it turned green, showed the name Iridium again. There were few options on here – it wasn't a smartphone, there was no internet, no apps; just 'MENU' and 'HELP'.

And some bars at the top right showing a signal.

Oh, thank God. With a surge of sweaty relief, he punched in the three digits – 911 – and hit the call button, sure he'd read somewhere that the emergency number here was the same as in the US. To his amazement, and euphoria, it worked – he heard the dial tone, and a woman answered after a short ring, in rapid Spanish that Ben barely caught anything of.

'*Hola*, hello, yes, do you speak English? I need help!'

'Yes, go ahead, what is your emergency?' *Thank you, thank you, Costa Ricans and your amazing language abilities.*

'I'm lost out in the rainforest – a few miles inland from

Rincon. There's a body out here, someone has died – and other people have been injured too . . .' His words came out in a rush; he knew he needed to slow down, but he couldn't get a handle on himself. It was as though, now that he'd got a glimpse of rescue, of safety, his brain and body were finally releasing all of the terror and grief he'd been consumed by since they'd found Hannah.

'OK, calm down, sir – I need you to say all of that again. And where exactly are you – do you have an address?'

Ben took a deep breath, tried again, racked his brains for the address Hannah had given him; he remembered the name, and the closest town, but the zip code, any other details – he had no idea. He'd just have to give this woman everything he did have. 'The retreat is called The Hideaway, and I'm stranded inside the property's private rainforest . . . there's a few hundred acres of it. I'm sorry, that's all I know.'

'OK, no problem,' she said. 'I can see that we've already received an emergency call for rescuers to attend this location today, but our helicopter was unsuccessful in locating you. However, your satellite phone should be able to send me your coordinates so I can see exactly where you are. I need you to go to the phone's main menu and find the option that says "activate GPS", or similar. Can you see that?'

Ben scrolled through the menu; sure enough, there was the option to 'ACTIVATE GPS AND SEND COORDINATES'. He pressed it. 'Done, do you see it?' he said.

There was a pause for a few seconds, then: 'I have it,' said the woman. 'I am sending another two rescue helicopters from Puerto Jiménez to your exact location now. Help is on the way – they will be with you as soon as possible,' she said. 'Please stay exactly where you are, don't move. If for any reason you walk elsewhere, you will need to call again and send us your new location. I will call you back in the next ten minutes to update you on their arrival.'

'Of course, I'll stay right here, whatever they need – thank you, thank you so much,' he said, starting to sob with relief as he hung up.

It was going to be OK; he was getting out of here. They'd find Hannah, they'd work out what must have happened to her, who hurt her – who *killed* her; the desperate search for an answer to that question had plagued him ever since they'd found her. They'd work out that it wasn't him – it couldn't have been him; he wasn't even here when she'd been killed. The murderer would be punished. Hannah would have a proper funeral.

I've made it.

He sobbed harder at the thought of being out of the rain-forest, at getting on the plane home. He'd been so wrong: he should never have snuck here, in some misguided attempt to get Hannah back – to admit he still loved her, to tell her how much he needed her. Getting himself clean and drug-free was never in Hannah's power – she'd never really had any influence over that at all. He saw it now, so clearly, what he must have heard them say in rehab and twelve-step meetings a thousand times:

I am the only person who can get myself well.

And that's what he was going to do: he was going to get well. As soon as he got back to that house and his suitcase, he would throw away the remainder of the pills; he'd flush them straight down the toilet. There would be another way; a better way.

He would do it this time; he'd do it for *her*.

A *crack* behind him – a branch snapping, a noise distinct from the warbles and cries of the small creatures that moved through the trees. This sound came from the ground, and it was somewhere just behind him.

Ben stopped in his tracks. *What was that?* He scanned from left to right, high to low. There was nothing out there. No jaguars prowling, no howler monkeys, no sloths – not so much as a tree frog, as far as he could see.

'Hello?' he called. 'Is there someone there? Naya, Scott – Carly – is that one of you?' He paused, licked his dry lips. 'Mira?' But there was nothing now; only silence. He shrugged, turned back to the phone.

He was safe; he was totally alone. He wondered if perhaps he'd imagined it or the snapping sound was one of the tropical birds the jungle was teeming with, raking through some fallen branches, rooting for food.

Yes, that's most likely all it was. I'm wired, is all. I need some sleep.

Snap.

Another branch, another footstep – and closer this time. He knew he wasn't imagining it now – it seemed to have come from only a few metres behind him.

A creeping sensation crawled across his skin; an absolute certainty, in that moment, that someone – or *something* – was coming after him. He held still, so still that he could hear the blood rushing through his brain in time with his pulse – perhaps, if it was an animal, some kind of predator, it would simply give up if it couldn't hear him or see him move.

Every cell in Ben's body wanted to run – *run, goddamn it* –

but he couldn't. If he moved too far from this spot, how would the rescuers find him? The phone operator had told him to stay in one place, hadn't she? Their best chance of finding him was if he stayed put.

There was another loud crack behind him; more snapping, faster now – and something else – footsteps. They didn't sound like those of any rainforest animal – these were decidedly human.

Ben, you need to start running!

He couldn't rationalize it, this urge to sprint; most likely, it was one of the others, deciding to follow the same path, stumbling across him. If they'd all been running towards that chopper earlier, that would mean he'd gotten close to them all. They'd mean him no harm, surely?

But he was gripped with fear.

Are they coming after me? Have they worked something out? Does someone know that I've turned up here uninvited?

That's it. I'm moving.

If he just tried to walk in a circle – he could keep watch on one of the taller trees, maybe, use that to navigate back to this spot – then hopefully he could lose whoever was after him and get back to the same place. It didn't need to be exactly the same spot, surely, for the rescuers to find him? As long as it was close enough, he'd hear them – or he could send the coordinates again, couldn't he?

The footsteps were coming faster and heavier towards him now – whoever it was, they were almost here. It was too late. He couldn't do it. He couldn't outrun whoever – or whatever – was following him. Better to turn and face it – them – head on.

Heart racing, hands clenched into fists, he turned to the source of the rustling, just as a figure emerged from the foliage.

He blew out a long breath and his racing heart began to slow when he saw who was standing there, watching him.

'Oh, thank God, it's only you!' he said, a smile tugging his mouth wide. 'I thought you were some kind of predator! How did you find me? Listen, I've managed to call—'

But Ben never finished his sentence.

His words were shocked from his mouth as the sharp sting of a knife slammed into his side.

He only just had time to register the look of pure desperation on his attacker's face, to see a series of fast-moving images behind his eyelids – Hannah's slow, lazy smile after he'd kissed her for the first time; his beautiful Blondie turning her chocolate eyes to him, excited for their morning walk; his mom staring vacantly out the trailer window, fried and zombie-like – before his body slipped to the ground and the world around him began to fade.

SCOTT

Scott hadn't been able to sit there waiting for Carly, or Mira – for bloody *anyone* – any longer. He'd decided he needed to focus on getting out of the rainforest; finding his way back to safety. Helping the others too, if he could. Helping himself.

He wasn't sure exactly how, at first. He was injured and totally alone; everyone who should have been there with him was gone. Hannah was dead; their supposed retreat was over before it even started. Naya was pretty much certain to be dead too. Ben had bolted off and left them – which might well have been for the best, if what they all suspected was true. Then Mira had gone to relieve herself some time earlier and never reappeared, and now Carly too had disappeared: she'd gone off to investigate the source of the sound he'd heard, *ages* ago now.

At least, it *felt* like ages ago, but he knew his sense of time was starting to get warped and strange. In pain and dehydrated and grief-stricken as he was, the hours and minutes out here seemed to be bending and contracting; earlier, for just a minute, he'd even forgotten what day it was. It was a disconcerting feeling: as though the jungle were turning him into an animal rather than a human being, some kind of creature without conscience, one that was only aware of the difference between day and night but nothing more precise than that.

Stop it, Scott. His thoughts were wandering again; rambling and rattling about in his brain. What was his point again? And why did it matter, anyway, now that Hannah was lying dead and beautiful, kind Naya had been taken down that stream? The image of her gulping at the air in panicked spurts, choking underneath the rushing current, flooded his brain again; made him gasp with sadness and horror.

Mira, Carly. That had been it. He'd been thinking about how long they'd both been gone, and what the hell had happened to them. However long it had been, he hadn't been sure either of them would be back any time soon.

And he sure as anything couldn't stay sitting still on that tree trunk, with what was most likely a broken ankle, waiting to die of pain and thirst. Not while he still had an outside chance of making it out alive and getting help for the others, anyway.

He'd decided it was time for him to start moving, to use what was left of his strength and energy to find his way out. Yes, he was heartbroken at the thought of leaving the others – Mira especially, who was so weak and vulnerable and might well be trying to make her way back to him right now. And Naya – *oh God, Naya* – his heart ached again at the thought of her.

But what good was he to any of them, just sitting here, injured and self-pitying? He had no choice but to try to escape. And the best hope of survival for all of them, not just him, was for him to use all of his knowledge and his half-decent navigation skills to leave this place behind.

He closed his eyes for a second; it always helped him to tune in, think more clearly, when he turned off some of his senses.

Yes. He could just catch the slightest rushing of the water; the stream was to the right of him. He'd make his way back towards it, then follow it closely until it led him out of the jungle. It had been dry out here for about twenty-four hours now – it should be possible to climb over the area the mudslide had hit, if he had to.

He could do this; he would do it. Hauling himself to his feet, using the stick as a crutch, he pushed himself forward, one painful step at a time, through the vines towards the sound of the water. But his brain had been playing tricks on him; the stream now sounded as though it were coming from a different direction.

He'd got it wrong – how had he done that?

His sense of direction was usually so strong. Now, instead of getting closer to the water's edge, he wondered if he'd moved further away from it – deeper into the interior of the rainforest.

Shit. What am I doing?

'Carly?' he yelled. 'Mira?' Perhaps one of them was still somewhere nearby; maybe he could get their attention. But his voice sounded weak – his throat was dry, and any sound he could make was barely audible to Scott himself over the chorus of the jungle.

There was no reply; of course not. Limping on, one agonizing step after another, he reminded himself why he needed to keep going. For Hannah, for his mum. For Naya. He needed to keep going. One more step. Then another.

He pushed on, the pain in his ankle red-hot now, searing

upwards through his leg, making him want to collapse onto the ground. *Don't lose focus, don't lose it.* The adrenaline surged through his chest, heart threatening to explode, hammering against his ribs.

He had to keep on walking.

Stop, start. One step. Another step. Scott didn't know where he was walking to, but something inside him was guiding him now. Driving him onwards.

A sound; a whimper. Someone moaning.

Someone in pain.

What was that? Did I just imagine that?

Another whimper; this wasn't just in his mind. It was real.

He needed to keep walking; try to find its source. He stumbled onwards, and then he saw it, and his guts lurched.

There was something there through the trees, in a small clearing, making the whimpering sound. It was lying on the ground.

Not something; *someone.*

A man; a man he knew.

Scott dropped to the ground. 'Ben! Holy shit, mate, I've got you.' Scott touched Ben's body gently, caught sight of the gash to the side of his chest, the blood that had turned the leafy mulch next to him dark.

What the fuck had happened to him?

He knew Ben had lied; that he was guilty of something. And it looked like someone had come to get their revenge on him for whatever that was. But attack him? Leave him here for dead?

Scott looked back at Ben's face, realized he was trying to mouth something – to speak. He leaned down, rested his ear just above Ben's lips, tried to make out the words he was mumbling, whispering, his voice weak and strained.

Scott heard a name – Ben muttered it once, twice.

'It was her. She . . . did this,' he croaked.

It can't be. He's wrong. Scott shook his head, baffled. 'But there's no way . . . she wouldn't. She couldn't have.'

Ben's eyes were closing again.

'No, no, come on – stay with me. Ben, please, you've just got to hold on – we'll get you out of here, we'll get help.'

Then Scott heard a sound that was so strange, so out of place, that he was sure he must be hallucinating; it was a ringing, the buzzing of a phone. His eyes roamed the ground; he couldn't see anything. Was he losing it altogether now – was he in so much pain and shock, so dehydrated that he'd formed the sound of something in his mind that wasn't really there? But then he remembered that Ben had taken the satellite phone; he'd had it with him when he ran off. Could that be what he was hearing? Could he have got it working somehow?

As he listened, the sound was getting quieter, then louder – he could hear it, and then he couldn't again – then it was back, louder.

He felt a squeeze to his hand. He looked down at Ben; the man nodded and whispered a few more words:

'I . . . had the satellite . . . called for . . . help. But she . . .' He fell silent.

'Yes – she? Ben, what? What did she do?' said Scott.

But there was no reply. Ben's eyes flickered and rolled backwards, opened again briefly, then fell closed one final time.

And then he felt it. The hairs on his arm standing up; a trickle of ice running from his scalp down to his heels.

He didn't know how he knew it, but he did.

Somebody was watching him.

He whipped his head round, scanned the trees beyond, tried to work out where the feeling had come from. Was that a shape, just there, behind that tree – a human outline? Was that some-body moving out there – or was it just the trees in the mid-afternoon breeze, a wind that seemed to be gathering steam now, as the day drew to a close?

It was impossible to tell; still the feeling of being stared at, surveyed, remained.

And then the leaves and branches shuddered and a figure emerged, walking towards him – slowly, with purpose – and a soft voice said:

'Ah. Here you are, Scott.'

CARLY

If there was one thing Carly had become an expert at over the years, it was *pretending*.

She had to do so much of it, all the time, relentlessly. *Pretending* to give a shit about people's dreary, humdrum problems; acting as if they were telling her something completely new and different and unique and special every time, when in truth, everybody complained about the same old crap.

They were all the same, really, people's wounds. You'd seen one, and you'd seen them all. She wanted to scream at the thought of it: the memory of the fifty-minute slots, one blurring into another, the same thing, all day, every day, without end.

Until she'd met Robyn. Robyn, who'd changed all that for her. Who'd been so beautifully unique, so different to anyone else she'd ever met. Robyn, who'd made Carly feel a kind of love she hadn't known was possible.

And then someone destroyed the best thing Carly had ever had. Someone took Robyn away from her. Someone killed her. *Hannah.*

Carly stared down at Scott, still crouched on the ground next to Ben. She gripped the now blood-soaked knife in one hand, the satellite phone in the other. She wondered why he hadn't said anything yet – perhaps he was in shock?

She'd hoped the source of the noise Scott had heard earlier in the trees was Ben, but it was still amazingly lucky that it was, and that she'd stumbled across him when she did – they must have all ended up close together when they were going after that helicopter. She'd not said one word before slamming the knife – which she'd snuck out of Naya's bag when she was looking for painkillers for Scott – hard into the side of Ben's chest. It filled her with guilt and horror – none of this was his fault – but what else was she supposed to *do*?

Then just a moment ago, she'd been lurking in the trees with the satellite phone, trying to find out how far away the rescuers were, when she'd seen Scott limp into the clearing, move towards Ben, lay an ear to his grey lips.

Finally Scott spoke. 'Did you do this, Carly? Did you stab Ben? And what about Hannah – was that you too?' He leaned over to one side, away from Ben, and retched onto the ground; nothing much seemed to come out, they were all too dehydrated for that, she supposed. Carly watched as he wiped his mouth, then turned to look back at her. 'But . . . I don't get it. *Why*?'

Carly pondered for a moment how much to tell him. He didn't need to know every detail, sure, but it might be good for him to understand some of it. She wanted him to know that she'd had a good reason for coming here to confront Hannah; for doing everything she'd done.

'I lost someone,' she said eventually, her voice soft, wistful – the way she always sounded when she thought about Robyn. Those three little words could in no way sum up the enormity of her pain, her grief. 'Then after I lost her, I lost everything else.'

And it was true. After Robyn died, Carly had spiralled. She'd found she could no longer be a therapist; could no longer listen to people talk about their nightmare dates or low self-esteem or how much they hated their boss. She could no longer kid herself that she was any good at helping anyone with their struggles; if she couldn't even save the person she loved most in the world, what the hell was she doing trying to support anyone else?

So, she'd stopped practising, found herself unable to work – unable to *function* – for months, until she'd defaulted on her mortgage. Eventually she'd taken a crappy customer service job at a local tech company, reading robotic scripts instructing people on how to set up their new devices, because it was the only thing her traumatized brain could handle.

Not that any of that could compare to the loss of Robyn.

Scott shifted then on the jungle floor; Carly turned to look at him. He was watching her, eyes full of confusion.

'But what's that got to do with Hannah?' he said.

Carly shook her head; a strange, bitter sound emerged from her throat, somewhere between a laugh and a sob. 'What's it got to do with her? Everything, Scott. Robyn's death was Hannah's fault,' she said. 'Hannah killed her.'

Robyn had told Carly about her bipolar disorder in Peru, the first night they met. Her diagnosis had come a few years earlier, when she'd ended up in a South London hospital after a manic episode that saw her survive on nothing but cigarettes and Red Bull for nearly two weeks, before collapsing at Denmark Hill station.

'There's no point in me hiding it anyway, not with those group leaders watching me like a hawk,' she'd said, laughing, in her South London accent. She'd been taking a mood stabilizer for eighteen months now, quite a high dose, and sometimes it made her a bit flat – sort of numb, she said, like she wasn't really feeling her emotions. But it was worth it. 'Keeps me from going doolally,' she said. 'Trust me, babe, you don't want to see me thinking I'm the next artistic prodigy or trying to buy the whole of the bleeding internet on my credit card again. Don't reckon you'd be so keen on me after that.'

But Carly would have been. She'd thought Robyn was wonderful: funny and clever and strong. And sexy as hell, with her hourglass figure and wavy balayage bob and deep, gurgling laugh. When they got back from the rainforest, things moved fast. Within a couple of months, fed up of long train journeys and unsatisfying Zoom sex, Robyn decided to rent out her studio flat in Camberwell and move up to Cardiff, into Carly's flat. Robyn worked remotely – she could do her web design job online from anywhere – so it was easier for her to move than Carly, who had rented her therapy room on a long-term contract and had clients to think of.

For one blissful year, they had everything: lazy Sundays in bed, scary movies on the sofa, laughter and fun and electrifying sex and a deep, heartfelt connection; a belonging. They fitted together; they were each other's person.

And then someone, one of her work colleagues – someone well-meaning but stupid, *so fucking stupid* – had told Robyn about Hannah.

Scott stirred from his spot sitting on the ground, winced

as the movement jarred his ankle. 'Hannah killed someone you loved – I don't understand . . . how?' he said.

Carly looked at him, saw shock, disbelief even – but also genuine sadness in his face. She closed her eyes for a second; saw Robyn's last moments on earth behind them, as she so often did. 'Robyn watched Hannah's videos. She actually believed all that rubbish Hannah preached – that stuff about how Western medicine shouldn't be trusted and antidepressants mess up your brain for ever. About how we should allow our bodies to heal themselves by coming back into energetic balance – all that shit,' she said.

Then she told him the rest of the story. About how it was as if Hannah had cast a spell on her; Robyn was enchanted. She'd taken Hannah's word as gospel when she said that mood-stabilizing medication was harmful and unnecessary. Hannah had even made an entire twenty-minute TikTok special on lithium carbonate, the drug Robyn had been taking for years, the medicine that kept her on an even keel. The day after she'd watched it, Robyn told Carly she was going to lower her dose; see how she felt. 'I've been on thirty mil a day for years, doll,' she'd said. 'It's the highest dose. God knows what it's doing to my body – or my brain. I reckon it's about time I give it a go, try to see how I am on a bit less. If I start getting a bit wobbly, I'll go back up.'

Carly had been terrified. She knew the risk of a manic episode was at its peak in the days after stopping or reducing mood stabilizers; she was afraid for Robyn, for what she might do. But she had no choice except to trust her; she knew it wasn't her place to force drugs down her partner's throat, or to speak to Robyn's GP on her behalf, asking them to break patient confidentiality, for simply cutting back her dosage.

Carly should have put more stock in her first instincts; she would never forgive herself for not having fought harder against Robyn's decision. Because when the love of her life had taken a flying leap from the balcony of their sixth-floor flat, believing the angels would save her, Carly had been the one to run to her, desperate and praying, ignoring the screams of horrified pedestrians floating up to her as she rushed down the stairs.

And then she had been the one to find her cracked and shattered on the concrete pavement, a mashed, bloodied pulp where her beautiful face had once been.

Carly hadn't known when, or how, she'd make Hannah pay for what she'd done to Robyn. She'd just known that she would. She'd waited, and watched, and *pretended* from the sidelines, following all Hannah's channels, offering nothing but heart emojis and comments like 'Love this – and YOU – so much!' as Hannah spouted her dangerous nonsense online to more and more unwitting followers on TikTok and Instagram and anywhere else people would listen to her.

She'd known it was time to act when she saw Hannah's giveaway. The chance to come here, to see Hannah in person, to confront her in the presence of people who admired her – it was too precious to pass up. She knew she had to at least try.

She'd spent hours planning what she'd say in her application video: describing the passion she had for healing, for spiritual discovery. She'd spoken about all her experiences with plant medicine; how comfortable she felt in the jungle; her love for the rainforest. How much she wanted to serve people, to make an impact on a bigger scale by learning from Hannah then spreading her message to help vast numbers of people at once, not just one struggling client at a time.

She could hardly believe it when it actually *worked*. Carly had obviously become much better at pretending than she'd realized; she'd been able to guess exactly the kinds of things that would win her a place on the trip. Hannah genuinely seemed to believe that Carly wanted to come and learn from her, be a part of her retreat. Unless, perhaps, Hannah's ego was just so big and so keen to be flattered that she'd simply *wanted* to believe it.

More fool Hannah.

'I'm . . . I'm so sorry, Carly,' whispered Scott, his voice a sad husk. 'For what you've been through.'

Carly startled; she'd almost forgotten he was there. 'I came here to confront her about it,' she said. 'My plan – my *intention* – was never to hurt her. But when I got here – early on the first day of the retreat, a couple of hours before we were meant to arrive – and she was waiting at the pavilion, I told her it was time for her to change what she tells people – to confess that what she preaches is dangerous.'

In fact, Carly had told Hannah that unless she admitted to it – then, when everyone else had arrived, right in front of her precious followers – Carly would tell them herself. She would expose her. She would hold up the photo of Robyn's beautiful face in front of them, and tell everyone who Hannah truly was: the kind of person that spreads dangerous, life-threatening lies while being worshipped by millions. And she knew she needed to do it face to face – Hannah's social media presence was highly controlled. She could easily have deleted any comments Carly had left on her posts, or dismissed her as mentally ill if she'd interrupted one of her online talks. No, this was the only way – in person, where she couldn't get away, where Carly would hold the cards.

'I even showed her Robyn's picture, her beautiful, happy face, to try and make her realize the impact of what she'd done – show her the real human beings behind her follower count, you know?' Carly's fingers grasped the edges of the photo in her pocket now; she'd felt such deep relief when she'd swiped it from Ben's backpack after he'd fallen to the ground.

To her disgust, Hannah had simply plucked the photo from Carly's hands, looked at Robyn's face, and then turned her back and walked away from her. Her words rung again in Carly's ears: 'I'm very sorry for your loss, hun, but this was *not* my fault.' She'd almost *laughed* as she said it; as if Carly's anger with her was so ludicrous it could barely be believed. 'I can't take responsibility for other people's actions – if someone I've never even met decides they want to die, you can't blame that on me.'

Decides they want to die. How fucked up was that? Carly felt the heat on her cheeks at the memory, the adrenaline pounding through her again now, making her muscles tense and flex – just like it had yesterday, in front of Hannah.

'I was fucking raging, Scott, and I yelled at her, and she told me to shut up and follow her. First, out of the pavilion, and then . . .' Carly thought back to when Hannah had led her away from her house and deep into the rainforest, far away from the ears of any staff. As she'd walked behind her further into the jungle, Hannah had been telling Carly that she was wrong, that she just needed to breathe more deeply and absorb the magic of the rainforest and allow the healing of nature's spirit into her heart – she was trying to *convert* her, for fuck's sake, and then – and then . . .

Carly didn't know how it had happened, exactly. She was behind Hannah, and listening to her spewing all her bullshit, and at the same time witnessing the scenes around her, this beautiful rainforest and Hannah's perfect resort, and all she could see – all she could think – was that Hannah had this amazing, wonderful life and was adored by this huge community of people, and Robyn was dead, alone, in the ground.

She couldn't bear it, all the pain and grief. 'And then I shoved her, and she fell over onto the ground,' she said. She felt a hot slice of guilt at the memory. But then she reminded herself: *I did the right thing – the only thing I could do.* Because how dare she? How dare Hannah have believed, so pompously, that she had the cure for illnesses that doctors had spent centuries trying to heal? The *arrogance* of her.

No, she didn't regret it. The world would be a safer place without Hannah, and other 'healers' like her, in it. Honestly, if she could, Carly would wipe out the lot of them.

'She fell over – but then how did she die?' said Scott.

Carly stared at the jungle floor. Even if the outcome was for the best, she didn't take pleasure in thinking about how it had happened. 'She banged her head when she landed. It was slippery on the ground. She must have hit a rock right on her temple, just on the soft part – anyway, it looked like she was gone.' She paused for breath. 'I panicked after that. I went on autopilot, thought the best thing to do was to drag her further into the forest.' It had been hard work – Carly was fit and strong, but pulling Hannah by the arms through dense vegetation, into the heart of the jungle – it had taken everything she had. 'I decided just to . . . let the rainforest do its thing,' she admitted.

'Do its *thing*?' said Scott.

'Yeah. I know it sounds bad,' said Carly. 'But I didn't know what else to do. She looked dead – I thought she was – I really did . . .'

'Hang on a minute, are you saying . . . she wasn't dead then?'

'When she was lying there in the forest, she didn't stir. But then, as I was about to leave her . . . her eyelids flickered a bit.' Carly had been torn between an instinct towards compassion and her all-consuming rage in that moment. Perhaps Hannah could have survived, and Carly knew the *right* thing to do would be to call for help.

But the fury in her had won out – this human being no longer deserved to exist; she should no longer have the right to cause devastation to gullible people's lives – and so Carly had scooped up as many leaves, vines and branches as she could carry, piled them on top of Hannah – and left.

And I think I'd do the same thing again.

She sighed. 'Anyway, when we all found her, she was long gone.'

'But someone might have been able to save her,' said Scott. 'Maybe she didn't have to die like that.'

Carly faltered. 'I doubt that – but in any case, I needed to move fast. I knew all of you were on your way here and that I'd hardly have any time before you'd all arrive, looking for Hannah.'

Her first plan, of course, had been to get the hell out of there: run like the clappers back to the main road, hitch a lift as far away as she could. She had her phone's GPS and the track she'd made dragging Hannah through the jungle to help her navigate, so she made her way out of the rainforest's interior easily enough – but she was too late. As she approached the pavilion, Carly saw Luisa waiting there to greet them, and then the first taxi arriving, with Mira inside it. She'd had to buy herself time, and the only thing she could come up with on the spot was pretending Hannah was safe and well.

'So, the messages – the photo – was that you?'

Carly nodded. She'd bought a Costa Rican SIM and cheap phone when she'd arrived in the country, just in case she needed a quick getaway. With her phone in her hand, all she had to do was send a few texts – timed to arrive later, when she wouldn't be using her phone, of course. She'd got hold of their numbers and details from the emails on Hannah's phone, which she'd then switched off before she arrived back at the pavilion, and thrown as hard as she could into a thick patch of trees.

Then, when the storm had struck that night, blocking her escape, she'd come up with the idea of creating a fake background to one of Hannah's plentiful supply of photos on her socials. She'd surprised herself by managing to do a decent enough job that no one doubted Hannah was really sending the messages. She'd used the opportunity to search the lodge that night too, finding the map and satellite phone – the thing wasn't charged, but she wasn't to know that – so she could make it look as though Hannah had planned every detail.

'I was supposed to keep it up until I could get out of here yesterday evening, or as soon as the flooding cleared up – I'd have claimed there was an emergency back home or something. By the time anyone found Hannah – if they ever had done – I'd have been miles away. And who knows? Maybe you'd even have got something worthwhile out of it if I'd taken things over here, because it was me leading it, an actual, qualified therapist, not some pseudo-psychobabbling bullshitter spouting life-threatening nonsense. So, yeah, that was the plan. Except, then . . .'

'Except then what?' said Scott.

Carly shook her head, the memory of it nearly felling her. The thought of how differently things could have gone . . . how much easier it all would have been.

She sighed.

It would all have been all right, except . . .

'Except we had to get bloody lost after that mudslide and find Hannah's body. Didn't we?'

MIRA

Mira had found a place to hide, and nothing was going to force her out of it.

She might have had almost no strength left, but whatever she had, she would use it to keep her mind alert; to stay alive as long as she possibly could. And her best chance of doing that had to be by staying right here, camouflaged beneath the foliage, listening to the shrieks and cries of the animals, and trying not to move a muscle. It was past the hottest point of the day, it would cool down soon enough, and here amid the undergrowth she was protected from the worst of either rain or heat.

Surely she wouldn't have to wait too long. Someone would have noticed they were off the grid as early as yesterday afternoon, when they didn't come back from the rainforest. Paola would have started a search for them; she'd have called for help – that helicopter could have been the first stage of a rescue mission. If she could just stay hidden here a little longer, surely someone would come and find her?

Yes, staying here, hidden under these fallen vines and branches, was the safest option, especially after being chased like that through the trees. She could no longer trust anyone out here – not even those she would have blindly followed only hours ago. After what happened with Ben, and now that Scott and Carly too had abandoned her, left her to fend for herself out here, she knew she could no longer rely on anyone. The only person she still held any faith in – her only true friend here – was most likely floating somewhere along the stream, or worse, lying at the bottom of it.

Her eyes had adjusted now to the murky darkness of her hiding place; she could see a bunch of thick, fleshy green leaves just to her right. Their surfaces were glistening. Mira stared at them: was that rainwater? It had to be – the plants here were so deeply buried under the canopy, they were protected from the harshest of the sun's rays. Rain from yesterday's downpour could plausibly still be sitting here untouched.

Gently at first, tentatively, and then more greedily, she allowed her tongue to dab the surface of the leaves, absorbing the fresh water droplets. They had to be the best thing she had ever tasted; she ran her tongue up and down the leaves, swallowing only the tiniest amounts but feeling somehow rejuvenated.

She was so taken over by her thirst that she hardly noticed the movement in the foliage in front of her.

By the time she caught sight of the figure looming above her, she only had time to yell out in fear, cover her head with her hands and curl into a ball, squeezing her eyes shut like a child afraid of a monster.

'Mira?'

She heard her name, recognized the lightly accented voice that was saying it. *That's it. I'm losing my mind from the shock – the dehydration*. She'd been thinking about Naya, and then her brain had told her that Naya was here. But she couldn't be; Naya was gone.

Perhaps Mira was dead then, and had been reunited with her friend in the afterlife? She'd succumbed to her thirst and tiredness; someone had attacked and killed her, maybe.

'Mira – it's me,' came the voice again. 'Are you all right? Come on, you're safe now. Open your eyes.'

She wasn't imagining it. She pinched herself on the arm; it hurt.

She wasn't dead, then. This was real.

Naya.

With her hands still clamped, inexplicably now, over her still-closed eyes, Mira tried to steady her breathing. One finger at a time, like she remembered her nieces doing when they were little, she peeled her hands away from her face, and half-squinted up into the face in front of her.

'Naya? Oh my God, it's you! I thought you were dead! But how did you . . . ?'

'I managed to cling onto a rock and climb out of the stream – I don't even know how,' cried Naya. 'I thought . . . I thought it was the end.'

Reaching out to her, Mira took Naya into her arms; both of them sobbing with relief, with joy.

'Mira, I am so happy I've found you, but we have to get going – we have to get out of here. We can't get stuck here for another night . . . Where are the others? Where are Carly and Scott?'

'I lost them,' said Mira, explaining how Scott had twisted his ankle and how she had managed to lose them when she'd nipped off to the stream. And how she had tried to find them again – before being chased by someone.

'It was the strangest thing – at first I assumed it was one of the others – Carly, Scott or Ben – but then I called out, and they didn't answer, and the way they were chasing after me, not saying who they were – it wasn't right. It felt . . . predatory somehow.' She shuddered.

She closed her eyes briefly, then opened them to look at Naya again, realized she was shaking – and was wearing only her jacket, underwear and shoes, by the looks of it. Then she caught sight of the blood-soaked fabric tied around her leg.

'Naya, oh my God, you're hurt!'

'I cut my leg on something in the water. It hurts like hell, but I'll be OK – honestly, I'm just glad I made it out alive. But the person who was chasing you – you didn't see who it was?'

'I didn't,' admitted Mira.

Naya looked in all directions, then turned back to Mira, rubbing at her temples. 'Well, whoever it was – they're not chasing you any more.'

Mira exhaled and glanced upwards. Above them, just visible through the canopy, she could make out thick, purplish-grey clouds gathering, and a new chill in the damp, close air. They couldn't have long, now, before it started raining again. They couldn't spend much more time here; not in the cold, with nothing to eat, no water – and a fresh downpour on the way.

Naya groaned and put a hand to the wound on her thigh, jolting Mira from her thoughts. Then she remembered: 'Your rucksack – I took some things from it, like the first aid kit! It's in my bag.'

'Oh, you found it – I thought it went into the water with me!' said Naya.

'It did – it got caught on a rock, a little way out from where you fell in. I waded out and managed to grab it.'

'Oh, thank you,' said Naya, pulling Mira back into her arms. 'I am so glad you did that. I can try and fix my leg up a bit now.'

'And let's find my towel for you to use as a blanket – your skin feels cold.'

Mira opened her rucksack and handed over the swimming towel, which Naya draped over her shoulders, then dug out the first aid kit. Its contents were damp but intact. Naya winced in pain as she removed the strip of fabric from her thigh, and the two of them examined her wound.

'It looks painful, but at least the bleeding has stopped,' said Mira.

Naya nodded, took a deep breath and gritted her teeth. Pulling the first aid kit towards her, she picked out a sterile wipe, tore it from the packet and dabbed it around the edge of the wound. The gash looked deep and nasty.

She sighed, turned to Mira. 'Can you help me to walk? I made it this far OK, but I don't know how much further I can go without support.'

'Of course – well, I'll try,' said Mira. 'Though I don't know how much use I'll be.'

'Let's just do our best.' Naya pointed back in the direction of the stream, whose rushing torrent was still just about audible. 'We should follow the water along in the same direction, as far as we can,' she said. 'It will lead us to something – somewhere – and we'll know that way that we're not going around in circles.'

Mira nodded her agreement and then, with Naya using her

as a sort of crutch, the two women began to hobble and stumble through the trees. They moved slowly and hesitantly at first, then more quickly as they got into a rhythm, Mira supporting Naya to keep going, even when the pain in her leg shrieked at her to stop.

They trampled on in silence. After a while, Mira halted and turned to face Naya, opened her mouth ready to suggest they rest for a short while – but Naya raised a hand to quiet her. 'Shh . . . what's that? Do you hear voices?'

Mira frowned; she hadn't heard anything.

'I don't think so, I—'

She stopped herself short.

Yes – I can hear them!

The rise and fall of voices – familiar ones – coming and going, through the trees.

Oh, thank God! They had found the others.

'It's them!' said Mira. 'I think it's Scott, and Carly – is it . . . ?' Mira was about to bolt through the trees to find them, had started to move, when Naya's hand yanked her backwards, a sharp tug that had her almost falling flat on the ground.

'Shhh!' said Naya. 'Don't move. I don't think . . . something doesn't sound right.'

The two of them halted on the spot, listened, tuned into the two voices.

They couldn't hear everything, but snippets, fragments of the conversation drifted through the trees to meet their ears. Words – confusing ones, sentences that made no sense, not in isolation.

And then, piece by piece, Mira started to put it together. Looking into Naya's eyes then, she realized that Naya understood everything too.

They knew what had happened and why. They knew who had killed Hannah.

And they understood, too, that their fight wasn't yet over.

Slowly, Naya knelt to the ground, stifling a groan as she moved her wounded leg. She gestured to Mira to hand over her rucksack, which Mira did, and began to rifle through it.

'What are you looking for?' asked Mira, voice low.

'The knife,' she whispered. 'It was in my rucksack with the first aid kit – but it's not in yours. Did you see it when you went through my bag?'

Mira shook her head.

'Then someone's taken it,' said Naya.

Naya dropped her eyes down, and Mira watched as she sifted her hands rapidly through the damp leaves of the jungle floor.

When she lifted them back up, her fingers were clasped around the sharp edge of a fist-sized rock.

SCOTT

Scott was terrified, but he was doing his best not to show it. His heart was battering his ribcage, the palms of his hands were clammy with sweat. He was almost grateful for the throbbing pain in his ankle, which was serving to remind him he was still alive. Still here. *Now let's make sure I stay that way.*

Perhaps he could show Carly he wasn't the enemy somehow; that she didn't need to get him out of the way. It was worth a shot.

'I think I understand,' he said, the words rasping in his dry throat. 'You wanted Hannah to know the impact of her work on Robyn – you wanted her to stop telling people to avoid proper medication.' Carly nodded; she looked relieved that he'd understood her. 'And then Hannah's death was a kind of tragic accident.'

He paused, then forced himself to make eye contact with her, trying to get across as much of an air of compassion as he could. 'It must have been really hard to know what to do after we found her body . . .'

Carly sighed. 'Yeah, I was gutted, honestly. I didn't want to have to hurt anyone else. But when Ben ran off, I realized that as well as the satellite phone, he took the photo with him.' She reached into her back pocket and showed Scott a crumpled photo – she must have taken it back from Ben when she stabbed him, moments ago. In a flash, he understood: it was the picture of Robyn that Carly had shown to Hannah when she'd confronted her.

'I'm glad Ben found it, to be honest. I thought I'd dropped it somewhere. Hannah must have been holding it in her fist – I didn't realize she still had it when she fell, and then when I noticed it was gone, it was too late to go back for it.'

Scott swallowed. 'I see. And if Ben had that photo on him when the rescuers came – well, the police would have figured it all out, wouldn't they? And you couldn't let that happen.'

The satellite phone, still in Carly's hand, started to ring again, giving Scott a quick rush of hope – but it was quickly extinguished as she pressed a button to silence it. 'I never meant for all this,' she said softly. 'But after we'd found Hannah, I thought if I could just get the rest of you to be injured or weakened in some way, I could get out of here without you following me. Then when you were navigating earlier, just before we saw that snake, I told you we were still lost so we'd stop going in the right direction . . . and then – I'm sorry about doing that to your ankle, by the way.'

'Ah . . . that was you?' *She tripped me up.*

'It was me,' she whispered. Scott thought he saw regret in her expression as she said that. But her eyes stayed rooted to the jungle floor, as another cold wave of realization washed over him. The snake that almost bit him – hadn't she edged him towards its lair? Could she have seen it – done that on purpose?

And Naya – no, not Naya. He had to know. 'Did you push Naya in the stream?' He almost choked on his words. Carly's eyes shifted; she dipped her head slightly, then said: 'No, but I could see she was too close to the edge, and I didn't warn her.' She at least had the decency to look shame-faced about that.

But does she feel bad about the rest of it? Does she wish she hadn't done this – to Hannah, to me, to Ben?

As if on cue, Scott sensed, rather than heard, a whimper from Ben, lying behind him, shielded from Carly's sight. Scott had done his best to stem the bleeding from the side of Ben's chest with a tourniquet he'd made from the swimming towel in his bag, wrapping it around the top of his shoulder – but in his own weakened state, Scott wasn't optimistic that he'd done much to help. Ben must be only minutes away from bleeding out.

'None of this was part of the plan,' she said. 'I thought we'd just go to the waterfall that first full day, make our way back in the afternoon, and then I'd make a bolt for it later on, once the road out wasn't flooded. I only had to resort to all this because we found her. But you have to admit, there was something odd going on with Ben. He knew Hannah somehow, I'm sure of it. And he ran off with that satellite phone and somehow managed to call for help for himself.'

Scott shook his head. 'So that was enough of a reason to shove a knife into him?'

'I had no choice. He had that photo – if he'd given it to the rescuers, they'd have pieced everything together in no time.' She sighed, brushed a strand of filth-encrusted hair from her forehead. 'And now you know too – so much more than Ben

307

did. I thought I'd be able to just disappear, leave you and Mira here in the jungle to fend for yourselves – you'd have hours left, at the most, with both of you so weak now and no water to drink. Naya's almost certainly already dead. I wouldn't have needed to do anything else – and I don't want to, really I don't – but you've found Ben now, and rescuers are on their way, they'll be here any minute, so . . .'

Scott swallowed. He knew what that meant. He would be next. In his usual state, at full strength, with his size and bulk, he'd have no issue fighting Carly off. But he was a long way from that. His ankle was twice its usual size; he was exhausted, and had hardly drunk a drop of water for over a day in the raging heat. He'd barely be able to fight off a toucan at this point. She had the advantage.

This is hopeless. You might as well just give up now.

'I'm sorry,' said Carly, walking closer to him. 'If there was any other way, I wouldn't do this. I know you're a good person. None of this was your fault.' Carly's mouth was turned downwards, and Scott thought he saw genuine sadness in her expression. 'But I can't risk you getting away and telling other people what happened here.'

'But you said it was an accident, right?' he said, panting now, his voice sounding unlike his own. 'You didn't mean to hurt Hannah. I'm sure if you tell the police that, they'll understand.'

Carly shook her head. 'Understand? The police – here? I don't think so – I can barely explain it in English, let alone Spanish. Besides, how would I make them understand everything afterwards – not coming forward sooner, not getting help for Hannah – and what I did to Ben?'

She was getting closer, one foot after the other, towards him. Scott was forcing himself to move now too; he found himself crawling backwards, away from her – but he was too slow, his ankle far too painful.

'There's no other way – I wish there were, but this is it. Naya's drowned, Mira's at death's door, Ben's got a couple of minutes left, if that. It's only you that stands in the way of me getting out of here.'

Scott could barely breathe; any second, he was going to pass out or vomit.

Just try to keep her talking.

'But what are you going to tell them – the police, I mean? How will you explain it?'

'I've thought about that,' Carly said. 'I've come up with a decent story – that we got lost, and Ben confessed to murdering Hannah after we found her body – then the two of you got into a fight and ended up stabbing each other with the knife. I tried desperately to find Naya and Mira – but they were lost and weak, and in the end, I was so weak too, I had to make my own way out of here.'

The world started to swim in front of Scott's eyes. So she was planning on stabbing him too, if she wanted her story to stack up.

'But look at me,' he said. 'I'm injured, I'm lost – I've got no food or water and I've not drunk anything for nearly an entire day. You leave me here, and I'll be as good as dead by tomorrow – you don't even need to finish this yourself. The jungle will do it for you.'

Those words had the right effect; Carly paused, cocked her head to one side, thoughtful. Then, slowly, she nodded. 'That's true – but think of it another way for a minute. That's a horrible, slow way to go. I can make it quicker for you.'

Shit, shit, shit.

Carly stepped forward again; she was almost in front of him now, close enough that he could make out the muscles twitching close to her jawline, see the flecks of mud and dirt – and something else, something dark, encrusted on her cheeks, her chin. He could see the grief in her eyes; the fear, but also a sad resolution, a solid determination.

Could this really be it – was this how he was going to die?

Carly's eyes flickered away from his face, then back to him. 'I'm truly sorry,' she said, as she lifted the knife, held it towards Scott's neck.

He squeezed his eyes shut and braced himself for the blow – he only hoped it would be quick, that she'd hit him in an artery or something, somewhere he wouldn't bleed out slowly.

And then, close to him, only a few feet away – a voice, hoarse but full of feeling, yelling 'NOW!', and the thundering crash of bodies – two of them, so much smaller than his but possessing a wild kind of strength, bursting out of the trees behind him.

He caught the wide-mouthed expression of shock on Carly's face as the knife was knocked out of her hand, and a small, thin body rushed towards him, made herself a shield between him and Carly, while someone else – someone half-naked and bleeding, a fierce rage in her expression – grabbed at Carly, yanked her backwards.

Carly shrugged herself free, eyes ranging across the three of them, measuring them. For one insane, terrifying moment, Scott thought she was going to come at him again, to launch herself towards them, to try to take on all three of them at once.

But then Mira – tiny, frail Mira – launched herself at Carly, winding her, and managing in the shock of it to push her down to the ground. Mira wasn't heavy enough to hold Carly for long, though, and Naya rushed forward to help, Scott lumbering behind her, slowed by his bad ankle.

In her haste, the rock fell out of Naya's grasp, landing close to Carly's foot, and Carly sprang forward, gazelle-like – dropping the satellite phone that she still gripped in her hand – grabbed the small boulder, and drew back her arm.

And then, too fast, before either Scott or Naya could get to her, Carly slammed the rock into the back of Mira's head, then turned and bolted past them into the nearest thicket of trees, vanishing into the wilderness before Mira's crumpled body had even hit the ground.

NAYA

'Where are they?' said Scott.

All four of them were collapsed, slumped on the jungle floor, Scott cradling Mira's bleeding head as she lay semi-conscious and whimpering in pain; Naya doing her best to keep Ben alive.

'They must be almost here now,' she muttered, with a confidence she didn't quite feel. 'It can't be long before they'll find us.'

The wound in her thigh was bleeding again; she had pushed herself too far, launching at Carly like that, and the dressing and bandage she'd patched herself up with from her first aid kid had almost come off. It was worth it, though. They had saved Scott's life. She'd do the same thing again in a heartbeat.

She couldn't tend to herself right now; both her hands were pressed hard onto the wound in Ben's chest as she did her best to stem his bleeding. She leaned in close to his face, checked for his pulse again. She could barely feel it now, it was so faint, and it was becoming slower. This was the worst possible sign. He'd lost too much blood; most likely too much to be saved.

Come on, come on. Ben and Mira can't hold on much longer.

She knew the rescue helicopter was on its way; Scott had told her what Ben had managed to say about calling for help with the satellite phone. Scott had it in his grip now; the handler had called again, just a moment ago, and reassured them that the location she had for them was still accurate, that the rescuers were entering the retreat on foot as they spoke.

She hoped they would be here soon – they could do nothing until then but wait. There was no hope of them walking themselves out of here, not with Ben so close to death, her injury and Scott's twisted ankle, and Mira now badly wounded, and all already so exhausted and dehydrated and weak. Naya knew, too, that Carly might still be lurking somewhere nearby – she no longer had the knife, thank God, but she was smart; resourceful. She'd shown that well enough. Perhaps she had more plans to take them down.

Their only chance of survival was being found here – and soon.

Naya looked around the group again, then at the blood still trickling down her leg, though mercifully less quickly now. She thought of Carly, so racked with a grief that led her to take such extreme revenge; she pictured Hannah, left to perish slowly and alone in her own rainforest, her dreams of creating a spiritual sanctuary for her followers as dead as she was, before it had even begun.

She thought of her beautiful children at home, of how proud she was of them, of their resilience in the face of all the challenges they had already been dealt. She thought of the life that was growing inside of her. She had raised two of them already, hadn't she? She could do it again – she could do it one more time. She was a good mother – good enough, at least.

When she'd got here, just two days ago – how was that possible? – she'd felt that her abilities as a mother were stretched beyond their limit; she was a rubber band that had lost its snap. But now she saw it – her true resilience. If she could cope with this, she could handle a third child – even if she would be doing it, essentially, alone.

I can do all of it, if I make it back home alive.

Naya thought of all this, and she did something she hadn't done for years, not since she'd stopped being forced along to the Catholic church in Armentières with Maman every Sunday until she was fifteen: she closed her eyes, and she prayed. Eyelids squeezed together, hands still clasped over Ben's wound, she pressed her knees into the jungle floor, no longer caring what crawled over her. She sat and she waited and before she knew it, she was drifting; the exhaustion and the shock and the blood loss taking over, all the adrenaline draining away from her.

'Naya?' A hand was rocking her gently, stirring her from her haze. 'Do you hear that?' It was Scott, his voice coming from close to her ear. 'I don't know if that sound is in my head, or if it's real.'

Naya blinked her blurry eyes, listened. Then she heard it too: a chopper, its blades whirring high above them.

'Oh my God, I hear it,' she said, as the shouts of the rescue team grew louder. 'They're coming – they're going to find us. Mira, Ben, stay with us, please! They're almost here—'

Mira made a sound; Scott shushed her: 'It's OK. Don't try to speak – save your strength.'

'Ben – Mira – they have to take them first,' said Naya.

Scott touched her arm. 'Don't worry. We'll tell them. We'll make sure they know.'

'And Hannah,' she said. 'They have to find her.'

'They will,' said Scott. 'I marked all those trees, remember . . .' But he stopped short as voices, calling out to them, started to reach them through the trees – quietly at first, echoing, but then quickly they became artificially loud – *of course*, Naya realized: the sound was coming through a megaphone. They spoke in Spanish at first, calling out for them, and then in English.

'They're here!' said Scott. *Thank goodness.*

'*Hola?* Hello? Help is here – please call out so we can find you.'

Naya took a deep breath, mustered her remaining strength and shouted: 'We're here! Over here! Please, we need help!'

'We can hear you – please keep on calling out to us, so we can find you.'

Naya and Scott did as they'd been asked, yelling out with cracked, hoarse voices, screaming to help the rescuers find them. The voices approached them, becoming louder every second, and the chopper above was tracking the path of the people with megaphones, circling lower and closer.

The rescuers burst through the trees towards them, a flurry of bright orange and olive green and khaki. A paramedic rushed to Ben's side; another ran straight to Mira.

'We are evacuating you to the hospital in San José,' said one of the rescuers. The chopper was still circling and it was low now, so close that the tops of the trees were blowing wildly, swaying from side to side; Naya's eyes were dazzled by the beams of its lights.

'Please,' she said, nodding to Ben and Mira, 'take these two first – Ben has a stab wound to the side of his chest, and Mira has a head injury. I'm a nurse – I've done my best to stem his bleeding, but he's lost a lot of blood. I think it might be too late . . .'

Two more paramedics rushed to Ben, and within seconds Naya was releasing her grip on him as they hauled him onto a stretcher, then carried him through the trees, directing the chopper to a large enough clearing where it would be safe to come lower. Two others raced to Mira, took her next, then Scott, and finally Naya, whose dry, heaving sobs now wouldn't stop as the strong arms of four men carried her, the stretcher bouncing her through the jungle.

Soon she would be leaving Hannah's rainforest retreat and its catalogue of horrors behind.

I've made it.

Cupping a blood-smeared hand across her stomach, she whispered the words to herself:

'We made it, baby. We have survived.'

She imagined the little bean inside her stomach, pictured Elodie and Marcus in her mind, told them silently:

It's going to be all right. I am coming home.

SIX MONTHS LATER

MIRA

'Well, I can't say our interview was everything I was hoping for – but I'm confident I can turn all this into a decent story,' said the journalist. 'You're sure there's nothing else – no final comments, no last-minute memories that have sprung back?' he said. 'You're sure you didn't bury Carly out there in the rainforest, and keep it a secret all this time?' He snorted, a bitter-sounding laugh, then in a mockingly deep, serious voice said: 'Come on, speak now, or for ever hold your peace!'

Oh, dear God. Mira cringed inwardly. She was feeling a little embarrassed for him. That this earnest freelance reporter had convinced the editors at *The Post* to pay them all a nice sum of money to hear an only slightly more detailed version of the events that had already been splashed over front pages across the globe. Through the computer screen, she could see his eyes were still hungry; even now, when their time was up and it was so close to being over, he was desperate for something more. And she couldn't blame him. But they had nothing else to give, and even he knew that.

'I'm sorry,' said Scott. 'That's everything we know. We can only assume Carly died somewhere out there in the rainforest – if she'd managed to escape the jungle, someone would have spotted her by now. No one can stay off the radar for that long – not with half the planet knowing what they look like.'

'I suppose so. Thanks for your time, then,' the journalist said, attempting to dredge up whatever morsel of enthusiasm, of gratitude, he could find. 'Best of luck with everything in the future – and if you think of anything else to add, you know where I am.'

He hung up, and the app made a sharp little bleep as he went. She must have done dozens of video calls since the start of the pandemic, and the sound was hardly unfamiliar, but the noise still startled her. She reminded her nervous system to stay calm: she was safe now; the worst was over.

'Well, thank God that's done,' she said, shifting in her chair and checking the time in the corner of the screen. She looked at the two other faces on her screen, smiling at her. 'Thank you – both of you. I don't think I could have got through this without you there – I was nervous, to be honest, doing this. I've never really spoken to a journalist before. If it wasn't for getting the money to help pay for my treatment, I'd never have agreed to it.'

Naya leaned back in her chair, rested a hand on the large swell of her belly. Behind her, in the blurred-out background, Mira could make out the shapes of her two children, lying on the floor on their stomachs in front of the TV, kicking their legs in the air behind them. It was a good job they were able to negotiate having the interview online rather than in person; it was too late in Naya's pregnancy for her to travel far, and she was insistent that she wouldn't leave her children again.

'I felt the same,' she said. 'I'm glad it's done too. I just wonder if he felt that he got his big story.' She shrugged. 'He seemed disappointed that we didn't know more about what happened to Carly.'

At the thought of Carly, Mira felt the familiar jolt of panic in her stomach; a pang in the ribs she'd cracked in the mudslide, a throb at the base of her skull – as if the now-healed wounds had memories of their own. *It's all right,* she told herself. *We're all safe now. She's gone – there's no way she made it out of the jungle. She can't hurt me any more.*

Scott took a sip of water. 'Well, even if he is, we've kept our end of the deal. We told our stories, and honestly, even though being paid for it doesn't nearly make up for everything we've been through, or bring Hannah and Ben back – well, it seems like we could all use the cash.'

At the thought of the money which was about to wing its way into her bank account, Mira's eyes filled. 'I can't even tell you how much it means to me, getting that payment. I'll be able to fly to the States for the new treatment they're developing – they're getting amazing results with it over there.' She smiled sadly. 'And if it doesn't work – well, then I'll have enough left over to take Ezra on one last beautiful holiday together. To do something special, before – before . . .' Her voice cracked.

'It's going to work, Mira,' said Naya, eyes bright and fixed through the camera on Mira's face. Mira felt the strength of her belief; wanted her to will it to be true. *It is going to work.* If she could believe it enough – if they all could – perhaps that would make it real.

Mira smiled. 'Thank you. And I'm so happy for you too, with the money . . . I'm sure it'll make such a difference to your family,' she said.

Naya beamed. 'Oh, yes. Did I tell you? I'm going to be able to get the kids into an amazing school – I can cover the fees for at least the next two years.'

'Oh, I didn't know!' said Mira. 'That's wonderful.'

'They have these really small classes, and they're outside in nature almost all the time – it'll be so good for them.' She paused, looked overcome for a moment. 'And of course, the money will help with this little one too.' She reached a hand down to stroke her belly. 'And if I can, I want to try and keep some of the money aside to go and visit Ben's grave one day – say a proper goodbye to him.' Naya's eyes glistened as she spoke.

Mira felt a deep pang in her chest at the thought of Ben; the guilt at having suspected him, wrongly, of Hannah's murder; of how hard he'd tried to hang on to life. His heart had still been beating when the rescuers arrived – but by the time they'd got him to the hospital, it was too late. If only it hadn't been too dark for the emergency services to send out a search party straight away, when Paola had called them that first evening after the group didn't come back. Or if only the first rescue helicopter that had flown out early the following morning had found Ben when it had been circling above their patch of jungle, not long before Carly stumbled across him. He'd have made it; things wouldn't have ended the way they did. They all could have been saved more injury; more trauma.

At the thought of how close he'd come to surviving, tears spilled onto Mira's cheeks. 'I'd like to do that too, one day,' she said softly. 'Maybe we could even all go together – a real tribute to him.'

Naya smiled, nodded. 'I'd like that.' She looked thoughtful for a moment. 'I just couldn't see it at first, you know? Ben and Hannah, in a relationship. But I think he really did love her.'

'And I'm sure she really loved him too,' said Scott. Mira had to resist rolling her eyes at that; in spite of everything that had come out about Hannah since her death – her history of alcohol and marijuana abuse; the lethal danger of some of her advice and claims – Scott was resolute in his loyalty towards her.

'And Scott, what about you? Have you thought what you'll do with the payment from the interview?' Mira said.

Scott shifted in his chair, looked suddenly uncomfortable. Mira wondered if perhaps she shouldn't have asked – was she being intrusive?

'Ah, yeah – there's a conservation project actually, over in Europe, that I'm hoping to get involved with,' he says. 'They've got an opening for someone to take over the management of it – so if I do that, the cash will come in handy to help me move and everything—' Mira wondered why telling her this would make him feel so awkward, as if he were keeping some big secret he didn't want her to know.

She decided not to ask any more. Her eyes flickered across the screen towards Naya, but her gazed seemed to shift away from Mira, over to the side of the room.

What's going on? Are they trying to hide something from me?

She looked at Naya again; her cheeks had turned a gentle shade of pink. And in a flash, Mira understood.

Of course – how could I have missed it before?

NIKKI ALLEN

Mira smiled. 'I see. And would that conservation project happen to be based in France, I wonder, Scott? Somewhere in the north?'

Scott laughed. 'Naya, it looks like we're busted,' he said. Mira glanced at Naya; she was beaming.

'Yes. We've been talking about it for a while, and we're going to spend some time together,' he said. 'See how things go.'

As Scott spoke, Mira saw on his face an expression of such sincerity, such depth of emotion, that her heart seemed to swell in her chest, filling her ribcage. It had been like this for her in all the months since she got back from Costa Rica – feeling everything more intensely, more deeply. Pain and joy, both amplified.

Behind her, Ezra called her name.

'Coming, *schatzi*. I've got to go – we've got family coming over for Shabbat,' she said.

'It was so good to see you, Mira,' Scott said. 'Let's stay in touch, all of us?'

She smiled at them both, nodded. 'We will,' she said. 'We're in each other's lives now – for good, I hope.'

Then she waved goodbye, closed her laptop and headed to the kitchen, where Ezra was waiting for her.

EPILOGUE

CARLY

Carly checks the view behind her in the computer's camera. This is the biggest risk she's taken since she's been here; she needs to make sure there's nothing in the cafe that might give away where she is.

To be fair, the likelihood of her being recognized – with the silver-grey pixie cut she's now sporting, coloured contact lenses and her skin several shades darker after so many months this close to the equator – is fairly slim. But she can't take any chances.

As she takes in the line of white sandy beach and the steep cliffs that line the Pacific coast outside the cafe's window, she feels her familiar pang of yearning for Wales. She misses home every day. Even the grey skies, the drizzly cold of winter. In Ecuador, there only seem to be two types of weather: rainy and hot, and dry and hot. Today, especially, she is longing for the dreariness of February back home.

You're lucky to even be here.

And it is true; it was a decent amount of luck – plus some

reasonable wilderness survival skills – that led to her ending up here. Hiding inside a giant kapok tree in Hannah's rainforest for three days, living off insects and rainwater collected in those giant leaves. Waiting until the biggest flurry of police and rescue workers had given up on finding her, presumably deciding she was dead and swallowed up by the jungle.

Then following the stream in the opposite direction to Hannah's house, making her way out of the rainforest to one of the local villages in the dead of night; bribing a local farmer to drive her to the bus station near Rincon where she gave herself a haircut and bought a change of clothes.

And then the treacherous journeys facilitated by drug dealers and smugglers, using up the last of her American dollars, in the backs of trucks and lorries, sneaking across the border to Panama, then into Colombia – and finally, months later, she arrived here, a tiny fishing village in the Manabi province of Ecuador.

For months she's lain low, barely leaving her beach hut, making some quick dollars helping harvest coffee beans at a nearby farm. None of it is ideal; her hands are torn to shreds, and some days she barely makes enough to eat.

But what choice does she have?

She is a murderer. Perhaps if she'd just confessed when she'd knocked Hannah down – if she'd called for help, instead of dragging her further into the rainforest – she'd have been forgiven; she could be back home right now, in her dead-end job, but at least she'd be free.

She hadn't done that, though; she'd *wanted* Hannah to die, be left to rot in her own sodding jungle. And then the others. Ben – she'd killed him in cold blood, for God's sake. If she had somehow got rid of the other three, she might have had a chance to come up with some kind of story about them all turning on each other, with no one left alive to contradict it. But there was no way she could have taken them all on by herself.

No, she is a criminal, and people know it. She could be on the run for the rest of her life.

But over the past few weeks, she has started to feel a touch braver. No one is coming for her. No one even has any idea she is alive. She'd made it to this internet cafe a fortnight back, did a quick check for herself online: *TWO DEAD IN SANCTUARY TRAGEDY. INFLUENCER'S MURDERER PRESUMED DEAD.*

She might just have got away with this. And it is a *good thing*, what she's done. Getting rid of Hannah, wiping out her dangerous brand of influence from the world.

But the thing is, she's only wiped one of them out. And that bothers her. In just a few hours of surfing Instagram and TikTok, she can see that these influencers seem to multiply, to breed like rabbits. Every time one of them disappears, another springs up in their place.

Another, like Olivia.

Olivia with her three million Instagram followers, and her reels on the healing power of affirmation. Olivia, who preaches about how modern medicine and traditional therapy just *can't get to the root of trauma* in the way that chanting and raising your vibration can.

Olivia, who is, at this very moment, offering her followers the once-in-a-lifetime opportunity to come and meet her at her retreat near Santo Domingo, less than two hundred miles away from where Carly is right now. It is fate – it is destiny. Surely it has to be. This is Carly's life's work now; her mission.

She has it all planned out. In her vlog, she will be Laura from Hertfordshire, a yoga teacher who's been travelling for some time but is now living simply on the Venezuelan coast after going through a tragic event last year. She'll make sure to bring tears to her eyes, to talk about her insomnia and her terrible anxiety. She'll say how, if she gets the opportunity to work with Olivia, she'll be able to pass her techniques on to other people, help spread her amazing work.

She'll even offer to come a day early and help Olivia get everything set up for the retreat. Make it all perfect for the other guests. Just say the word, and she'll be there.

Carly checks her reflection one more time, clears her throat, practises *hello* under her breath in her most clipped English accent.

She takes a deep breath, and hits record.

ACKNOWLEDGEMENTS

Thank you to my fabulous agent, Kate Burke, and the team at Blake Friedmann for encouraging and supporting me in writing and editing this book. Your editorial insight and unwavering belief in me made this book possible, and I am so grateful.

A huge thank you to my dream editor, Raphaella Demetris, as well as Rosa Watmough and her fantastic colleagues at Pan Macmillan, for loving *The Hideaway* and its characters from day one.

Thank you to the incredible writing coaches and editors at The Novelry, who taught me so much and have championed me and my writing every step of the way.

Thank you Amy Durden for answering my myriad, ridiculously detailed questions about Costa Rica with endless patience and love.

To my writing bestie, Bella Blissett, and my dear author friends Natasha Boydell, Dex Stacey and Anna Brooke-Mitchell – thank you for holding my hand and believing in me.

To my family and friends: your pride and excitement are contagious and mean the world to me. I'm so grateful.

Thank you to my children, for being my greatest teachers

and inspiring me to grow into a woman who pursues her dreams so that you can be inspired to pursue yours too.

And with all my heart: thank you, John. This book, and indeed this author, could never have become what they were meant to be without you.